DESIREE, *death in a small southern town*

Joseph Inge, Jr

"I loved you." – Adrian Carlton Edwards

Prologue

She stood in the doorway framed by the most radiant light I'd ever seen. The white dress she wore was reminiscent of the one worn by Marilyn Monroe, the wind blowing it up, and her luxuriating in the breeze caressing her supposedly bare buttocks. The light reflected off perfect honey-brown skin. Her hair, a shade lighter than copper, was immaculately sculpted; shaved at the nape.

She gazed at me the way she had a thousand times in the past. Only there seemed an urgency that had never before been present. A pleading, I thought, that she could not yet express. Those large light brown eyes, reflecting shards of emerald, beckoned.

From my bed, I called to her. "Desiree'?"

She smiled a smile that was as flawless as any rainbow. And it hurt to look upon her, to remember our past, the longing, the wanting... The lusting!

Tears welled in my eyes. "I've missed you, Desiree", I said.

Her smile seemed to fade a bit. She nodded slowly as she responded. "I know Adrian, I'm sorry." She batted her eyes, and then smiled with her lips only.

I always hated when she did that. Next she would start working her magic on me. Of course, I'd been powerless to resist. All I could do is hope she wouldn't ask me to lie down in the middle of Highway Seventeen at

3

midnight, swim a 'gator hole naked, or some such nonsense. You see? I'd have done it.

"Come closer, Desiree," I pleaded. "It's been so long,"

She shook her head. "I can't," she said sadly.

"It's always the same, isn't it, Desiree?"

She lowered her eyes, seeming to stare at her feet. I followed her gaze, noticing for the first time that she wore no shoes and her feet were wet.

"Please, Adrian. I need your help. Don't let them get away with this."

"Let who get away with what?" I asked.

She merely shook her head. A tear rolled down her cheek. She was usually so strong and self-assured. But now she was weakening. I wanted to go to her; to comfort her. But something held me back. I thought of all the time I wasted. Wanting and waiting. …All in vain. And suddenly, I wanted to hurt her; to kick her while she was down.

"Why should I help you after all these years?" I asked. "After everything you've done to me? I loved you. And you ruined by life."

"I'm sorry, Adrian," she sobbed. "Don't be cruel. Not now. Please."

She glanced over her shoulder as if startled by a noise from behind.

"Adrian, I've got to leave."

"Humph. That's always the way. Desiree, I loved you." I wanted her to suffer.

"No. Don't…" she pleaded.

"I loved you," I whispered through clenched teeth.

"Adrian? They're coming, Adrian. I've got to leave," she said urgently.

"I loved you." I wielded the admission like a knife.

"No! Not yet! Please!" She had turned and was shouting into the light. Turning back, she pleaded. "Adrian, you're the only one who can help me. Don't let them get away with this! Please!"

"I loved you."

She shouted. "Oh, my… They're coming for me! Help me, Adrian! They're coming! Help me! They're… No! Don't… Help me! Adrian!"

"Ace, you're making a mess." – Juliette Edwards

CHAPTER 1

I awoke to what amounted to a battery of Bradley armored track vehicles firing in succession inside my head. Each round bounced off the back of my skull to ricochet interminably, causing me to wince with every movement, breath or thought. I lay still, hoping to will away the pain of too many Chivas Regals, straight up with water back. Some hangovers can nauseatingly attack the stomach, while others attack the brain. Still others cause the muscles to ache as if the previous evening was spent trading body blows with the next heavy weight contender. But scotch hangovers are a triple threat. They twist your muscles and stretch your gut like a pair of gigantic hands working an enormous pretzel. The headaches were the worst. A team of a thousand heavy-footed dwarves with pick axes work inside, prospecting for any brain cells that may have escaped the evening's libacious assault.

I steeled myself against a wave of nausea. As it subsided, the hard-on that I was leaning into told me how badly I needed to pee. I squeezed myself through baggy sweats, trying to remember the last time I had been laid. …Hmm? What year was this? That long? No. But it seemed like it.

I squirmed out of bed and followed my erection to the bathroom. On the way, I staggered into a pair of doorjambs and a wall while trying to get that first-of-the-day stretch. Standing over the commode, I let go a stream that caused me to rock back on my heels, splattering the edge of the porcelain bowl. I regained my balance and scratched. I peed for days, closing my eyes, enjoying the release and allowing the rush of the waters to relax me as wind chimes on the front porch.

Standing at the washbasin, I examined my face in the mirror. Not bad for a fortyish alky. But time and stress and booze were beginning to take their toll. Soon I wouldn't be able to pass myself off as twenty-eight. And the ronies that I scarcely get now would become non-existent.

My mind tallied the mental hit list I had compiled. It was ten names deep and getting longer every weekend. I really had to get off my behind and put some serious effort into nailing some of these babes.

But lately, I just couldn't seem to raise the interest. …Among other things. Not that I couldn't get hard. It just wasn't getting as hard for them. …Only for her. But she wasn't mine anymore. She never had been.

As I allowed my thoughts to drift, they rested upon her and the dream I'd had the night before. "Ahh," I groaned. I had been cruel to her. I had never had the nerve to mistreat her before. How could I? I leaned my head onto the mirror, enjoying its glassy coolness like a cold compress, easing my cloudy mind.

But now, I had a different pain; a mixture of loneliness, regret and loss. Tears began to fall down my face. I raised my head from the mirror and for an instant gazed into her eyes. There had been her most perfect face with its enchanting smile; and those eyes. They were the most beautiful eyes I'd ever stared into. Then she was gone. "Desiree," I moaned, and sank to the bathroom floor sobbing. "I love you!"

I sat on that bathroom floor for fifteen minutes crying my eyes dry. I cried as if I had seen Desiree for the last time. Love should never hurt this badly, I thought. But it did. Suddenly, I understood very well, the meaning of the term 'crime of passion'. I would have killed for her had she asked.

They say 'crying never helps anything,' but I did feel better now. My hangover was subsiding and the dream was becoming a faded memory. But that was before the phone rang.

I took a sip of the scalding coffee before asking Deputy Hicks what they expected to find in the submerged automobile.

He shrugged. "Dope... a body... who knows?"

Well, someone surely knew. This case was high profile already. And they didn't even know what the car looked like yet.

The phone call had been Bill Cook, the editor at the Courier. He told me to hustle down to King's Ferry Landing to cover this story of a car that had plunged into the river overnight. It seems some fishermen had hooked into it and used their fish finder to determine something wasn't exactly right. I hurriedly, cleaned up the best I could and swung by a drive-thru for coffee with a hash brown potato cake and breakfast sandwich I couldn't eat.

When I arrived at the scene, everyone was just kind of milling around like they had been waiting for me. Hicks intercepted me as I got out of my car. He said they hadn't attached the winch yet. That I should stay back out of the way. Let the divers and the guys with the wrecker do their jobs.

"No sweat," I said. "Probably just a stolen car some kids abandoned whey they got tired of it."

He grunted something unintelligible and gave me a suspicious sidewise look.

I dismissed his glance and we spent the next ten minutes shooting the breeze. We debated the Braves' chances of winning the pennant this year. I personally didn't care. Football was my game, and I guaranteed him the

Falcons would not win their division—not until they put together a decent linebacker corps.

Hicks nodded his head, and motioned, as if responding to some predetermined signal.

"Looks like they're about to pull it out," he said.

We walked over to the bank of the river. I watched its lazy current carry a twig away. I wondered just how many souls had been extinguished in the depths of these black waters. I had a weird feeling about this. My stomach began to boil again, and my knees trembled. It was almost as if I knew what was on the other end of the cable. An instant before the car's trunk broke the surface, I had a premonition.

"No," I whispered, shaking my head.

Hicks was staring at me with a frown on his face. "You okay?"

I couldn't speak. I just stood there shaking my head.

"Ace, we want you to do a preliminary I.D. on the body."

I shook my head. "No. Desiree," I whispered.

Hicks nudged me. "Ace, you hear me?"

I turned to the cop. "You knew," I said accusingly.

Hicks nodded. His face was cold granite, void of emotion. "…The only gold Bentley in the county."

9

There I was again alone in my two bedroom apartment. Smack in the middle of Hinesville's low budget district. Small town newspaper reporters don't make a whole lot of money. It was hours since I watched that four-wheeled luxury coffin being dragged from the bottom of the Ogeechee River. Funny thing... I remembered how the water flowed from all the cracks and crevices. I recalled stepping over to peer at a bundle that had been placed on the ground for me to see. I even remembered saying, "Yes, that's her: Desiree Simone McKensie." But, for the life of me, I could not remember actually seeing her body. I know that I did. I even wrote the story for the Courier. The headline read *"Prominent Local Business Woman Drowns in Late Night Auto Plunge."*

The details were sketchy. But foul play had been ruled out. It seemed that I wasn't the only one to have gotten drunk on the night before. Desiree had drunk nearly seven Long Island Iced Teas. At least, that's how many had been bought for her by different guys throughout the night.

I had seen her that night at the Stewart Non-Com Club. She was in the middle of her element. Brothers had been shooting game at her all night long. Most went down in flames. Some got big play, but none stayed at her table for very long. Desiree enjoyed the game but bored easily. I watched her for as long as I could stand, and then found some honey to help pass time. I couldn't even remember what she looked like.

By most accounts, Desiree appeared to be as sober as a judge, despite the number of Iced Tea glasses that littered her table. I'd always admired that about her. I had never seen her drunk. In fact, I don't' recall ever seeing her take more than a sip from any drink I'd bought her.

The more I thought about the police report, the more I began to question its accuracy. For instance, Desiree lived thirteen miles from where she went into the river. What in the world was she thinking; going out there at four thirty on a Sunday morning?

I thought of the dream again. She'd been dressed in white. She was also dressed in white last night. I wondered if they had found her shoes. She had no shoes in the dr....... "This is ridiculous," I said to myself. "You're reaching. She's dead. ...Never coming back. You can dissect this thing anyway you want. The answer's the same. Desire drove her car into the deep end of the river."

But something just didn't fit. I fixed myself a scotch and sat back in my favorite old easy chair. I took a sip and let the liquor lubricate the rusted and tight spots in my head. I shut my eyes and let my thoughts drift.

I'd had a family. ...But not anymore. ...Kids. ...A beautiful wife. ...A family. ...A career. ...A family.

When I opened my eyes again I was eight years younger, standing in line waiting my turn to enter the Non-Com Club. A not-too-well-dressed brother took my I.D. card, and then returned it motioning me past. I smiled at the attractive cashier, but she simply took my two singles and blew me off. As I made my way through the lobby, it occurred to me that I was over-dressed in a tan, worsted wool suit and silk tie. Kicking sneaks and shorts that hang to the knees never seemed to work for me, though. I liked the edge a well fitted suit gives you.

I pulled open the door to the crowded disco lounge. Extreme bass-beat, smoke, attitude, and dark assaulted my senses. I paused a moment to let myself adjust to the vibe. I allowed the music to kick around inside my head while my body fell in synch with the undulating night rhythm.

Once acclimated, I shouldered through the crowd and made my way to the bar. The line was way too long for my liking. So, I caught Totsie, the cutie pie waitress who always made eyes at me. She smiled. "Hi, Baby," she said. "What can I get you?"

I ordered my usual Chivas on the rocks and waited for her to return. As I watched the partiers on the dance floor move to some rump shaker-booty grinder, I wondered what anthropologists might write about the American clubbing sub-culture. Would they consider this syncopation some form of worship? It could, most certainly be considered some type of mating ritual. I personally always thought of old Tarzan movies when I saw a group of young brothers gyrate and twist around a lone pelvis-thrusting sister in the middle. But then that was simply the overactive imagination of a writer at work.

Finally, Totsie returned with my drink. I paid her, and kicked in a healthy tip so she wouldn't forget to check on me from time to time. I watched as she melted into the crowd. She had a nice behind. She was kind of short, but maybe one day, I thought, we'll raise the stakes on our little friendship. Who knows? It might turn out to be one of the best times I ever had.

I went back to checking out the crowd. So far I hadn't seen anyone I knew. I'd been stationed at Fort Stewart for ten months and I still didn't feel quite at home here. It really wasn't a friendly place for newcomers. Everyone had to carve his or her own niche. No one ever gave up any ground here. Even at my job, I was forced to hack away and hack away at barriers, resistance. …Resistance from superiors, subordinates and the doggone job itself. But I was the man for the job. I was the expert. …The best. I assumed that's why I was chosen as editor of the "Victory" division's Patriot newspaper.

I took a drink from my scotch. That's when I met her. The room was small, and people were close on one another. She brushed by as I tipped the glass to my lips. Her shoulder bumped my elbow causing my face to be bathed in liquor and ice.

"Hey!"

"Ooh! I'm sorry," she said. She seemed to sing it.

Without looking at her, I attempted to brush scotch from my suit and tie. "Look… why don't you…." I saw her for the first time. She was smiling, her eyes twinkling in the half-light.

"I said I'm sorry," she admonished. "Why don't you let me buy you another drink?"

I was dumbstruck. I couldn't speak. She just smiled, then took my hand and guided me to the bar. Standing in line, I found my voice. "You don't have to buy me a drink," I told her. "In fact, let me buy you one."

"No," she replied. "My treat... You can buy the next one."

...Next one? This could be good, I thought.

"What's your name?" I asked her.

"Desiree." She smiled. No teeth, just a warm, open, glowing smile. Her eyes sparkled.

"Hi, Desiree. My name is Ace."

"Ace?" She kind of screwed up her face like she had a whiff of something that didn't smell so neat. "Is that you real name: Ace?"

"Um... Well...uhh. No. But it's the one I like"

"What's your mother call you, Ace?"

"I, uhh," I stammered uncomfortably, and then leaned to whisper in her ear.

She laughed softly, and then repeated my name.

"Adrian."

I had never liked my name. I had always been teased about it, but there was no teasing in the way Desiree pronounced it. She made it sound manly and proud.

"Adrian what?" she asked, smiling.

"Adrian Carlton Edwards," I replied.

"I like that. Very classy."

"Well, thanks," I said. "Anything to please."

She chuckled. "Careful, Adrian. I may hold you to that."

I grinned. "Please do."

Our eyes locked for a moment; then we looked away self-consciously.

"Are you married?" I asked.

"Are you?" she volleyed.

"Afraid so," I said, as I twisted my wedding band. "And you?"

"Yeah….. It gives me perspective."

I nodded. I wished I had said that.

Conversation faltered and our eyes searched the crowded room as if seeking a subject to help maintain the connection that was slipping away. Just then the Deejay fell into his slow jam set. "Would you like to dance?" I asked.

She looked at the dance floor, then at me.

"Sure," she said. "Why not?"

On the dance floor, she was warm and graceful. Our slow drag was stimulating but not overtly sexual. Her arms squeezed my back as her pelvis did a slow grind with my own. I squeezed her in kind and felt the beginning of an erection in response to the pressure of her hips against mine.

Self-consciously, I attempted to move away from her. I only succeeded in improving the angle, increasing the stimulation. I needed to so something to take my mind off my situation.

I closed my eyes and concentrated on sports scores. I'd danced with a lot of women and never felt the least embarrassment about a hard-on pressing up against them. It was a part of the game. I'd felt that it was expected. …Sort of a compliment. For some reason I thought it would offend Desiree; though I don't know why. She seemed sophisticated enough that a normal human response wouldn't send her screaming from the dance floor. But, she was just so glamorous that I wanted to do everything right and on time where she was concerned. And that meant staying cool and not rushing anything.

She whispered something in my ear. "You're stiff."

"Huh?"

She looked into my eyes. "I said you're stiff."

I blinked at her, pretending not to comprehend.

She smiled. "Your dancing is stiff. Maybe you're not comfortable. Let's find a table and talk."

"Oh," I said dumbly. Then, grinned, grateful to have been such an awful dancer. "Yeah, I think that would be a good idea."

We located an abandoned table in a dark corner of the room. Only one chair remained though. So, I borrowed one from the people guzzling champagne at a nearby table. Along with the chair, they forced me to take two glasses of the bubbly wine. I asked them what the occasion was, and they told me the financier of the party had won five hundred dollars on the pick three lottery.

Poor guy… At the rate his buddies were ordering booze on his tab, he was going to need two more lotteries to pay the bill.

I set down the drinks and pulled over my chair. Desiree was already sitting. I joined her and she smiled. I returned her smile, wishing I had something James Bond-like to say. Instead, I made small talk.

"So, tell me about yourself," I started.

"What would you like to hear?"

"I don't know," I said. "How about where you're from."

"Louisiana," she replied. "…A little parish, called Saint Luke, about a hundred miles southwest of New Orleans."

When she said New Orleans, she tied it all together so you couldn't tell it wasn't just one word. "Nawlins". Suddenly, in my head, I had a picture of her in some backwoods bayou village with her hair all wild and loose. Her dress, two sizes too small, clinging to her lithe form, was dirty and ripped at the armpit so that just a hint of her fleshy breast was exposed. Her feet were bare. And they were dirty; as was her face. Her legs were spread apart and uncovered as she knelt and dipped the chicken she was cleaning into the tub of hot water between her feet.

I grinned.

"What?" she asked.

"You're not into voodoo are you?" I asked, thinking of Lisa Bonet in the movie, "Angel Heart."

She laughed. "Why? Do you have someone you'd like me to work roots on?"

"Are you serious?"

Now she grinned.

"No. I'm only joking," she said.

But that closed mouth smile remained.

I only half believed her.

We watched the crowd awhile, and talked about everything from sports to the weather, but nothing about ourselves.

"Adrian, I've got to go," she said after a time.

My heart sank. "Okay," I said. "It was nice meeting you." I offered my hand. She took it.

"I'm sorry I didn't get to buy that drink."

I shook my head. "Not a problem."

"I'll make it good next time."

...Next time? "That'll work."

"Can you walk me to my car?" she asked. "You know. ...Protection."

The crowd had thinned. And what remained were mostly the arm snatchers and the "can-I-go-home-wit-chew" brothers.

I grinned. "Sure."

We left the wine mostly un-drunk, and made our way through the sparse crowd. I followed her to a gleaming gold Bentley. Huh, I thought. ...Impressive. Alarms rang in my head. ...Officer's wife out slumming.

She got in, put the key in the ignition, and then turned over the engine. When she let down the tinted window, the mingled aromas of spring gardenia and new car escaped from within. And there was that smile again.

I leaned to speak though the open window.

"Can I see you, again?" I asked.

"If you like..." That smile.

"I like," I replied.

She produced a pink card with teal print.

"...Desiree's Boutique?"

She nodded, obviously, proud of the shop that bore her name.

"And you're Desiree, I take it."

She smiled. "That's me."

"Well, I'll call you," I told her.

"I'd like that." Smile.

Our eyes locked and I knelt to be closer to her. She leaned forward and inevitably, we kissed. ...Tentatively, at first. ...Then with ardor only possessed by strangers intent on becoming lovers. Inwardly, I cursed the door between us and longed to once more feel the warmth of her form pressed against the length of me. My hands searched for and found hers, and our fingers entwined. A moment later, the kiss was over, and I awoke to deafening pounding at my apartment door.

"What! Who is it?" I shouted from a throat that seemed caked with chalk dust.

The pounding continued.

I winced, my head throbbing from each knock at the door. The pain reverberated behind my eyes as I shut them and attempted to massage them into focus.

I ran my tongue around the inside of my mouth, hoping to draw moisture to lubricate my dry throat. "Oh, geez!" I croaked. My mouth tasted as if I'd been chewing used sweat socks.

And the pounding continued.

"Go away!" I shouted.

"Ace, you open this door!" The reply from the other side.

It was Diana, come to console me, no doubt.

"No! Go away!"

I forced my body to move from the chair. My glass from the night before was at my feet on its side. Picking it up, I hoped that I didn't waste any of my scotch. Shame and embarrassment washed over me; then were gone. Aww, man! I went to the kitchen where I'd left the scotch bottle.

"Ace! Ace! Open the door! ...Now, Ace!" She was kicking as well as knocking.

"Shut up! You got a key. Use it," I shouted at the door.

"You've got the deadbolt on!" she said reasonably.

"Then wait," I shot back.

I heard her shout. "Open this door! Now!" Then she muttered something I didn't quite understand. I chuckled.

I reached for the scotch bottle and found it empty. Twisting off the cap, I turned it up. Not even fumes escaped the bone-dry container. I must have used that trick last night, I guessed.

I tossed the bottle into the trash can, and went to open the door for Dee. The day was glorious, radiant. I squinted and shielded my eyes from the bright sunlight.

Dee didn't say a word, but pushed pass me and stalked the middle of the floor. She finally stopped. Crossing her arms, she glowered at me. Mentally, I braced myself for what would come.

"You sorry...." She shook her head struggling to maintain control. "That's why Julie left...." Her voice trailed off. She wasn't playing fair. Her speech was very calm, though each word held an edge as sharp as any razor.

I sat down and prepared for the full treatment.

"Poor cry baby," she said. "Another man's woman dies and you grieve as badly as he does. You are sorry. What gives you the right....No! You don't have the right! I won't allow you to mourn-not like this. Not when that man has lost a wife. You spent a few chosen hours together. ...A few hours out of a long lifetime. You had only the best of her. You didn't... You couldn't have known her the way you think you did. You weren't with her through sickness and quarrels-and whatever. You couldn't know her deepest fears. ...Her regrets or sorrows."

"You spent hours of passion, maybe love. …Definitely laughter and pleasure. But, you did not share a life together."

"I would have," I said. A tear fell to my chest.

"I know, Baby," she answered. "But you didn't. Don't tarnish your memories of her by grieving this way; locked alone in a dark apartment, killing yourself by slow degrees."

She held out her arms. "Come here," she whispered.

I stood and went to her, my feet, suddenly, blocks of lead. She enfolded me with her arms and I allowed my entire weight to rest upon her. Surprisingly strong, she held me and stroked the back of my neck.

"This is the way, sweetheart," she said softly. "Grieve to me."

She held me as if my life depended on it. As if, to release would send me, helplessly, careening into the jaws of a bottomless chasm.

And I wept.

"Dee?" I called her so softly, I wasn't sure she'd heard me.

"Yes, Baby?" she whispered.

"I'm sorry I made you wait at the door."

She chuckled and we moved together.

"I thought you might be," she replied.

We laughed. And holding each other gently, we cried. I cried for Desiree, and I supposed Dee cried for my grief.

And she was right. This was the way to grieve.

Diana held me until I no longer required the reassurance of her embrace. She touched my face with her fingertips, wiping away a tear. "Better, now?" she asked.

I tried to smile. "Slightly," I replied.

She gazed into my eyes. "Well, that's better than nothing," she said.

I nodded.

"Ace," she whispered. "Would you do something for me?"

"Anything," I whispered back. "…Whatever you need."

Her face had a look of serious concentration.

"Could you, please, go take a shower?" She fanned her nose, laughing.

"Humph. Excuse me," I mumbled. I coughed, attempting to clear my dry throat.

She stopped laughing. "B.C. has given me your assignments," she said.

"Why? Is he firing me?" I asked, walking into the kitchen. I coughed again.

"No, he's not. It's just that he felt sorry about the last one he gave you. He thought you might like to take a little time off. …To clear your head, maybe?"

I picked up my scotch glass and filled it from the faucet. "Is there anyone in this whole town who doesn't know about Desiree and me?"

I turned up the glass, swished once, and spat the water into the kitchen sink.

Dee pulled a face; then replied, "Well, you were rather vocal back then."

"Yeah," I said. "And all that did was get me laughed at and ruin my life."

Neither of us spoke. We were reflecting upon events of the past.

Dee shrugged. "Oh, well," she said, breaking the silence.

"Yeah," I replied, wistfully. I sighed and shrugged. "I'll shower."

"Okay. When you're done, I've got something I think will interest you."

She produced a manila folder from her purse, and smiled. I gazed at it, frowning.

Comprehension seeped into my brain. It was a confidential report. Dee knew just how to cheer me up. "Oh," I said. "Oh! I'll be right back."

As I showered, I thought of Diana. How could I not be in love with her? Why is it she had never affected me the way Desiree did? With her chocolate brown skin and long raven-black hair, in many ways, she was even more beautiful than Desiree. ...In most ways, in fact. Man, that body! She was tight and well proportioned with a tiny waist and generous hips and bust.

There was no denying that we loved one another in some way. But, our relationship had always lacked intensity, fire. We were comfortable. It was the type of friendship that grows out of constant proximity. It seemed that we had never been without one another. Not since our very first year in high school.

Diana Flanders and I had met in our freshman year. Although we were both English majors, it was unusual that for the entire four years, we would

24

have every class together. Every class but gym, that is. And even that was during the same class period.

For spending so much time together, we became one another's greatest adversary and ally alike. When life or love beat one of us down the other would step in and work to set things right. Whether we provided an inspirational word or lent refuge in the waning hours of the night, we were steadfastly devoted to each other.

Despite our symbiotic relationship, I owed Dee a great deal. As the years went by I withdrew increasingly more from our emotional bank account than I could ever hope to repay. In college, she had more than once bailed me out when I blew my rent money on drugs or babes. She would even take notes for me if I decided to skip a class or two.

Dee had been the perfect roommate. Still, it was amazing how well our friendship had endured. I had thought we had ruined everything that night we got high together. Finals were over, and we were relaxing before going out to blow off steam. She was sitting on the couch when I walked into the room tokin' a seriously fat blunt.

"You're not going to share?" she asked.

I took a long hit, holding in the smoke.

Taking the joint from my mouth, I exhaled.

"Sure," I said, passing her the cigarette.

I licked the taste of the strawberry flavored rolling paper from lips.

She hit the blunt, and then passed it back.

"Shotgun?" I asked.

"Okay," she replied after licking her own lips.

I turned the cigarette around. With the lit end in my mouth I held it between my teeth. Leaning over her, I placed my lips against hers, and then blew the intoxicating vapor into her mouth. She leaned back while accepting the smoke. I rested my hand on her shoulder to help maintain my balance. Unconsciously my fingers began to stroke her shoulders, neck and then her ear. She brought her hand up to my chest, and gently pushed me away. I took the joint from my mouth, and attempted to back away.

Dee shook her head slowly, and pulled me by the front of my shirt. Our lips met, and she opened her mouth. As I opened mine, she blew the smoke into my lungs. I inhaled, and then returned it.

She took a deep breath, and shuddered. I had been trembling the entire time. Our tongues met, seeming to battle for a position of dominance, until we managed a mutual exchange.

I lowered myself to the couch. And she positioned herself so that I could lie on top of her. We made love on the living room couch, not fifteen feet from either of our bedrooms. I suppose we didn't move because the living room was neutral ground. And so no one's territory would be desecrated by this forbidden act.

Anyway, it happened. We did it. It was over. It was good. And we never spoke of it. Not ever.

Not even when I met Julie and we started dating. Not even when Julie became pregnant. Not even when I left school to marry Julie. …Nor when Julie and I divorced, and Dee came to comfort me.

Never… Not ever….

Diana completed college and became a very successful freelance writer. She had even published a book. A fictional piece called "Toast to the Fools." The book enjoyed marginal success, and I teased her about selling out and producing gossipy, commercial, soap opera trash. What I didn't say was how proud of her I was. …And how lucky I was that she was on my side.

All cleaned and dressed, I joined Dee in the living room. She sniffed the air. "Ahh, much better," she said. "Cologne. …A good touch." She grinned.

"Thanks," I said, smiling. "Let's see what you got."

We took seats at the dinette table. She passed me the folder. I opened it, and quickly scanned the papers inside. …Nothing. I continued studying each page more carefully. …Still, nothing.

I glanced up, into Dee's eyes. She nodded. I resumed poring over the documents. I scoured the papers for fifteen minutes, searching for clues that may lead to any conclusion but suicide. Dee had brought me this file for a reason. I must be missing something.

Once more, I read over the file. I read each word; studied each photo, measurement, or statistic twice. Finally, I gave up. Looking into her impassive face, I raised my hands. "What?" I asked.

"Nothing new, is there?" she asked, shaking her head.

"Nothing I didn't already know," I replied. "Except that her shoes weren't listed in her personal effects."

Diana cocked her head to one side, pondering, and then dismissed the statement. She took the file.

"Ace, this is trash, unremarkable" she said. "There are significant omissions to this report."

"How do you know?" I asked her.

"Ace, please," she snorted.

Of course, she had her sources. I apologized.

"Anyway," she began. "An autopsy was done."

That was quick. I waited for her to continue.

"Well, Ace, from what I could gather, Desiree was active that night."

"Yeah... I know," I confirmed. "I saw her out."

Dee shook her head. "I know. ...Um Ace, there was semen inside of her."

I took a deep breath and released it.

"So, you're saying that she was raped?"

Coldly, without expression, she replied, "Hardly."

"What?" I asked. "You want me to believe that after having consensual sex, Desiree decides to try and swallow the entire Ogeechee River?"

28

She didn't answer. We stared at one another, over the meaningless file. I wasn't handling this well.

I broke the stare. Glancing down at the file, I shook my head. "It doesn't make sense. It could've been rape."

"Ace," she said. "You don't understand. When I said, 'There was semen inside of her," I meant, that there was semen *inside* of her."

I shook my head, not getting it.

"Inside…her…stomach," Dee spelled it out.

My eyes watered, and I felt a flush of heat flow through me, as I clenched and unclenched my hands on top of the table. "So…. I guess that kind of eliminates the question of rape."

She nodded. Then said, "Not necessarily…….. I guess. It certainly doesn't eliminate the question of murder," she said.

In spite of myself, I was relieved. Diana was giving me a purpose. ...Something to fight for. ...A reason to go on. I waited for the rest.

"Ace, Desiree did not drown. She was strangled to death. Chances are the guy she had oral sex with killed her."

I didn't say it. But, she probably read it on my face. I doubted that the guy Desiree had been with could have killed her afterwards. I knew from experience.

Desiree was that good.

"You got to be kidding me!" Bill Cook nearly fell from his swivel chair as he laughed behind his paper-cluttered editor's desk.

I glanced at Diana whose face wore a crest-fallen expression. She looked at me and I shrugged.

"I'll tell you why that information was left out of the police report," he said. "That is, if your snitch can be trusted, Diana."

Dee opened her mouth to answer the insinuation. I shook my head, halting her. I wasn't convinced, myself, that her lover/killer theory was dead on. I wanted Bill's slant on all the information we gave him.

He continued, stabbing his index finger forward, giving accent to each word. "The cops omitted that information from the report because they didn't want to taint their investigation. They want everyone to think the case has been solved, and the matter closed."

Diana nodded. I didn't get it. That report wasn't smoke screen. It was legit. We were all missing something.

Bill spoke to Dee. "Diana, I think you're wrong about this blowjob guy. I think he's just a wild card. It was Saturday night, after all. Folks were getting laid and whatever all over the place. Besides, the way McKensie looked, the last thing a man would do is ki…..

"Bill," Dee broke in.

She glanced at me.

"Sorry, Ace," Cook apologized.

"It's alright, Bill," I said, frowning.

"But, Diana, you get my point here, don't' you?" he asked.

She shook her head. "What I'm getting here, Bill, is a bunch of macho crap. You're telling me that a man can't get violent with a woman after sharing a tender hummer."

I suddenly felt warm, and hoped Dee hadn't noticed me wipe the back of my neck.

"Well, I'm telling you that sex-especially oral sex-can be used as an expression of dominance. And men are often violent, not only after, but during. Thank you, very much."

I sat very still, blinking.

Bill shuffled uncomfortably in his chair. It squeaked when he moved. "Ah…yeah," he managed. "So, where are you going with this?" he asked, more professionally than I'd ever seen him.

"I thought Ace might want this one, actually," she said.

Bill looked at me. "…Ace?"

"Well…uhh…well, yeah. …I do," I stammered.

"So, what's your angle?" he asked, avoiding Dee's glare.

Dee had not convinced me, but I said falteringly, "I guess…I'm looking….for a very satisfied killer."

Dee glowered. And I did not meet her gaze.

I sliced into the bloody steak laying on my plate. The red juice mixed with the kernels of corn; then was dammed by the mashed potatoes with brown gravy. I loved a nice rare cut of beef. But this meat was absolutely raw… and cold.

Diana was a much better cook than this. She'd done this on purpose. She was still pissed from our meeting with Bill.

Sheepishly, I glanced up from my meal. From across the table, her eyes found mine then locked in. …Threatening. I nearly cringed.

"Diana, I can't eat this," I said softly, through a half smile.

Her eyes narrowed. I half expected her to leap across the table. I'd seen her this way many times. She was a very practical person. If I remained calm, she would soon, become reasonable. The trick was not to say anything that would further piss her off.

"Why didn't you back me this afternoon?" she asked.

"Because I don't believe Desiree was killed by a lover," I answered flatly.

"What do you believe?" she asked.

I didn't have an answer.

I frowned, staring at my plate, as I shook my head.

"I don't know," I said. "But something's not there. It's just too easy to use that lover scenario.

"Dee, all we've got is an official police report. …And hear-say. We don't know one thing. …..Not really."

"Ace, I have a reliable source who says that your girlfriend had oral sex and was strangled that same night. How many men do you think Miss Desiree was with that evening?"

Diana tapped the table with the nail of her middle finger as she spoke. I bit my lower lip before answering. I took a deep breath.

"Diana, I was at the scene," I said. "I identified the body. I should know whether or not she was strangled."

She pressed. "So, what did you see?"

I thought for a moment, and could not recall. The entire scene was all haze. No details. It was as if I hadn't seen her at all. Had I seen her, I should have noticed the bruising of strangle marks on her neck.

I shook my head.

"I don't remember," I admitted.

Dee mocked me. "You don't remember."

"Dee, what's this about?" I asked. "I know you never liked Desire, but..."

"I never had anything against Desiree, Ace," she defended.

I went on. "What is it, then? Is it about you and me?"

"Hold up a minute, Adrian," she said. "There has never been any you and me, nor me and you. Nor us. There is me. And there is you." She pointed for emphasis.

"What is the problem, then!" I shouted.

"The problem is that you can't believe that any man was capable of boning this tramp, then killing her!" she shouted back.

"That's it, Dee! That's enough!"

"It's not enough!" She continued. "She was a slut! A common slut! If she had you, she had five more like you!"

"That's not fair! You've had men!" I countered.

Diana calmed. We stared at one another across the table.

"How dare you try that?" she spoke. "I have never had men the way Desiree did-or as many. I have never used men the way she did. Besides, it's not only the quantity I'm talking about. It's the quality. Her standards were low by anyone's account."

I sneered as I spoke. "Diana, if you were a man, I would beat you down."

Slowly, she shook her head.

"No," she said. "If you were a man, you would get beat down."

She stood and came around the table. "I'll fix your steak," she said, picking up my plate. Blood spilled onto the table in front of me.

As I watched the crimson stain soak into the white tablecloth my stomach churned. I don't know if I was made ill from the sight of the raw meat or the kick in the gut I'd just gotten from Diana. But nothing was going to stay down that night. I sat, allowing Dee's words to echo in my mind. 'A common slut' she'd said. 'She had five more like you.'

They were harsh words. I knew that Desiree had had other men. That had never mattered to me. It never mattered either that she was married. I loved her. And she loved me-in her way.

Dee was jealous, I thought. And it wasn't right. Suddenly, I was very angry. I rubbed my temples with my fingertips and drew a deep breath. Releasing the breath, I rose from the table and made my way for the front door.

Dee entered the dining room with my repaired meal. "Where're you going?" she asked my back.

"Home," I replied over my shoulder.

"We're not finished!" she snapped.

I turned. My eyes narrowed and watered with emotion. "Oh, yes," I said quietly. "We are finished."

"Ace…. Please stay." She was still holding my plate.

I shook my head slowly.

"No."

"What about your dinner?" she asked.

"It's ruined," I replied flatly.

She glanced at the plate then set it on the table.

"Don't leave," she pleaded, her eyes searching my own. "I need you."

At that moment my anger began to subside. Diana was as beautiful and vulnerable as I had ever seen her in my life. I wanted to hold her. To comfort her in spite of the pain she had caused me that night. I moved for her, and she closed the distance between us. Holding her, I stroked her hair and patted her back slowly. Through her clothing, her flesh was warm and firm. Her breasts against my chest were warm and inviting. I raised my head from her cheek to place small tender kisses upon it. When I moved to kiss her lips she brought her hand to my mouth.

"Ace," she whispered, "you're way too easy."

Dee reached behind her and removed my arms.

"Let's sit on the couch," she said while guiding me by the hand.

As we sat, she held my hands. She gazed into my eyes.

"Sweetheart," she began, "you need to solve this case. But sleeping with me will not make it happen. We've handled this badly from the beginning and I don't intend to make things anymore complicated than they already are."

She had been wearing her professional reporter face. But now she smiled a bit.

"I love you," she said. "You've been my best friend for as long as I can remember. That will never change for me. But if we're going to accomplish anything, we need to back up and start thinking and behaving like professionals."

I didn't answer.

"Do you think you can manage that?" she asked.

She was challenging me now. I resented that. And I resented the ploy she'd used to keep me from leaving. It wasn't fair that she could manipulate me that way. I thought back. Had I always been this susceptible to her will? ...To any woman's? ...Or maybe to every woman's. I couldn't remember. I always seemed to get what I wanted.

But, perhaps, I was only getting what they wanted to give me. Maybe all the women I'd bagged were not actually my conquests, but I was theirs. I didn't want to believe that. It would mean admitting to a weakness I never knew existed. And I wasn't prepared to do that. I resolved to answer her challenge, to regain control. In my mind, our friendship had met a pivotal juncture. Now we could either withdraw or conquer. But we could never again be totally at peace. ...Perhaps truce, but never peace.

"Okay," I said. "Where do you propose we start?"

"All over," she answered. "We need to ask ourselves some basic questions."

I could see it coming. We had avoided this one from the jump.

"Who stands to gain the most from Desiree's death?" Dee asked.

I shook my head, and she understood.

Dee nodded.

"Yes. He had motive enough-more than enough. He had ability. He's trained to do it. And he had the best opportunity."

What she had said was correct. ...On all counts. But I refused to believe that Colonel Alexander 'Bud' McKensie had killed his wife.

Diana frowned.

"Here we go again," I thought. This was not going to be easy.

Diana wheeled her car off the dark highway into the parking lot of Kings Ferry Landing. The area was pitch-black except for the light extending

37

from the power pole illuminating the boat ramp. She parked facing the river, killing the engine, but leaving on the headlights. The mists rolling over the warm waters reminded me of just about every Twilight Zone episode I'd ever seen. The eerie vapors seemed as wraiths come to life to dance and chase one another across the slow moving currents of the Ogeechee.

I thought of Desiree, alone in her sinking automobile as those wraiths watched on. Had they tried to save her, reaching for her with vaporous hands that could not grasp beings existing in the realm of the living? Or had they cheered her demise, grateful for the company of yet another soul before it drifts away to meet with those claimed by the River Savannah?

Diana whispered. "...Ace?"

I turned to her.

"Maybe this wasn't such a good idea." She said.

"We're here now," I replied.

She nodded.

Just then an engine roared and the night was filled with the glare of headlights as they descended upon us from the driver's side of the car. The sound of tires spinning in gravel mingled with that of the racing engine as the car sped toward us.

Paralyzed, we stared, wide-eyed in disbelief. Suddenly, the car veered away, jetting for the exit. An instant later, the vehicle was just a memory on its way up Highway 17.

In the dark, we stared at one another. I shrugged; then opened the take-out sack with cheeseburger and fries inside. Dee watched as I bit into the sandwich.

"I could have fixed you something else to eat," she said.

With my mouth full, I mumbled, "I don't think I want you to fix me anything else to eat, Dee. ...Ever!"

She shrugged. "I think you just like drive-thru food."

I ate.

"Suit yourself," she sniffed, turning away.

I chuckled, watching the black waters flow by.

Diana and I had made up as best we could after our disagreement. She shared my opinion that Desiree's husband was an unlikely suspect in her murder. That didn't put us any closer to solving the case, however. We still didn't have any concrete clues. And we had no one to place at the scene of the murder. We didn't even know where the scene was.

Dee figured that the most logical place to start our investigation would be where the body was found. I didn't relish coming back to this place with memories of the day before so fresh. But we had to start sometime and someplace. Here and now were as good a time and place as any. I just hated it. This park was so familiar. ...So many memories. I didn't allow myself to think. I finished my fries; then slurped the last of my orange soda.

Dee turned to me.

"Are you ready?" she asked impatiently.

"Just about," I said, then belched and patted my belly. "Ahhh."

She turned away, sighing as if attempting to maintain composure.

"Let's go," she ordered.

When she turned off the headlights, the river went black except for the area near the boat ramp. We got out of the car, and met at its trunk. Dee opened the trunk and the light washed over us.

She reached in and without searching found exactly what she needed. Dee was so organized that, sometimes, it was sickening. She thrust a large black metal cylinder at me. Her hand was wrapped around the flashlight with the lens in her direction. I pretended not to understand.

"Dee, I don't think this is the time or place for that sort of thing," I teased.

"Afraid of a little competition, Ace?" she chided as she turned the flashlight around and pressed the button.

The beam in my eyes caused me to squint.

I laughed, taking the phallic facsimile from her hand. "I'd call this more than just a little competition," I answered.

She laughed. We looked at one another, smiling. Then we remembered that we weren't close friends anymore. She turned and reached into the trunk, removing another flashlight. Who keeps two flashlights in their car? She was really starting to piss me off. She pressed the button and nothing happened. I was tempted to cheer. But, of course, she had spare batteries. She tested the flashlight; then shut the trunk.

That's when we noticed him standing at the front of the car. We both swore and drew back our flashlights, preparing to use the heavy aluminum cases for clubs.

The man was standing with one hand resting on his hip and the other on what appeared to be a holstered pistol.

"Hicks, is that you?" I called.

"You two sure know how to mess up a guy's night," he replied.

We shined our lights on him. He put up his hand to shield his eyes.

"What're y'all doing out here?" he asked.

"We're on a date," Dee replied.

I might have come up with a better answer. I assumed Dee just didn't care. Hicks eyed the flashlight in her had and grinned. I could almost read all the dirty thoughts playing across his face.

"Must be some date. Huh, Ace?"

I ignored the insinuation.

"What are you doing out here, Hicks?" I challenged.

"…Just on patrol, Ace. That's all," he answered.

I didn't believe that anymore than he believed Diana's date alibi. He was out of his jurisdiction. I shined my light around the parking lot. The reflection of glass and chrome shot back at me from the direction that speeding car had come. I turned the light back on Hicks. He grinned.

"Okay," he said. "I sneaked up on a couple of lovers, and decided to have some fun with them."

41

Diana and I stood, waiting for the rest. He continued. "They were both women. I tried to pressure them into lettin' me join in, but you blew that for me. They're probably in Effingham by now."

"I'm sure you can catch up if you hurry," Diana offered.

"Naw," he said. "I think I'd rather hang around here and watch you and Ace, Dee."

"Humph," I snorted. "Alright... Well, let's get started, then."

They both watched me. I walked around to the front of the car. Shining the light up one side of the riverbank then the other, I turned to Hicks. "We're looking for clues," I told him.

He nodded. "Naturally," he replied; then gave Dee a sidelong glance, shaking his head. "I'm disappointed," he told her.

"Give me a break, Hicks," she said, walking around the vehicle herself. I chuckled.

He turned to me. "Ace, I'm really sorry about Desiree. I had a lot of respect for that lady."

I wasn't watching Dee, but I could imagine her rolling her eyes skyward in disgust.

"Thanks, Hicks," I said. I decided to pump him for information. "She had a lot of friends. ...Seems like she had everything to live for. Why do you suppose she'd kill herself?"

He shrugged; then glanced at Dee, who remained impassive. "I don't know, Ace. I been a cop for a long time and the only thing you can be certain about is that you'll never figure folks out completely."

Not quite the answer I had been fishing for; so I decided to try the direct approach. "Some folks are saying that she was murdered. …That the cops are hiding something. Protecting an investigation, maybe?"

He laughed. …A downright belly laugh with his head thrown back, and tears coming to his eyes. When he finished, he shook his head, saying, "Hot dang! You writers got one heckuva 'magination. There ain't no investigation, son. It's all over. Nobody wants this case open. Not the colonel. Not the sheriff. Not Old Royce. And, especially, not you, partner. You see, in my book, you're the prime suspect."

I drew a breath to steady myself. I was certain that Hicks was bluffing, putting up smoke screen for whatever he was hiding. I didn't buy it. I glanced at Dee, who remained calm. I could tell that she was analyzing everything Hicks had to say. I had to keep him talking.

"Well, that's just trash talk," I told him. "First off, why would Dillon give two cents one way or the other about Desiree's murder?"

He shook his head. "Ace... Ace... Ace... Think man! He owns the doggone town. And prominent people gettin' murdered is bad for its "Safest City in the South" image. Shoot! It's bad for industry. Everybody suffers: Kids. Shop owners. Newspapers. …And their reporters. You get the idea?"

I suddenly felt threatened. And that pissed me off.

"Deputy, if you got something to say, just spit it out."

"Okay," he said. "Here it is, Ace. If you start digging around in people's business, you might bring up a few things that would be better off buried. You know the Colonel don't want his wife's business out in the open. Start people to saying out loud what they been whispering all of these years."

"So, you expect me to just go home and wait for you to make up evidence against me," I offered.

He grinned.

"No... No, Ace. You misunderstand. If you walk away from it now, there won't be not evidence or nothing," he said. "Think about it. You done got away with murder." He looked at Dee. "This would be a good spot to celebrate. What do you think, Dee?"

Diana had been taking it all in quietly. I wondered what she thought about Hicks's accusation.

"Good night, Hicks," she answered.

He chuckled. "Good night, Dee. Better enjoy that date, Ace. Women are going to be kind of scarce where you're going."

"See you later, Hicks," I snapped. He chuckled as he strolled away.

We watched his tall, lanky form fade into the darkness, then reappear as a silhouette shadowed by the interior light of his patrol car. A moment later, the car was on its way up Highway 17 in the direction of the other one.

"So what do you think?" I asked Dee.

"I think you need the name of a good lawyer," she teased.

I shined my light in her face.

"Dee, this isn't funny," I whined. "Hicks is trying to pin a murder on me."

Diana clucked; then sighed. "Well, did you kill her?"

"Of course not!", I shouted.

"Then stop worrying," she said, reasonably. "Besides, you wouldn't have all these problems if you weren't such a *ho*."

"That's not helping, Dee. Hicks is measuring me for a frame." I was nearly hysterical.

She laughed.

"I don't believe so, Ace," she said. "I think maybe, he wants you to solve the case for him."

I looked at Dee as if she'd lost her mind.

"How do you figure?" I asked.

"Well, let's think about it," she said. "Old man Dillon wants this thing buried and if the old man wants this to be a suicide, you can believe Sheriff Lindsey; good old J.L.; wants it to be a suicide, as well."

"So?" I asked impatiently.

So, as bad as Hicks is, he's an honest cop-as honest as a cop can get around here."

"You're saying he's using us to do his investigation?" I asked, finally catching on.

She nodded.

"I think that's a real stretch, Dee," I said.

Without missing a beat, she asked me, "Would you think it was a stretch if I told you that Hicks is my snitch?"

I thought about that revelation for a moment, grateful for the darkness that hid the shocked expression on my face.

"It could make sense," I thought aloud. If the sheriff wasn't allowed to investigate Desiree's death then it stands to reason his staff was not, as well. But Hicks wasn't your run-of-the-mill honest cop. He was ambitious, as well. So, what did he stand to gain by going behind everyone's backs and launching a stealth investigation?

"This is a hard one," I told Dee. "What's in it for Hicks? Why does he want this case solved?"

"Those are good questions," she said. "Maybe he's planning to expose Dillon's operation."

I shook my head. "No. Not likely. Hicks is the old man's only nephew. …So he'd probably not expose family secrets. There's got to be another angle."

Dee sighed. "All we have are questions, no answers. Ace, I'm tired. Why don't we call it a night?"

I shook my head. "Uhn uhh. I want to check out the bank. You can stay here if you like. It'll only take me about fifteen minutes."

"Okay," she said. "But you'll be quicker if I help. Where do you want to start?"

I laughed. Her competitive streak wouldn't allow her to give up as long as I was going to continue. I pointed down river.

"You can take that direction. I'll work up stream," I told her. "Watch out for 'gators."

"Humph!" she snorted. "Funny guy."

"……And snakes."

"Snakes?"

I started up river, the flashlight beam cutting through the thickets only a few feet before me. I hadn't a clue as to what I was looking for. Maybe I'd know it when I saw it. Perhaps, subconsciously, I was hoping to come across a pair of women's shoes.

I thought of the dream, with Desiree pleading for me to help her. "Don't let them get away with this," she had said. It seemed that people were determined that I would be involved in this case. …Desiree's shade in my dreams. Dee and Cook both encouraged my participation. And even Hicks, by dropping me a list of suspects who didn't want the case investigated. I was beginning to feel manipulated, powerless.

I'd felt that way, almost, from the beginning. I'd never had control over Desiree and eventually lost control of myself where she was concerned. Now here I was reacting to circumstances and hearsay. Something would have to give. I did not intend to spend the rest of my life beating back weeds, trekking through Georgia swamps in memory of ungrateful Desiree.

"Forget this!" I said, stopping in my tracks. "I'm sorry, Desiree. But I don't owe you a single thing." I turned and started for the car.

Then I heard her. I thought it was Diana at first. But her call was coming from the wrong direction.

"Adrian."

Her voice, carried by a light breeze, wafted from the river.

Stopping cold, I looked about. I called out, "Dee?" No one answered. After a moment of indecision, I started in the direction of the call.

"Diana, where are you? Did you find anything?"

Silence.

I halted. Once again the voice called to me. It had a child-like quality; but a strong, resonant undercurrent.

"Adrian," the call came. Not shouted, nor loud, but the woods around me seemed to vibrate with its force, nonetheless.

The mists from the river began to roll through the brush.

Once more... "Adrian." I wheeled around, searching for the source of the mournful beckoning. The fog thickened, blinding and disorienting.

"Here I am, Adrian," her voice came.

"Desiree?"

There she was gliding through the mists, her long white dress flowing. A tear escaped the corner of my eye. I took a deep breath and released it slowly.

As she came, the fog thickened further, hiding her for a time. Impatiently, I waited. When her form was visible again she had changed. Where I had expected to see Desiree, there stood a small child, a boy dressed in a white choir gown.

His presence seemed as natural as the night. Though I'd never seen him before I knew exactly who he was.

He came to me, stopping some fifteen feet away. "Hello, Father," he said, his gown billowing in a breeze I did not feel.

"Hello, son..." I answered without thinking. I had no son. Why was it so natural to claim this child, this apparition, as a child of my own?

I knelt and beckoned him to my outstretched arms. I loved him and wanted to embrace him as my own. I wanted to teach him. To play catch in the backyard, to push him along on his first bike, and watch tearfully as he climbs on the bus for his first day of school.

He shook his head slowly.

I mouthed the word *why*. As if in answer, he extended his palms to me. Recoiling from the streams of blood that flowed from his hands, I sprawled on my back to the ground.

"Father, help me!" he called.

I struggled to regain my balance. Then I fell backwards. I'd lost hold of the flashlight. The entire area had gone black, and the vision of the child vanished. Crawling around on my hands and knees, I searched through the forest debris. At last, my hand, finding the black cylinder, lifted it and pressed the on button in one motion. Nothing happened.

"...Father! Father, help me!"

I reached for the son that I'd never had. "Son," I whispered, taking him into my arms. I held him close to my heart, kissing his brow. My lips were warm and sticky with the blood that hemorrhaged from his every pore. I licked them. The taste was strange, but not unpleasant.

"...My son! Hold on! We'll get you some help!"

I attempted to rise and he moaned with the pain of my movement.

"No! Father, no!"

Tears began to stream down my face as my son's blood soaked my arms, chest and legs.

"Son! No! Please! No! I won't lose you! Not again! I won't!"

Juliet was absolutely radiant. I had never been more in love with her than I was at that moment. I watched from the den as she moved about the kitchen. Whenever we thought her parents weren't watching, we'd blow one another kisses or smile and gesture to meet in another part of the house to fondle.

While she prepared Sunday dinner, I tried to make myself comfortable watching the basketball game with her father. I smoked cigarette after cigarette and guzzled beers while he droned on officiously, waving his pipe and sipping twelve-year-old scotch.

"I tell you, Ace," he'd say. "This year's 'Sixers is the best basketball team ever."

I would pause and think about his statement, preparing an argument. But I thought better of it. Respectfully, I'd nod my head. And he would go on to some other nonsense that I was dying to debate. I kept my opinions to myself. You know, when your boss is also your landlord you learn a good deal of humility.

Juliet smiled at me from the kitchen. I grinned then rolled my eyes, indicating my boredom with her father. He went on talking, never noticing. I tuned him out as I concentrated on Juliet.

Man! She was beautiful; in her seventh month of pregnancy, her belly swollen and tight. She was even lovelier than the day I met her. Or rather, the day I noticed her.

It seems that she'd known who I was in high school. She was a freshman and I, a senior. She held a crush on me through that year. I barely remembered her as a boyish little ragamuffin in school. But, by the time she reached college, she had sprouted into some kind of babe.

She caught my eye at the freshman icebreaker where I was hanging out with the fellas. We were checking out the new talent on the yard. She brazenly walked up to me and introduced herself. I remembered her after we had talked for a while.

Julie was a real cutie pie. I decided to go ahead and tap it. Maybe wrap it up and put her in the stable. She was even fine enough to sport full-time.

Well, everything moved pretty quickly. Before I knew anything, I was explaining to Dee why I had to leave school, that I was in love and having a baby.

Dee laughed.

"You're having a baby?" she asked. "You don't look pregnant."

She hugged me, congratulated me, and was the "best man" in my wedding. That took a lot of work, convincing Juliet. But, she finally bought it.

Juliet was cooking a special Sunday dinner for our fifth month anniversary. I thought that this would be as good a time as any to break the news. Maybe there was no good time. But, I had to tell them. And maybe the entire thing had been a bad idea. But that was only hindsight. It would do me no good to question my decision now.

Halfway through dinner, with Terry, Juliet's father, at the head of the table, across from me, I told them. The ladies sat opposite one another. I was working on my second helping of dressing, ham, and yams (the kind with marshmallows melted on top). I took a long swig of brew; then cleared my throat.

"Ahem." They had all been talking and eating. But they stopped and looked at me. I began to feel very self-conscious. "I…. umm," I began.

"I've got something to tell you all." I didn't know how to start, or how they'd take it.

"I've ....uhh," I stammered. "I want you to know, Terry and Sheila... ...That I really appreciate what you've done for Julie and me. ...Everything. ...The job, Terry. Letting us stay with you until we can get ourselves together..."

Terry cut me off. "Ace, boy, you're family, now! What else could we do?"

He wasn't making this easy. I nodded and drew a big breath. Releasing it, I blurted out, "I joined the army last week!"

Silence prevailed. I think the television that had been left on even stopped working.

"...The army?" Juliet repeated.

I nodded, watching the puzzled expression on her face.

"You're leaving me?" she asked

"Well, in a sense. But..." I tried to explain.

"Why?" she asked pitifully.

She was so young. I was so young. I tried, again, to explain.

"Julie, we'll only be apart for a couple of months."

"...A couple of months? That's not true. I know how soldiers live. You'll find someone. And you'll send me a 'Dear John' letter."

I tried very hard not to laugh at this. But, the tension of the situation wouldn't allow it. I snickered. Fighting for composure, I quipped. "Maybe, a 'Dear Julie' letter."

Though he remained silent, Terry closed his eyes, and slowly shook his head.

"You think it's funny?" she screamed. "Do you think it's funny that you're deserting you're your wife and unborn baby?"

I sighed. I was becoming frustrated. I turned to Terry who appeared to wish I'd leave him out of it.

"You understand don't you, Terry?" I was pleading for his support, but he looked as uncomfortable as I was.

I suddenly felt very sorry for him. Here was this guy he barely knew, about to take his only daughter away from home. To top it off, I was breaking her heart in the process.

"Well..." he started slowly. "Of course, I understand, Ace."

"Daddy!" Juliet was near hysteria.

"Well, sweetie pie, I think it's a great idea. Ace is a man. He wants to live like a man and support his family on his own. I'd probably have done the same thing if I was in his position."

She didn't like that at all. She pushed her chair from the table so violently I thought she'd fall backwards. Instead, she rose more quickly than she had in several weeks.

She raced upstairs to our bedroom. Fearful that she'd trip in her excitement, I followed.

"Excuse me," I said to Terry and Sheila, embarrassed by the scene I'd caused to occur.

When I caught up to Julie, she was lying across our bed sobbing.

"Sweetheart…" I said, reaching for her.

"Get away from me," she said, pulling away. "You don't want me anymore. I'm fat and ugly and you're going away to find yourself another woman."

Her accusation was stinging. Funny thing is, had it been anyone but Juliet, she may have been right. I had never been the most faithful lover in the world.

I shook my head.

"No, baby. You're my wife," I told her. "I've never been in love before and I'll never love anyone but you. This is for the best. Believe me, please."

She turned her face to me, the tears subsiding somewhat.

"Look at me, sweetheart," I said sitting close to her. "This is me. Juliet, I'm your Romeo. I'll always be your Romeo."

She smiled; then sniffled once.

"I want to believe that," she said.

"You know it," I replied. I was holding her hand now. "All you have to do is look at me. You can see how happy you make me."

I leaned close to her ear. "Juliet," I whispered. "Juliet, I love you. I love you. I'll always love you."

Julie turned her face to me. She kissed me lightly on the mouth. She took my face into her hands; then gazed into my eyes. She was lying on her back and I lay close to her now.

"Will you come to me as soon as the baby's born?" she asked.

"Just as soon as you begin labor, I'll be there, Juliet." I had no idea if I could keep that promise or not. But I did intend to try. That's as much as I could do, I thought.

We kissed and I held her. And that night we made love, tenderly, carefully.

It was about 2:30 am that I felt the warm liquid flow over the mattress to my side of the bed. At first, I'd thought she had peed the bed.

My eyes sprang open.

"Julie?"

She didn't answer.

Suddenly, I realized what was happening. I turned on the lamp next to the bed. Juliet was sitting at the side of the bed with her back to me. I reached for her.

"Oh, Rome... Romeo..."

She sat there in shock. I called for help and we rushed Julie to the hospital.

At the hospital, I was a total klutz. I couldn't fill out the papers. I couldn't answer any questions about Julie's medical history. And I was absolutely hopeless at consoling her.

I felt guilty and found a vacant corner of the waiting area to be alone. Julie's mom had gone to the treatment room. I barely heard when the familiar voice came to me from across the room.

"Thank you, Terry. I'll see what I can do with him."

My head was turned away as I didn't want anyone to see the tears that welled in my eyes.

"Hello, baby," came the voice.

"What do you want?" I snapped.

"Aren't you going to ask me to sit down?" she replied.

I glanced at the chair beside me, and nodded once.

"Help your self, Dee," I said.

She sat.

"It's nice that married life has matured you so," she teased.

"What do you expect?" I asked.

"I didn't cause this to happen," she said, patiently. I could tell she was trying to get me to think reasonably but I wasn't having it.

"No, I did."

Diana shook her head.

"It simply happened, Ace. She'll be fine," Dee consoled me.

"No. I should have found another way to tell her I was leaving."

I was pitiful.

Dee took my hand.

"If you insist," she said. "We can go with that. It was your fault. You're an insensitive bastard."

I frowned; then looked at Dee.

"You're not being very cheerful, Dee," I said.

"No. I'm not," she replied. "You're not in a cheering up mood."

I smiled-barely.

"Sorry. I'll try harder."

"Good," she said. "Let's go. It's times like this that family should be together."

I looked over at Terry across the room pacing. I suddenly felt very immature and selfish.

I squeezed Diana's hand and nodded.

And we stood and joined Terry. He took my hand then pulled me to him for a big embrace. At that moment, Terry seemed more like a father to me than if he'd been my own father.

We had been waiting for nearly four hours when Juliet's obstetrician walked in with an unreadable expression on his face. Terry and I were both beat. We were red-eyed and crumpled. Terry's beard was a dirty shadow that aged him ten years, with its gray flecks. I wondered if his own mouth offended him as much as mine did me, tasting all sticky and sour. Regardless, we were both wrecked.

Diana, on the other hand, was daisy-fresh. I watched as she moved to greet the doctor. He was tall, with big hands and he wore glasses that made him look smart and very successful. A pang of jealousy rode through me. This man had touched my wife. …My woman. Touched her in places that I wanted to believe I was the only man to ever touch. It didn't matter that when he touched her, it had never involved candlelight, wine or caresses, that it was clinical. He had touched her with those great big fingers and who knows what kind of weird metal utensils.

"Ace…"

"Ace…"

It was Dee, getting my attention. I had zoned out.

"This is Dr. Henry," she said.

I shook those big hands of his. They were soft, fleshy, and kind of clammy. You can tell a lot about a guy from his handshake. And I could tell that Dr. Henry was no threat to me. If he wasn't gay, he was definitely soft.

Inwardly, I smiled.

"How's my wife," I asked.

He touched the corner of his glasses with his left hand and then drew a breath before answering.

"Can I call you Ace?" he asked.

I nodded.

"She's fine, Ace," he said. "There were complications, however."

I didn't speak, preparing for the worst.

"There was a cyst on her left ovary. All tests for cancer were negative."

"Cyst? Cancer?" I was trying to comprehend.

"What about our baby?" I asked.

He shook his head.

"The child was dead when she arrived," he said. "We had to take it from her. That's when we discovered the cyst."

I trembled. I wanted to hit him but it wasn't his fault. I took a deep breath and closed my eyes. Someone was holding me up. I never saw who or heard their words. I did hear Dr. Henry's words before he left.

"For what it's worth, you had a son. I'm sorry, Ace."

I had a son.

I had a son.

I had a son.

I found myself on my hands and knees in the dark woods, vomiting. The vision of the hemorrhaging child had vanished. The mists had withdrawn to the river. I picked up the flashlight and struggled to my feet.

I recalled how Julie had taken the news of our loss. Although, she did mourn, she was in much better shape than I was. I blamed myself and resolved to do better with our next child. I quit smoking and began an intense fitness regimen.

And I was fawning and attentive throughout each of Juliet's next two pregnancies. Both of the girls were healthy, strong and beautiful. But I always regretted the loss of my only son.

As I made my way back to Dee's car, I searched my pockets for gum or mints. My fingers came across a half roll of candy breath fresheners. I peeled back the paper and took all of the "O" shaped confections into my mouth. The wet coolness chased away the taste of bile and regurgitated burger and fries.

I pressed on through the woods. The ground seemed to pull at my feet, holding them down and impeding my progress. I moved along in a trance-like state, afraid to believe what had just occurred. The two dreams I'd had of Desiree could be reasoned away as alcohol induced. And of course, I had been asleep. I tried to think. Had I fallen? Hit my head, perhaps?

No. I was not injured. I was dead sober and awake. There was no way to explain the visitation. Well, no way for a sane man to explain it. And I was a sane man.... ......maybe. I decided not to try and explain it to anyone. As far as I was concerned, there was no bleeding child in he woods. No mists. No Desiree.

Presently, I came clear of the woods. Diana was sitting on the passenger side of her car waiting for me. She let down the window. I could see that she had been crying.

"Do you mind driving?" she asked. Her voice was low and lacked energy.

I shook my head. "No problem," I said.

Diana stared out at the river as I slid into the driver's seat. She turned to me.

"Did you see anything?" she asked softly.

I stiffened as my breath caught, and I prayed silently that she hadn't noticed.

"No," I lied. "Did you?"

She shook her head and turned away. "No," she answered. "No, I didn't see a thing."

I watched her for a moment and turned away. I nodded slowly. "Not a thing," I whispered and started the car.

Neither Diana nor I spoke as we made our way back to town. Highway 17 was dark and winding. The road was deserted but for the occasional semi-truck that raced pass with its payload and critical delivery deadline.

Dee broke the silence when lights from the gasoline plaza came into view. "Pull over, please. I need something to drink."

I nodded and headed for the convenience store slash fuel station slash fast-food oasis. Automobiles, semi-rigs, vans and vehicles of all sorts were jockeying for position to either enter or exit the plaza.

As I wheeled into a parking space, I cut off a shiny chrome-rimmed monster pickup truck. The cowboy in the driver's seat shot me the finger. I returned the gesture, hoping he'd stop and escalate our encounter. The events of the last day or so were beginning to work on me. Before I'd been grievous and sorrowful, but now I was really starting to boil and my anger simmered just under the surface.

Instead of getting out of his truck, the cowboy gunned his engine and burned rubber as he raced from the plaza. Several motorists veered and dodged to clear his way, and the blue lights of a highway patrol cruiser sped by in pursuit.

I grinned and slowly nodded my head.

Dee never seemed to notice the brief excitement. Without a word, she got out of the car and entered the store. Moments later, she returned with two bottles of spring water. She passed me a bottle before cracking the seal on hers. After taking a sip, she tipped the bottle into her hand. She patted her face and neck with her damp hand.

Closing her eyes, she took a deep breath and released it slowly.

"Oh, my God!" she whispered.

I remained silent, hoping Dee would explain her mood.

The radio was on and she reached over and turned it off. She turned to me. "Ace, I've got something to tell you."

I watched her face. Her voice sounded very serious and strained. She had found something in those woods after all. …Another body, perhaps? I doubted it. But something had shaken her and it seemed that it was sure to rattle me.

Blinking back tears, I prepared for the worse.

"We've always had an unspoken pact," Diana began. "We have never mentioned or referred to the night we had sex in our apartment."

She looked away.

People were passing on their way to the store or their cars. I watched them, wondering if I should respond. Wondering what was the proper response.

"Dee, I never thought it meant that much to you."

"It meant as little to me as it did to you, Ace," she replied.

Our encounter meant a great deal to me, although I had never told her. I often thought that I should have. That if I had, she and I would have been married instead of Julie and I.

"That hurt, Dee," I responded.

She ignored me.

"Ace, I shared my body with you. You were, always the single constant in my life."

She shook her head.

"What you must think of women," she said.

"I was waiting for you to say something," I asserted my alibi.

"And I was waiting on you," she said. "It's such a shame. We missed out on a great deal."

"Maybe, someday we can recapture it," I tried, encouragingly.

"You mean: Now that *she's* gone." She was referring to Desiree.

I brought my hands to the top of the steering wheel and squeezed. After the initial pain, I rested my forehead on my hands.

"I didn't mean it that way," I said. "I'm sorry."

"No," she said. "I owe you an apology. I…I had an abortion."

"You what?" I lifted my head.

"I killed our child!" She said it in a rush of emotion. "Ace, please forgive me."

"You… An abortion?"

She nodded.

I turned away to watch the cars passing by. Taking a big breath, I nodded slowly. She'd had an abortion.

I lay in bed reflecting on the events that had occurred since Saturday night:

Desiree's death

My ensuing investigation

Diana's startling (frightening) revelation.

Diana… Diana! She had been pro-choice since I don't know when. But I never thought that was the choice she would actually use. She had asked my forgiveness. I didn't need much time to think about it. Of course, I'd forgive her. She was my best friend and I loved her in a way that I'd never love anyone else ever. That included Desiree.

I rolled over to see the clock on the night table next to the bed. The numbers blazed out at me, green and glowing. They were way too bright for three o'clock in the morning.

I closed my eyes and turned away. But the digits remained etched on the backs of my eyelids. Three o'clock.

"Three o'clock already?" she murmured.

I whispered into her ear between nibbles. "Closer to four, actually."

Juliet released a breath and wriggled closer to me.

"Did you have a good time?"

I pressed myself into her hip. She reached for me.

"Not as good as if you'd been with me…mmm."

She rolled over pressing her body into mine.

"Let me make it up to you."

Juliet had never been much of a night owl. But, since we came to Stewart she had all but abandoned any nocturnal activities that kept her out past midnight. But she insisted I got out-if that's what I wanted to do. The only stipulation was that I bring it home to her at the end of the evening. I had no complaints with that. I could manage any extracurricular activity on my own time. Besides, Julie did her best to ensure that every homecoming was well worth my while.

I nibbled at her neck and she moaned, squirming against me. She gave herself to me, and I was asleep before my head rested on the pillow beside hers.

I was jolted awake by Juliet's startled squeak.

"Eek!" she screamed as she gathered the bed covers in a buddle to hide our naked bodies.

As I lay there, my eyes sprang open to stare into the angelic face of our four-year-old daughter, Janice.

"Morning, Daddy," she said with just a hint of laughter in her voice.

I returned her greeting. "Morning, Precious," I said, too embarrassed to say more than that.

Just then, her older sister, Sheila, came into the room.

"Morning, Dad. Morning, Mom."

"Morning, sweetheart," we said in unison with the covers bunched about us.

Janice giggled.

Julie spoke quietly. "Sheila, why don't you take your sister into the kitchen and fix her some breakfast?"

"Okay, Mom," she answered. Guiding her sister by the shoulder, she ordered, "Come on, Janice."

"Sheila, I saw Daddy's pee-pee."

Sheila hushed her sister. "Shh!" But she couldn't resist the urge to peep back over her shoulder. Feeling strangely violated, I flinched and pulled the covers tighter to my body. Juliet fell from the bed to the floor in laughter.

"Julie, that's not funny," I complained. "The child could be scarred for life."

Through her laughter she replied, "Nonsense! I've seen my father naked on numerous occasions and…"

"Not recently, I hope."

She stopped laughing and simply gazed into my eyes.

"Juliet?"

"No. Of course not," she answered.

I shook my finger at her. "You see? That's my point. She'll develop a sick sense of humor."

"If she does, sweetheart, I guarantee it'll come from your side of the family," she giggled. "Relax. The girl will be fine."

She stood and walked over to close the bedroom door. After pressing the button and checking the knob to ensure the room was secure, she smiled. Standing at the door, splendidly naked, she said, "Now, why don't you let down those covers and let *me* see your pee-pee?"

I thought I heard giggling from outside the door, and I held the covers tighter.

The rest of the day passed rather uneventfully. Sunday's were that way around the Edwards's house. If we didn't go to church, Julie and I would lie around all day and do practically nothing. Sometimes we'd barbeque out back or rent videos. But normally, we'd spend the day in monumental laziness.

Today was one of those lazy days. I lay sprawled across the living room couch with a ballgame playing on TV. As I dozed, I'd awake from time to time to catch the replay of a particularly dramatic play or score. Through sleepy eyes, I watched Julie stroll in from the kitchen. The apple that she held to her mouth looked cool and juicy.

"That looks good," I hinted.

"It is," she mumbled while chewing. "Want some?"

I grinned. "Uhh huh."

She came over and laid herself across me. I caressed her as she held the fruit to my lips for me to take a bite. After I chewed and swallowed, she kissed my mouth.

"Mmmmm, that tastes even better," she said.

"Where're the girls?" I asked.

"…Next door playing."

I nibbled her neck and stroked her with my fingertips.

She giggled and hunched her shoulder pushing me away.

"You'd better stop. You'll get yourself in trouble. You know you're not that young anymore."

"Well, you didn't say that last night-or this morning," I teased.

She kissed me again.

"That was last night and this morning," she whispered. "…The night and morning before this afternoon."

She giggled. "Besides, I don't think you're going to be able to pitch a triple header today."

I kissed her lips, and then answered. "You may be right," I admitted. "I guess I'll just have to call in a relief pitcher."

The tip of my tongue found her ear as she squirmed against me.

"Umm hmm," she purred. "Yes. That's my boyfriend."

That night, as Julie went through the ritual that women go through in preparation for the next day, she produced the business card that Desiree had given me the evening before. She turned from her dressing table with the tiny placard thrust towards me.

"Where did you get this?" she asked firmly.

Lying in bed, I was frozen with shock. How could I have been so careless? I searched my mind for an excuse, but none came. The pink and teal card, held forth, proclaimed my guilt like a banner across Main Street.

"Umm..."

"Don't waste your time trying to deny it," she said, accusingly. "I just hope you haven't bought a gown for me yet."

70

"Huh?"

"Darling, it's a sweet gesture, but you know we'll only end up taking it back."

"Umm..."

"Close your mouth," she said. "You're busted. You didn't buy me a gown yet, did you?"

She got up from the dressing table and searched our closets.

"Umm... No."

I had forgotten all about the military ball. It was two weeks away. Besides purchasing tickets, my own preparation was minimal. After all, the only thing I ever wore to formal functions was dressed blues. So naturally, the event was pushed to the back of my mind.

Julie sat on the bed beside me. She kissed me as I sat up dumbfounded.

"I'm sorry I spoiled your surprise."

"It's okay," I mumbled.

"Well... I don't know," she said. "You obviously want to be part of this. I'll tell you what... We'll take extended lunches tomorrow and go shopping."

"Okay."

"Now, stop pouting. I promise I won't buy anything you don't approve of."

"Okay," I said.

I didn't trust myself to say much more than that. I was afraid I might confess to something I hadn't done yet. So, without saying another word, I slid my head under the covers and tried to sleep.

I spent a restless night tossing and turning. I just knew that when Julie and I rolled up into Desiree's shop tomorrow, my world would come crashing down. In my dreams, I saw myself taking a long surreal walk to the gallows. Janice read gibberish from a thick black Dr. Seuss book. Sheila escorted me up the steps to my doom. She stood guard at my side as Juliet placed the noose around my neck.

I looked out over the crowd to see Desiree's smiling face everywhere. She was mayor, the blacksmith, the little boy with a spotted dog on a leash. They were all smiling or laughing up at me. They were all beautiful.

Julie stared into my face.

"Any last requests?" she asked.

Tears welled in my eyes. I couldn't speak. She mistook my silence for a "no".

"Very well, then," she said.

She moved to release the lever. I watched as her hand grasped the wooden handle. The crowd's laughter grew louder. Janice's reading filled my brain. I heard Juliet's faint voice in the distance.

"For sins committed…love… sentence you… hanged by the neck until…"

She pulled the lever. I heard the mechanism grind and the trap door fell. The dead weight of my body followed; then was stopped cold, as the rope snapped taut.

"No!"

"No! No, Specialist! This paper does not cover your garden variety retirement ceremony-especially Air Force type retirements.

"I suggest you get back with those people over there and make that clear to them."

I had yelled at the specialist, but I was angry with myself. I was supposed to meet Julie at Desiree's in thirty minutes. All morning, I prayed for some national emergency to keep me away from that dress shop. A small personal emergency would do the trick just as well; maybe an auto accident on the way.

I took a breath.

"Hey, listen. I'm sorry," I apologized. "Do what you can for them and come on back to the office."

He left and I placed my hands over my face.

"Man. Oh, man," I whispered. "I am going to be in so much trouble."

I glanced at the clock on the wall. It was nearly eleven-thirty; time to get going. Julie would be waiting. I signed out to lunch and headed for my car.

The drive to Desiree's Boutique was way too short. There was Julie in her car, waiting for me. She was smiling. In spite of my situation, I smiled back. She always made me feel good when she was happy. I prayed that she'd still be smiling after our little excursion.

We got out of our cars.

"Been waiting long?" I asked.

"Not very long," she answered. "How was your morning?"

I kissed her on the cheek. "Pretty good," I lied.

Desiree's shop was located in a small upscale shopping plaza. The sign, designed in Old English script, proclaimed the name of a highly tasteful establishment: Desiree's Boutique. The other businesses displayed just as much panache. Their facades were quietly stylish and fashionably understated.

I glanced around the parking lot and recognized the Bentley Desiree had driven the night we met. There were several other expensive automobiles, as well. People were doing very well in this little plaza.

As we walked through the door of the shop, a tiny bell tinkled, signaling our entrance. The delicate fragrance of a light potpourri wafted in the air. Smooth jazz played in the background, barely audible. The lighting was complimentary, designed to enhance the colors and flow of the gowns and dresses that the customers would try on.

Desiree was at the rear of the shop assisting a fairly buxom sister who wore a silver lame` number that seemed to have been created especially for her.

"Hello," she said. Or did she sing it? "Welcome to Desiree's." There was that smile. "As you can see, I'm a little tied up, right now. But feel free to look around. There's coffee and tea, if you like. I'll be with you in two minutes."

Julie nodded and smiled; then began to search through a rack of gowns. I poured myself a cup of coffee, and moved to sit in one of two wing-backed chairs that were provided for husbands who were dragged along on similar shopping tours. Before I could sit, Desiree was gliding towards Julie.

"Hello again! I'm Desiree."

"Hi. I'm Julie." The two ladies shook hands. They looked like sorors; as if they'd known each other for ages. "And this is my husband...."

"Sergeant Edwards," Desiree broke in.

"You said you'd bring your wife. I like a man who keeps his word."

She *was* good. I was taken aback and could only smile and nod.

She returned her attention to Julie.

"Julie, I take it you're looking for something for the upcoming ball."

"Yes, I am. But I haven't really seen anything that works for me yet."

Desiree smiled that beautiful smile; then reached into the rack. As if by magic, she held a sheer white gown, accentuated with shimmering sequins.

"Why don't you try on this one while I finish up with my other customer?"

"Huh," Julie said. "This just might work." Julie winked at me. "I'll be right back, Romeo."

As Julie made her way to the dressing room, Desiree completed her business with Chesty. When the woman left, Desiree called to Julie.

"Is everything alright, Julie?"

"Yes, Desiree. I'll be out in a minute."

She looked at me and smiled. I returned her stare, smiling. Suddenly, I was very warm. And began to think back on the kiss we'd shared two nights ago. I felt myself responding to the shopkeeper. Just then, Julie stepped from the dressing room. I was still holding a half cup of coffee. Startled, I released the cup and the liquid splattered at my feet.

Julie scolded. "Ace! You're making a mess!"

Desiree laughed. "Don't worry about it, Julie. Just be happy you still draw that type of reaction from your man when you enter the room." Then she began straightening the gown around Juliet.

She was very good!

The dress was magnificent! It sparkled and glistened with a brilliance that softened and intensified in a pulsating rhythm that seemed to match my heartbeat. The sight of Julie standing before me; the sheer fabric revealing the tops of her breasts, melding to her form and gently tapering away reminded me why I loved her so much. She was literally breathtaking!

Julie smiled. "Do you like it?" she asked.

"Oh Yeah," I answered, standing there with what I could only imagine was the dumbest expression ever.

She chuckled.

"Ace, I think you ought to clean up that mess you made."

"Umm. Okay. I'll get right on it."

Using some napkins I found on the table next to the coffee, I patted the carpet dry; then wiped my shoes.

"So Julie, what do you think?" asked Desiree.

Julie glanced at me. "Ace?"

I paused before responding. "How much is it?"

The women glanced at one another, smiling.

"It's very reasonable," Desiree answered.

"We'll take it," said Julie.

I might as well have never asked the question. That dress was sold the instant it left the rack.

Julie left to remove the gown. Desiree smiled at me once more. She was taunting me. She never said a word. And her expression was benign. But she was taunting me, all the same.

I was uncomfortable, and she knew that. She coyly toyed with me in a way that no one could notice but me. I was powerless to acknowledge her game. And it would have been down right foolish to expose her there in the shop. So, I endured the torture.

Julie changed out of the dress and we left it with Desiree to accomplish some minor alterations. She had said that it was very reasonably priced. It definitely was not. But it did do exactly what it was designed to do. I phoned into the office and asked my assistant to cover for me. I told her I was feeling *pretty sick* and was going home to bed. It was only half a lie and I was certain she knew it. I would hear about this for some time. To top it off, she became *pretty sick* four afternoons the following month.

So, Juliet and I spent the rest of the afternoon doing just about the same thing we had done half the weekend.

We were dressing, hurriedly trying to finish before the girls came home. I was I still a little paranoid about being seen naked by my younger daughter.

"Do you think she's attractive?" Julie asked the question while she examined her thighs in the mirror. This was very dangerous ground. There is a list of 'no-win' questions women seem to pass down from generation to generation. There's no right answer. But men, being men, of course, we attempt to answer anyhow.

"Huh?" Good answer. That will satisfy her.

She looked away from the mirror. "So what do you think is most attractive about her?"

"About who?" I played dumb. Desiree, of course.

"Don't play dumb, Ace. Desiree, of course."

Of course. Okay, why didn't she just ask me if I thought she was getting fat? Or what was her worst feature? These were perfectly good questions to have a fight over. This Desiree question was going to get me sent to the couch for the night.

Of course I thought she was attractive. She was buxom and narrow at the waist, and tall enough to carry that full-figure with class and grace. And she was stylish, yet low key. She was probably the most beautiful woman I had ever met, I thought.

"She's alright, I guess. I never really noticed her in that way," I lied.

"Well, I think she noticed you."

I hoped she hadn't notice me flinch. "Julie, I think she was just working to make a sale."

Desiree really didn't pay very much attention to me at all. Julie couldn't possibly have picked up on any vibe between us. I dismissed the matter. She was only fishing-or was she? Besides, I wasn't guilty of anything-not really. I felt very uncomfortable. As I lifted my leg to put on my pants, I stumbled and spun to my back on to the disheveled bed.

Julie giggled. "I still got it," she said.

"I guess you do," I replied.

I threw the trousers into a corner of the room.

"I'll just take a nap," I said, slipping beneath the covers.

She came to me, tucked me in, and gave me a kiss. "The gown is beautiful, Sweetheart. Thank you very much."

"You're welcome, Julie. I love you," I said, just before I drifted off to sleep.

I awoke from the nostalgic dream feeling melancholy and regretful. The realization had come to me that I'd thrown away everything real in my life to pursue an unattainable fantasy.

I reached for the phone on the night table. In the dark of the room, I pressed the numbers. Part of me hoped I had dialed the wrong number. The phone rang in my ear. Feeling a wave of panic, I thought to hang up. Then her sleep-groggy voice echoed across the line.

"Um….. Hello?" she sighed into the phone.

I didn't speak. I wanted to, but I just didn't. I'd lost my nerve.

"Hello," she said again.

I hung up the phone without speaking. I felt embarrassed and lost. What could I have said? How could I tell her, after all these years that maybe-just maybe-I'd made a mistake?

I was startled by the ringing of my own phone. Once more the tone sliced through the darkness. The phone continued to ring. Sitting up in bed, I turned on the lamp. It rang again. I reached and lifted the receiver to my ear. My hand shook with emotion. And my voice quavered as I tried to sound as though I'd been asleep.

"Ace?"

Aww, no! It was her.

"Yes," I answered. She had used the call back feature. It's a shame the things you can do with a phone these days.

"Ace, I heard about Desiree. I hope you're doing alright."

I sighed heavily. "Julie, I'm…" She cut me off before I could finish the apology.

"Ace, why don't you sleep on that, and call me in a couple of weeks?"

"Uhh…. Okay."

"Good night," she said; then hung up before I could reply.

I glanced at the clock. Three-Oh-Eight. I'd only been asleep about three minutes. It had seemed like so much longer. Suddenly, I was very sleepy. But I dreaded closing my eyes. Like scrooge, I feared a visitation from some ghost of my past, present or future. There must be a beer in the refrigerator, I thought. Then I thought better of it. That would surely trigger some type of depressing recollection.

I lied there straining to keep my eyes from closing. I knew that eventually, they would, and sleep would wash over me. Then I would once again plunge into a dream world more real than my waking hours.

I'd experienced these moments once. They were painful enough the first time. I whispered into the night. "Why do I have to live this all over again?"

If there was a reply, I never heard it. Sleep had overtaken me and I awoke to the buzzing of my alarm clock. I turned it off, grateful that I had slept the remainder of the night with no further disturbances.

I dragged myself from bed and accomplished the morning ritual of preparing for work. The entire time, my mind drifted between thoughts of Desiree and Julie. My stomach grumbled. But I didn't feed it. I had a belly full of guilt, mourning and regret. And the thought of breakfast on top of it all just wasn't that appetizing.

As I drove into work, the news anchor on the radio announced that Desiree's funeral would be held on Saturday morning. That announcement added to a progressively worsening stomachache.

I pulled the car into a parking space and made my way to the office. As I entered, the entire staff watched me with a kind of deer-in-the-headlights stare. There was the type of silence that makes you suspect you were the topic of conversation.

The normal buzz of gossip continued after I seated myself at my desk. I closed my eyes and rubbed them for a moment.

"Did you hear about the funeral?"

I uncovered my eyes and opened them slowly. It was Dee. She looked as though she had not slept all night. I wouldn't say her hair was a mess, but to say it was off wasn't a stretch. And her eyes had that just-been-crying puffiness.

I nodded. "Uh huh."

"Are you alright?" she asked.

I chuckled. She actually looked worse than I felt-and that was mighty bad.

"Considering the circumstances, I suppose I'm doing pretty good," I answered.

"Well," she corrected.

"Huh?"

"Well," she said. "You're doing pretty well."

She was in a mood; and I felt her pain.

I grunted. "I'm doing pretty well. What about you, baby girl? How you doin'?"

"Not so good," she said.

I wanted to scream.

"I've got a headache. I did not sleep all night long. I'm starting to have very vivid hallucinations. And to top it all off; my feet are swollen!"

I tried not to laugh.

"Oh," I said. "Does one have anything to do with the other?"

She shook her head. "Ace, I sure hope so. If not, I'm losing my mind."

It was going around.

"You said you were having hallucinations?" I urged her to talk about it, though I had no intentions to share my experiences.

She took a seat next to my desk. She looked around to be sure no one else was in ear shot.

"Ace, I told you that I didn't see anything in the woods last night."

I nodded. I had not believed her. But I was so shaken from my own experience that I didn't have the energy to get involved with whatever was bugging Dee at the time.

She continued. "Well, I don't think I was totally honest when I told you that."

I tilted my head to the side, not quite comprehending. "So, you did find something?"

She shook her head. "No. But I did see something."

Now she really had my attention. I looked around. Everyone was caught up in their own little office activities. It was not unusual for Dee and me to spend time at one another's desk, comparing notes or exchanging advice. They all ignored us now.

"I saw a child," she said.

"A what?" I was caught completely off guard.

I must have shouted because everyone stopped what they were doing and looked at us. When they returned to their business, she went on.

"A small boy. Our aborted son," she whispered, emphatically.

Although, I believed her, I stared as if I didn't. And I didn't tell her about my own experience with the vision of a little boy whom I was certain was my own lost child. I waited for her to continue. And she waited for my reaction, which I refused to let show.

Dee mistook my silence for disbelief. "I know it sounds crazy," she said. "But, he spoke to me. I held him in my arms. I knew it when I saw him. I knew he was ours."

I remained silent. I wanted to ask her how she could be sure he was ours. I wanted to ask her if ours was the only child she'd killed. I just didn't speak. It would have been too cruel.

She went on. "In his eyes, I saw myself abort him. There I was on that table. Ace, it was awful." Her voice broke. I was afraid she would break down right there in the office.

I stopped her.

"Dee, maybe we'd better do this someplace else."

She shook her head. "No. I'm okay."

"Well, I'm not." I didn't want to hear anymore. I was afraid I might sympathetically tell her my own ghost story. I changed the subject.

"I'm hungry," I lied. "Why don't we go get some breakfast? We can talk at the diner."

Dee and I signed out and walked over to the diner across the street. The place bustled with activity of the normal breakfast crowd. I felt a nudge of paranoia as we searched the room for an empty table. Some folks looked up and nodded. But, most ignored us as though we were completely invisible. Sometimes you can get so caught up in your own life that you forget other people have a story to tell-if they chose to tell it. Even as small as Hinesville was, it was conceivable that there were people who didn't know-much less care-about mine and Desiree's story.

We sat in an empty booth in back of the place. This was our booth; Desiree's and mine. We'd shared many breakfasts here. We'd shared our dreams. …..Told our life stories……. …Shared secrets.

One morning when she was particularly playful, Desiree massaged my crotch underneath the table with her nylon covered feet. I had tried to act as

85

if nothing was going on. She didn't quit, even when the elderly waitress, Lucy, came over to check on us. She continued as she told Lucy we had everything we needed. If Lucy noticed what was going on, she sure didn't show it.

Desiree smiled and chatted between bites of toast or bacon and eggs. I tried to remain as calm as she was but found my arousal increasingly difficult to contain.

"Ace!"

"Yes, I like that." I must have whispered it.

"Ace, Lucy asked you a question."

"Huh?" I grunted, blinking through blurry eyes.

"She wants to know what you're going to have," Dee said.

I must have drifted to sleep for a moment. "Uh… Just coffee, Lucy. Thanks." At that moment, I wasn't sure if I was awake or dreaming.

Lucy scribbled on a pad and walked away.

Dee stared at me, skeptically. "Where were you?"

"What?" I felt an uncomfortable stiffness.

"Don't try that," she said. "You left."

What did she mean, I "left"? Did I physically disappear? If so, this was way beyond anything I was prepared to comprehend.

"I did not leave. I've been sitting right here in front of you since we sat down." I really needed to adjust myself.

She agreed. "Yes, you were. But, where were your thoughts?"

"No place," I lied. "I was listening to you."

She challenged me. "So, what did I say?"

"You said that you......." My voice trailed off as she glared at me. "I can't remember. I don't have to tell you what you said. You know what you said." I was embarrassed, and was trying to play off the situation.

She clucked. "Uh huh. I didn't say anything at all."

That wasn't fair. I frowned and took a deep breath, releasing it slowly. I really didn't need this crap.

Dee continued. "And you just sat there with a dumb expression on your face. It was as if you were looking right through me. Like there was someone else sitting in my place."

Then comprehension seeped into her face. Her voice softened. "Was it her you were thinking of?"

We stared into each others eyes. I saw the pain in hers, and felt the tears as they began to well in mine. I nodded slowly. "Yeah," I said. "I'm sorry. I guess I *was* a little preoccupied."

My erection had passed now, and I hoped Dee wouldn't press me to tell her what I had been thinking about. I guess this was my lucky day, of sorts. She was a bit preoccupied, herself. She sighed, and nodded slowly. Then, dismissing the matter, entirely, she changed the subject. I was grateful.

"Okay. What do you think of my hallucination?" she asked. "Do you suppose I'm losing my mind?"

I chuckled. "I suppose you could be." Dee frowned. "But I doubt it.
I've known you a long time. And Dee, you're as pragmatic as they come.
Do you think maybe you've got a little fatigue working there? I mean,
maybe you're just stressed. You've never experienced hallucinations
before, have you?"

She shook her head. "Uh uh. No. Never."

Lucy brought our coffee and left.

"Well." I hesitated a moment before finishing my thought. "There's
definitely a little guilt at work here."

Dee considered what I'd said. She sighed then agreed. "Yes. I guess so.
But why now?"

I didn't answer.

She broke the silence with an apology. "I'm sorry, Ace."

"You don't have to apologize to me, Dee. I can't imagine how awful it
must have been for you." I touched her hand.

She nodded. "Thanks. We've got work to do. Why don't we forget about
it? ...For now."

There was nothing I would have rather done more. Though dismissive of
Dee's vision, it struck me as strange-relatively-that she would experience
visitations. I wondered if the entire town would begin receiving visits from
ghosts of their past. Had Desiree's death opened some bizarre door-way for
the dead? Now that was crazy.

What was most likely was that Dee had experienced a sympathetic reaction from my own hallucinations. They say people can become so close that they finish one another's sentences. Or communicate complex thoughts without speech. Perhaps I had, unconsciously, communicated my experiences to Dee.

Whatever the cause, we agreed to shelve the subject for a while. After all, we were already deep in the middle of an existing mystery. If Dee really was going mad, we figured we would find out sooner or later. I barely suppressed a grin. In a kind of sick way, I was glad Dee was seeing visions. I was grateful I wasn't the only one losing his mind.

"Ace?" Her voice cut into my thoughts.

I answered her, startled. "Yeah?" She frowned.

"You know we've got to back to the crime scene."

I released a heavy sigh and shook my head.

She nodded. "….In the day time, I mean."

I rationalized my reaction. "Dee, we've been there. We didn't find anything."

"It was dark," she said. "And it was late. We were stressed out-and even a little angry at one another." When she said that last part, the trace of a smile played at her mouth and her eyes twinkled a bit.

"We don't even know if that is the crime scene," I reasoned.

"Ace, that's the only lead we've got until we can place Desiree with someone at three o'clock Sunday morning."

I frowned.

She really was a glutton for punishment. And I did not want to go back to that river bank another time. I was afraid of what I'd see. The memories of that place had become hurtful. Desiree and I had even used it as a rendezvous spot once or twice. We had made love on a concrete picnic table beneath the pavilion.

I recalled how she had responded to me as she sat in my lap. I could almost taste her kiss; feel the heat of her body against me. Smell the scent of her perfume.

"We're going back," Dee declared, firmly.

I groaned and hoped she'd misunderstood its origin.

"Sergeant Edwards, you're a very lucky man." – Lt. Col. Alexander "Bud" McKensie

CHAPTER 2

Once again we pulled into the park. I eased the car over the gravel drive, wincing the entire way. Little two-seater sports cars don't handle dirt driveways very well. Dust and rock flew from beneath the over-sized tires. And I thought I heard a ping from one of the stones hitting the passenger side fender.

"Hope I don't scratch my new paint job," I whined.

"You really should sell this super charge phallus," Dee advised. "Get yourself a car more suitable for a man your age."

"As far as I can tell, a red sports car is completely suitable for a man my age."

"You think it impresses the babes, don't you?' she chided.

"Doesn't it?" I countered.

She shook her head. "Not if they're about anything-no one of substance, anyway."

"Huh. Do large breasts qualify as substance?"

"No, Ace. They don't," she answered going along with the joke.

"…Unless there filled with silicone, of course."

I laughed.

She continued. "Really, you'd do just as well if you drove something more conservative."

"Well, my goodness, Dee. Was that a compliment?" I teased.

She thought for a moment. "I suppose it was," she answered. "I didn't mean too. It just slipped out."

I grinned. "Well…. Thank you, anyway. But, I'm keeping the car."

"Never doubted it," she said. "Suit yourself, Romeo."

I nodded. "Suit yourself, Romeo" she said. It's funny. That's the same thing Julie had said when I pulled up to the house in that brand new *candied-apple red* sports car. She came out to the driveway in response to me blowing the horn like a mad man. It was an early spring afternoon; but it felt just like Christmas morning to me.

I sat behind the wheel making *vroom-vroom* sounds with my mouth. The girls had both piled in and were already practicing breaking all the gadgets and buttons they could find.

"What do you think?" I asked, grinning.

"Where is your car?" she asked.

Julie stood there with her hands on her hips like an exasperated mommy.

"Can I keep it?" I asked. "I'll feed it, and walk it, and clean up after it. You'll never know it's around."

"Ace, it's a car; not a puppy." She said flatly.

"Please."

"Ace, where's your car?" She asked more sternly.

"At the dealer," I replied, my heart sinking.

She crossed her arms. "Did you sign anything?"

"No, Baby," I said.

"Get out," she said.

"Huh?"

"Get out!" she repeated.

I got out of the car and she replaced me behind the wheel. She turned the key and the engine roared. I watched as she changed gears and backed to the end of the drive. Then she pressed it forward. The car lunged ahead.

The girls tumbled over one another in the back seat, giggling as she jerked to a stop.

She looked up at me from behind the wheel, smiling.

"You're going to need another job," She said.

"Not a problem."

"Suit yourself, Romeo. Let's go sign the papers."

"Thanks, Sweetheart." I leaned through the window and kissed her. But when I reached for the handle to open the door I heard the automatic lock click.

"I'll drive," she said.

Strapping into the passenger seat, I mumbled my disapproval. The girls giggled in the backseat.

That car was my only remaining asset from the marriage. It was old. It needed constant repair. The insurance coverage was too high. Tires were too expensive. And it seemed that someone was always trying to write me a ticket for one thing or another. But it was paid for. And it was a link to what may have been the happiest time of my life.

As a matter of fact, the first time Desiree and I made love was in that car. I'd had it for exactly one day. Julie had asked me to pick up her gown from the shop during my lunch hour. Naturally, I forgot.

I was actually one block away from home when it occurred to me. I turned around and fought rush hour traffic back into the business district. When I pulled into the boutique's parking lot, I noticed Desiree's car was missing. I felt a pang of disappointment. I didn't know if it was for the fact that I couldn't get the dress or that I wouldn't get to see Desiree.

Just then, I noticed the open sign in the front window. Great! I could still pick up the dress. Desiree must have an assistant running the place. That disappointed feeling persisted.

"Hello! May I help you?" sang the young woman's voice as I passed through the door.

"Umm, yes," I said, producing the claim ticket. "I'm here to pick up my wife's gown."

"Sergeant Edwards!"

That lovely voice was followed by one of the most beautiful visions I'd even seen. Desiree glided through the curtains of the storage room to greet me at the counter. I attempted a Billy Dee in Mahogany vibe. I wasn't sure if I was pulling it off or not.

"Good afternoon, Desiree. How have you been?"

"Fine, thank you," she replied. "And, yourself?"

"Oh. Fine."

"And, how's Mrs. Edwards?" she asked.

"Oh. She's... Fine... Fine! Everybody's fine."

Desiree smiled as she took the ticket from my hand and passed it to the young woman behind the counter. "Lisa, would you get the sergeant's gown for me?"

"That's my wife's gown, Lisa," I said.

94

"Of course, Sergeant Edwards," Lisa replied, respectfully. But it didn't come across that way.

Desiree chuckled. Her laugh was soothing.

"You did that on purpose," I accused.

"Perhaps," she said, hinting that she could possibly be guilty.

And I knew that by no stretch of imagination was she possibly innocent of anything.

She smiled. And I grinned. It was a conspiratorial exchange that I hoped Lisa would not notice when she returned.

"I didn't notice your car outside," I said. "Is something wrong?"

"No," she replied. "I just didn't like the stereo system. I'm having it replaced."

"The car?" I asked.

She laughed.

"No," she said, smiling. "But I did consider it."

I stared into those brown eyes. Small flecks of emerald sparkled. Hypnotic. Mesmerizing. I was lost in those eyes. But it did not matter. I was exactly where I wanted o be.

"Here's your gown, Sergeant Edwards," Lisa said.

"Um…thanks, Lisa."

She slipped a cellophane cover over the dress as she pretended not to notice that something was going on between Desiree and me.

I took the dress from her. "Thank you, ladies," I said. "I appreciate all your help."

"You're quite welcome," Desiree replied. "Hopefully, we can do business again in the future."

"Oh, no doubt about it," I said smoothly. I turned to walk out as I said goodbye.

Before I reached the door Desiree called after me.

"Oh, Sergeant Edwards.... I wonder if you could do me a favor?"

I turned around. "That's Ace," I corrected.

"I believe that's Adrian," she corrected me.

I allowed a low chuckled. "Huh. Okay... Adrian," I conceded. "What can I do for you, Dez?"

"That's Desiree," she said, smiling.

"Never Dez?" I shook my head as I asked the question.

"Never Dez," she answered, shaking her head slowly, still smiling.

"Oh. Excuse me." I tried to throw a little Denzel in as I apologized. "What can I do for you... Desiree?"

"Much better," she said. "I like the way you say my name. You can give me a ride home-if it won't be a problem."

My mind said, "No! No! Absolutely, NO!"

But I heard my mouth say, "Of course. Not a problem at all."

The voice in my head said, "You are already late getting home. You are trying to catch a beating!" But there was another voice which said, "Do this

96

thing, Man! Do this! Don't you dare pass up this fine opportunity! Julie will understand. Anyone would. DO IT!"

"Good!" she said. "Just give me a moment to get myself together."

She stepped into the storage room, leaving me standing uncomfortably with Lisa. A moment later she returned carrying a large purse. And she was stunningly dressed. She had been wearing a generic looking white smock. It was neat and very professional. I didn't have a clue that she was so well dressed beneath it. The charcoal-gray pin-striped business suit was a statement of stark contradiction. The jacket was form-fitting and flared at the waist. Her sheer black blouse, layered with dazzling gold chains, revealed the slightest hint of her voluptuous breasts. The skirt, which would have seemed way too short on any other woman, helped to accentuate long shapely legs. And sheer black panty hose guided those legs into stiletto-heeled patent leather shoes that captured and released rays of light as she walked. The shoes gave the effect, with each step, of intermittent explosions of lightning, flashing from beneath her feet. To top it all off, her collar was flipped up in a street-tough manner that belied her pure femininity.

Desiree was, without qualification, the most beautiful woman I had ever met. Though she was thoroughly sensual, she had an ability to mask her sensuality. Or rather to tone it down to whatever level the situation required. At that moment, the volume was all the way up. It seemed that I could feel an electric current flow between us. My skin tingled and my mouth was, suddenly dry. I felt a bead of perspiration trickle down my back as I struggled to appear composed.

She pretended that my staring made her uncomfortable. "Is something wrong?" she asked.

"No. Not a thing," I answered, my gaze alternating between those long tight legs and her full, barely concealed bosom.

Lisa giggled as she slowly shook her head. Desiree smiled.

"Good night, Lisa," she said. "Thanks for locking up."

"You're welcome," she replied. "Good night, Sergeant Edwards."

I nodded to Lisa as I watched Desiree stroll pass me to stop at the door, waiting for me to open it.

"That's quite an outfit," I remarked, opening the door.

"Thank you," she said as she allowed her lashes to flutter just enough. "I wore it just for you."

Now she was teasing me. "You did not," I said, exposing the lie.

"No, I didn't," she confessed. "But I will wear it again. ….Any time you'd like me to."

She was very good at being very bad!

I laughed. "In that case, you may need two or three more just like it."

She laughed. "Hmm. On the other hand, I just may be able to come up with something that you'll like much better."

I gazed into her eyes. And she returned my gaze. I didn't comment. It's not that I didn't have anything to say. In my mind, there was only one logical reply. But I wasn't feeling as confident as I normally would have in a situation like this. She was obviously in control here. And I was absolutely powerless. I had the sense that was about to take a very long and perilous ride. My only hope was to get away before it began.

"Where do you live?"

"Not far," she replied. "Is this your car?" She pointed to the red speedster.

"Yeah, it is," I said, shuffling over to open the door for her.

I helped her in. And as she adjusted to make herself comfortable, her skirt moved up to reveal even more of her thigh. If I thought I'd seen all there was to see, I was wrong. She pulled the skirt down when she was settled. It was a wasted effort. The hemline, merely, slid up another fraction the moment her hand went away.

Watching her attempt to discreetly manage her skirt gave me a thrill I never would have expected. I took a long deep breath, and hoped she hadn't noticed that my hands were trembling. I also hoped I would be able to drive without killing us both.

After carefully placing the gown in what passed for a back seat, I slid in. Desiree inhaled deeply. "New car?"

"Yeah," I said, grinning. "I got it yesterday. What do you think?"

"I like it. It looks good on you."

"Thanks," I said.

I stared at her seated next to me. She was feline-like; relaxed with a confident awareness that indicated she could be dangerous with the least provocation. Her beautiful legs flexed as she pointed her toes in the high-heels. And she released a low moan while sinking into the seat.

"Ummmm."

I started the car. She turned on the radio and tuned in a jazz station. The cut was slow, sultry, and sexy.

"I love jazz music," she said. "It's so relaxing. It let's you settle down and do quiet things. There are no expectations. It let's you just...be."

I chuckled.

"What about Hip-Hop?" I asked.

She shook her head. "No. It's okay, but Hip-Hop tries to force you; to make you be and do what it wants you to."

I thought about that for a moment; then determined that she had a point. Hip-Hop was in your face telling you what to do and how to do it. It even boasted about who, when and where. Jazz, simply, puts you in the mood. And let's you figure out the rest.

By now I was getting some pretty good ideas.

"I really haven't had an opportunity to see what this car can do," I said. "Why don't we go for a little ride?"

"Sure," she said. "Whatever you like."

I put the car in gear, and pulled into traffic.

When she eased her seat into a reclining position, I imagined myself lying on top of her. An involuntary moan escaped my throat. She smiled at me; then closed her eyes.

I drove through town with the tinted windows raised so we wouldn't be recognized by anyone who may have decided to meddle. It was well after five now, and people were scurrying around, shopping and getting hair done, and paying bills-and rushing home before spouses could realize they had been hold up in hotels with lovers all afternoon.

The music played, and she hummed along with each song, seeming to claim it as her own. Though her voice was not particularly musical, it affected me in a way that no one else's ever had. I'd have paid to hear her sing-as long as I was the only audience present.

I turned onto a deserted highway and punched the accelerator as I shifted into high gear. The car responded by smoothly, gliding forward. The engine purred as if this was the work out it had been waiting for. The trees of the dense woods were a kaleidoscopic blur, barely noticed as we raced along.

Desiree stretched and opened her eyes. She commented about the time, wondering if my wife would be concerned about my coming home late.

I grinned nervously.

"I think she'll understand," I said.

"She most certainly, will not", I thought.

Desiree laughed. "I doubt that she will."

101

I laughed along with her. "Probably not," I agreed. "What about your husband? Will he mind my giving you a ride?"

"No, he won't mind."

"He won't?" I asked.

"He might-if he knew. But, I'm not going to tell him. Are you?"

"Oh, no!" I replied. "I am not!"

And we both laughed.

She raised her seat.

We had whizzed past dirt roads and goat paths for some time. We'd passed several other vehicles and left them well behind. By my reckoning, we had entered and left three counties in less than an hour's time.

Desiree looked around. She seemed to be getting her bearing, as if she had been disoriented.

"There's an intersection about three miles up. Make a right and follow that road for a while."

I followed her instructions. Turning the corner, I kicked the gas and watched the heart stopping image of blue lights fill my rear view mirror.

"Ah, man!" I moaned.

The siren whirred, and I pulled over. A tall, lanky deputy got out of the sheriff's car. The early evening sun stretched his shadow several feet before him. I watched in the mirror, as he sauntered up. His "Smoky Bear" hat and reflective sunglasses hid his eyes and any sort of emotion.

"Nice car," he said, as he stood looking down at me.

"Thanks," I replied. "Just bought it yesterday."

"Uh huh."

He looked the car up and down. The brilliance of candy-apple red reflected in his shades. I couldn't help admiring the image of myself sitting in that beautiful machine with a beautiful woman by my side.

I must have looked too satisfied, because he sneered when he asked if I knew why he stopped me.

"Uhh….yeah. I guess I do." I handed him my license.

"You were goin' kinda fast."

He reached behind him and pulled out the familiar ticket pad. Just then, Desiree stretched over me and looked up at the deputy.

"Hello, Deputy Hicks," she said.

"Ms. Desiree? Is that you?"

He stopped writing and put his pad away.

"What are you doin' way out here?"

He was grinning like a fool now. And I could tell they were old friends.

"Just taking an afternoon drive," she replied.

"Yeah? Nice day for it, too," he said

"Deputy, this is Sergeant Edwards," she introduced us.

"Glad to meet you, Sarge."

He shook my hand and passed back my license.

"Well, I'ma let ya'll go'one 'bout ya'll business. I gotta git," he said.

"Sarge, you take care."

"Yeah… You too, Deputy," I said.

"Hicks, you be careful," Desiree offered. "And don't be a stranger. You give me a call sometime. Alright?"

"Alright… I'll do that. You have a good evening now, Dez."

"Never Dez," she had told me.

I watched Deputy Hicks get into his car and drive away before pulling back onto the road. Desiree commented about my driving so slowly.

"In case you hadn't noticed, I just nearly got a ticket," I told her.

"Humph," she snorted. "He couldn't have written you a ticket had he wanted to."

I asked her why.

She grinned.

"He's out of his jurisdiction. He was just playing with your head. He probably has a little honey stashed out here someplace. He saw your car speeding, and decided to throw his weight around."

"You think?" I asked

"Yeah," she replied. "It gets him off. Men! Always trying to run things."

She laughed at her joke. I didn't think it was funny. But I had to admit that she had a point. Since then, Hicks took care of me like I was his own brother. And if anyone else in the area wrote me a ticket, he got it squashed. I had Desiree to thank for that.

I followed her directions and we ended up at a small fishing park. The place was a mile down a dusty back road. It was less a park than a clearing in the woods. A stream flowed by the grassy area and widened considerably there. Desiree told me that folks come and cane fish off the bank there. But, usually, it was deserted.

It was certainly peaceful, I thought. Then wondered how often she parked her-and with how many others.

"Come here often?" I asked.

"Yes," she replied.

I remained silent.

"But I've never brought anyone with me before."

I smiled.

"So, I'm your first?" I asked.

She laughed.

"You like being the first?"

"Well, if not the first, at least the illusion that I am," I confided.

"I'll see what I can do about maintaining that illusion," she said, earnestly.

The sun was setting, and bright diamonds of light danced upon the water, as shards of green danced in her eyes. I stared into them. It was a moment that could have lasted forever, total bliss. And I required nothing else.

For the first time in my life, I was complete…happy.

I must have made her uncomfortable.

"What's wrong?" She asked.

"Nothing," I replied. "I just…" I paused, searching for the word that would best describe my affection for her. "I just like you."

She grinned.

"I certainly hope so," she said seriously, those eyes still shining though dusk quickly approached.

"There was once a boy in my life," she said.

She stared out the window at the water as she spoke.

"We were so young then," she went on. "And he was so beautiful. Not feminine, the way some young men are beautiful. He was straight and tall and strong. And he was good."

I wanted to hold her now. I was puzzled at her mood, unsure what to say. I was unsure if I should say anything at all. I waited for her to go on.

"We were young. And we were lovers," she said. "We'd meet at a little clearing near a stream; a lot like this one. One night while he was on his way home, they stopped him. They beat him. And they killed him. And they cut him into pieces. It was awful. He was so beautiful. He was gone. I loved him so much. But I never cried."

She continued to stare out the window and I took her hand. She squeezed mine in return. Then there was that smile.

"Can I kiss you?" I asked.

She kind of giggled.

"You didn't ask last week."

She was right. I didn't ask that Saturday night. It was impulsive and I was bold.

I didn't feel that way that this moment. I was unsure of myself. A part of me hoped that she'd say no. That she would save me from myself. Prevent my going down a road from which I knew I would never return.

"I know," I said. "I think I may have been out of line then. I don't want you to think that I'm assuming anything. I really like you. I want your permission."

She leaned towards me. The sun had set. She was a beautiful silhouette cast in green by the glow from the car's dashboard lights. Sensual jazz played neglected for the moment.

I suppressed the urge to reach for her.

"Yes," she said, simply.

We kissed.

It was tender and gentle. She reached for my hand. I held hers. Time stopped. Then, as if responding to some pre-determined signal, together, we were swept away by a torrential passion. In its wake, the wave of emotions left us clutching and grasping, as if struggling to stay afloat. Powerless to resist its force, we gave in.

Gasping for breath, she panted, "I need you."

I held her and kissed her and touched her.

"Forever," I said. "Forever." I was unable to manage more.

The pain of wanting was becoming unbearable. We arranged ourselves into positions that allowed us better access to one another. The tight confines of the small automobile proved all the space we required.

The car seemed as big as a universe. Our movements were fluid, as if choreographed and practiced for a lifetime. I'd never made love with such intensity. It was, at once, pain and ecstasy. I had heard it described that way, but only now, understood the meaning.

I strove for fulfillment, but prayed it would never end.

Somewhere in the distance, I heard myself call her name. And that same voice declared love so empathically that it frightened me to hear it.

I kissed her face and tasted the tears that rested there, as tears of my own welled in the corners of my eyes.

I loved her. There was nothing I could do to prevent it. I loved her. And that was going to ruin my life. I knew that, as surely as I knew my name. I loved her.

It had lasted an eternity, it seemed, but was only minutes.

We talked while we dressed. There was no mention of a future together. Nor alibis. Nor plans. We spoke as casually if we had only just shaken hands.

She applied make up while I drove. We talked about our families. I told stories about the girls. And she told me about her daughter.

Her little girl was 13 years old and lived in Louisiana with Desiree's aunt. I didn't ask why. It wasn't important. And it wasn't any of my business. That part of her life didn't really exist to me.

Desiree's house was situated in back of the town's most exclusive-and expensive-subdivision. It was the largest in the area, and sat well back from the street. The enormous lawn was very well cared for. I felt a twinge of jealousy as I pulled into the driveway. She had explained to me that her husband was away on temporary duty, so I was fairly at ease about dropping her off.

It was a beautiful palatial mansion. "Dress makers do pretty good in this town," I said.

"I get by pretty well" she said. Then she gave a little laugh, as if she'd told a private joke.

"Yeah? More than just well, I'd say."

"Yes," she said cryptically. "We dabble in a little real estate. We've been blessed. Perhaps, you'd like to get in on one of our deals-if you're a good boy, that is."

"How am I doing so far?"

She laid her hand on my thigh. "You're off to a good start," she said.

But I couldn't shake the feeling that this should've been my home; and my wife.

I didn't know her husband. But I thought he must have been an awful man to neglect a woman like Desiree. Why else would she have sought comfort in my arms? I had nothing to give her. I could never have supported her the way he could.

He took her for granted, and he was a fool, I thought. He deserved exactly what he was getting.

"Well," she said. "Thank you for the ride home."

I resisted the urge to laugh. "You're welcome," I said.

She smiled.

"What's the deal with you and the deputy?" I asked her.

"Hicks?"

"Uh huh."

"We're friends," she answered.

"Close friends?"

"I guess you could say that," she said. "Fairly close. I've known him a long time. We have.....History."

"He called you Dez," I observed. She had corrected me when I called her that.

"Well... Hicks is different. He doesn't play by the same rules as everybody else. If it will make you feel better, you can call me Dez, too."

I suddenly felt childish and petty.

"Just me and Hicks?" I asked.

"Just you and Hicks."

"No. That's okay. I like Desiree better," I said

"Good." She kissed me. "Don't worry about Hicks. You'll be glad you met him. He's a very good man to know."

"I'm sure he is," I said.

I had already forgotten the deputy.

She opened the door to get out. The car's interior light made me feel exposed and vulnerable to the world.

"You know we've wrinkled your wife's dress," she said.

"Oh, my! Julie's gown!"

"Don't worry," she said. "I'll iron it. No one will ever know that we......rumpled it."

I laughed. "Rumpled it?"

"Well...You know," she said.

"Yeah. I know."

Rumpled was probably the most appropriate word. But I could have come up with several others.

"Come on," she said, taking the gown from the car.

"What?" I was astonished.

"Come inside while I iron the gown."

I looked at the front door with the porch light glaring; then looked at her, standing outside the car holding her oversized purse and the gown.

"I'm not going in there," I said.

"Why not? It's better than waiting out here."

She genuinely did not understand.

"What if your husband comes home?"

"I told you," she said. "He's away. He won't be home for days."

"You're sure?" I wasn't convinced.

"Absolutely," she replied; then started towards the house.

I got out of the car and rushed after her. I imagined the entire neighborhood peering at us from between drawn curtains. The walk to the door was excruciating. I felt myself relax slightly, sighing as I closed the door and locked it behind us.

Her home was as beautiful as I had imagined it would be. Expensive and fragile curio items were tastefully deployed throughout the expansive living room. The furniture had a decidedly unused look about it. The absence of a television or stereo was as conspicuous as a bathroom without a commode.

All and all, this part of the house was unlived in. It was a show case, a museum of art and niceties to be admired on the way to more functional parts of the home.

"I work upstairs," She said in a rather business-like tone. "Why don't you take the gown up? I'll be up in a moment."

"Okay." It was all I could think to say. She was in total control.

I made my way tentatively, as if feeling my way through some carnival house of horrors. At the top of the stairs, I followed a night light into one of the rooms. I found the light switch on the wall, just inside the room. I'd guessed right. This was her work area. And it certainly did look lived in. Not at all like that antiseptic living room.

There were baskets of clothes barely stuffed into one of two crowded closets. The ironing board and iron were already set up. A sewing machine, which seemed to get considerable use, dominated the room; not in size, but in presence.

The room was comfortable. And was made more so by the overstuffed easy chair and console T.V. in the corner. I draped the gown over the board

112

and let myself fall into that big chair of hers. In moments, I had fallen asleep.

"Well, that certainly is typical."

I imagined she was referring to the typical joke about men falling to sleep immediately after amorous activity. I straightened myself into the chair.

"It's been a long day," I complained.

"Indeed, it has," she countered.

I smiled. "Touche."

She placed a silver serving tray on the table beside me.

"Perhaps this will help restore your energy," she said, as she held a strawberry to my lips.

I bit it and she kissed me as I chewed. Sitting in my lap, she served me a grape from the tray. I swallowed it quickly; then reached for one of my own. I held it to her mouth, and she took it from my fingers. I stroked her lips with my fingertips and she licked them sensuously before drawing one into her mouth.

I felt myself respond as I caressed her through the nightgown she now wore. Pressing her tightly to me, I inhaled the light fragrances of soap and perfume.

"You smell so......umm," I whispered.

She giggled, adjusting herself under my touch.

"Oh...that feels so good," she sighed. "I don't want you to stop; but I've got to iron that gown."

She stood.

"Why don't you shower?" she said. "The bathroom's right across the hall."

I showered. And as I did, I heard someone enter the bathroom. I stood immediately at attention, worried her husband had come home early. The shower door opened and there she was.

"I got lonesome," she said, and stepped into the shower, under the steaming spray.

After my shower, we returned to the sewing room, and ate fruit and cheese she had prepared. We washed it all down with a just sweet enough, Chablis.

We talked and simply relaxed, enjoying each other's company.

It was well after two in the morning by the time I left Desiree's house with my wife's gown. I hung it up in the foyer closet when I got home. I crept into our bedroom, undressed in the dark and eased into bed.

If Julie awoke, I never knew it. The next morning, she was cool but cordial. She never asked me about that night. She never asked where I had been. She never asked what I had done. I had often wondered if our marriage would have turned out differently if she had challenged me about that night and many more that would follow.

Regardless, something changed that night. Whether it was Julie or me, it didn't matter. Our marriage was damaged, and neither she nor I attempted to repair it. She turned to community involvement and charity work. And I chased a fantasy.

"What about her daughter?" Diana asked as she fanned a swarm of gnats from her face.

I shrugged. "…Don't know. I Haven't seen her in years."

I had driven to Louisiana a couple of times with Desiree. We stayed with her grandmother, who didn't seem to mind that we were both married to other people. In fact, she had commented that she had never seen two people more right for each other. We laughed, as young people often do when older people impart wisdom.

Her daughter, Elizabeth, was pretty, but had none of Desiree's sensuous qualities-not then, at least. Her hair was light brown, and shifted shades in the sunlight. Her skin was a toasted honey color; just like her mother's. But she was very plain in many ways, quiet and polite. She was, obviously intelligent, but not brilliant. Her one engaging feature, though, was her eyes.

Her mother's were a light brown. And they captured your attention by sparkling green when the light was just right. Elizabeth's were straight up green. A bright hazel that, I was sure would learn to steal hearts someday.

"Oww!"

I swatted a mosquito.

"There wasn't a bug for miles last night," I told Diana. "Now every biting critter in the state is hanging around."

"Yeah. I know," she replied as she slapped one of her own. "So, the child still lives with her grandmother?"

"Well…I suppose so."

"Do you think they'll come to the funeral?"

We had been walking along the river bank. Looking for clues and sorting things out. I stopped.

"You know, Dee, I hadn't considered it. To tell the truth, I don't know if Colonel McKenzie even knows that Desiree had a daughter. So Elizabeth probably doesn't even know yet."

"You must be joking," Dee replied.

"No." I shook my head. "I always had the impression she had kept quite a bit from her husband."

"I've no doubt that she did. But that?"

Dee had a point. But I stood my ground.

"Especially that," I answered. "I don't think he would have approved."

We were silent for a while, walking along searching for anything that might be linked to Desiree.

"You really don't think it was him, do you?"

The question hung in the air. I wanted to fan it away or squash it as I did the insects that had annoyed me all morning.

Dee waited for a reply and the question wouldn't go away.

"No, I don't think he did it. I wish it was him, and that I could prove it. I hated him. He had what I wanted. I would love nothing better than to catch him dirty."

Dee shook her head.

"That's sad," she said.

She meant to say: "sad and petty."

I didn't apologize. It was the way I felt.

We headed for the car, satisfied that there were no clues to be found here. As we walked, we brainstormed a list of people to interview. People who may have seen Desiree leave the club with someone. Or who may have observed someone showing her an unusual amount of attention.

It was a start.

He was leaning up against my car, waiting for us as we cleared the brush.

"Don't you ever sleep, Hicks?" asked Dee as we approached.

"Too busy to sleep, Dee."

The lanky deputy pushed himself off my new paint job.

"Ya'll on another date, Ace?" he asked.

"Yeah, Hicks. And three's a crowd. Why don't you step off?"

He chuckled. When he did, Dee and I danced in his mirrored sunglasses.

"Did ya'll find anything?" he asked.

Dee answered. "No, it would help if we knew what we were looking for."

He got serious.

"You're looking for something to keep your boyfriend here out of the gas chamber. There are a lot of people in town who'd like to pin Desiree's death on him."

"You know as well as I do he didn't kill Desiree."

"I know it," he replied. "But whether it was suicide or not, sooner or later, fingers are going to start pointing at Ace. They did have...." He paused for effect. "You know...... How da'ya say it, Ace? ....Hist'ry? Yeah, that's it... They did have hist'ry, after awle."

They were carrying on as if I wasn't even present. I was innocent, but they were making me really uncomfortable. If I had to take an educated guess, given the facts I had at this point, I would have to say that I was the prime suspect. I needed and desired Desiree to obsession. I had acted irrationally at times, perhaps, even violently.

Hicks was right. Even if the courts didn't convict me, sooner or later, public opinion would. If a killer wasn't found, the rumor mill would invent one.

I just had some questions that needed answering. "Hicks, what's the big deal with you feeding us tidbits of information? What is it that you know? And why aren't you giving us all of it?"

He was cool. I had struck a nerve, but he seemed torn between opening up and stringing us along more.

"You know Desiree and I had hist'ry, too? ...To overuse a word."

I nodded. She had used that term herself. History: I wondered just what in the world that meant. She had never quite explained it.

"Yeah" I said. "That's exactly the way she put it: History. What's that mean anyway, Hicks?"

"Not what you think. That's for sure" he replied. "Anyhow, we'd known each other a long time. I don't want her memory fouled any more than you do, Ace. …Nor does the old man, for that matter."

"Old Man Dillon?" Dee asked.

Hicks nodded.

"Yeah. He wants this whole thing buried, though. He…."

"Let me guess," I broke in. "He has *history* with Desiree too."

"Yep. Afraid so, Chief." He kind of chuckled.

Dee had a sort of 'I-told-you-so' expression on her face, as if to say 'Desiree really got around.'

"Well…why not," I sighed. "So, he doesn't want folks to know about his and Desiree's past. Is that it?"

"Pretty much," he answered.

"So the old man wants it squashed. You want justice. But you can't investigate because you're under orders not to. So you kill two birds by feeding us crumbs of information. We do the hard work, you get the case solved. And you get to keep your job-and stay in the will."

Hicks grinned.

"He really ain't so dumb. Is he, Dee?"

119

The guy never let up.

Dee looked up at me, grinning. "No Hicks. He really *ain't* so dumb," she said.

She turned to Hicks. "So why don't you give us everything you have?"

"Because I just don't know how much I can trust you, yet."

I was just becoming disgusted. "You can trust us as much as we can trust you."

He was unflappable. "My point, exactly," he laughed. "C'mon. The old man wants to talk to you. And when you talk with him, the less you know, the better. He knows a lie when he hears one; no matter who tells it. So, if you don't know nothing, you can't try and hide nothing."

Five minutes later, I found myself on the way to the Dillon Farm. Dee drove my car back to town. She promised to start interviewing some of the people from our impromptu list. She would start with Colonel McKensie, Desiree's husband. We decided he would most likely, respond to her more favorable than to me. That was an understatement.

My investigation would continue with the old man. This was our version of leaving no stone unturned. Normally, these two men would have been a pair of the absolutely most unlikely murder suspects anyone could conjure. But each had motive, if Desiree's death was indeed a crime of passion. She was a cheating wife. And if she actually did have an affair with Old Man Dillon, she was probably a cheating lover as well. They were proud powerful men who just may have lost control in a moment of anger.

It was obvious why Dillon didn't want anyone digging around in Desiree's past. If his relationship with her was brought to light, he might even be revealed as her killer. He had money and power enough to cover the whole thing up. He owned the Sheriff's Department just as he owned a part of every small business in town-including Desiree's.

I finally had a target to shoot for thanks to Hicks.

Even as the idea came to me, I dismissed it. The old man was a lot of things, but I doubted he was a killer. Not any longer at least. The story goes that he had done a whole lot of things in his youth. Royce Dillon was a shrewd and ruthless businessman. He had, no doubt, cheated his share of people in his life. But I had never heard anyone speak ill of him. Not anyone worth anything, anyhow. The man made his money the hard way. He had done just about anything for a buck.

He had traveled around the world, working oil rigs, diamond mines, smuggling, mercenary, whatever. With every nickel he made, he bought up swampland in southeast Georgia. Folks had joked that he had lost his mind. They finally got the joke. And they weren't laughing when the punch line rolled around. But it was too late. He had property that the U. S. Government wanted. Uncle Sam paid him ten times what he had paid and twelve times what that useless land was worth. He had outsmarted a lot of people. And he secured his future along with the future of the town he loved. The military moved back in and businesses started popping up all over the place. Most required financing or a wealthy partner.

That's where he came in. With his new assets, he bank rolled just about every business in town. …..And, it was said, the politics, also. They say that a councilman had opposed him on a question of zoning. When re-election time came up, the guy swallowed a fish bone and choked to death. Some say it was a chicken bone. Others claim it was a straight razor, and he didn't swallow it. Whatever…. In a nutshell, Dillon was Hinesville. And nothing substantial happened in town, or on Stewart for that matter, without at least, a concurrence from him. Sure the town had a mayor, sheriff's department, city council. But they were all beholding to the old man. …The town's father. Best I could tell, he was a tough but honest businessman; these days. No. I doubted he was a killer. Not now anyway. They say he was a lot different when he was young. He had been smart, tall, and good looking. And he did exactly what he wanted. There was a rumor about a certain killing, they said it was justified. But like so many others, no one could give details. It was probably a lie. It was just something to go along with building the legend, to extend the lore surrounding Old Royce.

"So, Hicks, how long was your uncle involved with Desiree?"

Hicks turned the steering wheel and the cruiser left the highway. The road up to the Dillon place was paved as well as any freeway.

He glanced at me from behind those ever-present mirrored glasses.

"I never said they were involved."

"Of course, you did," I continued. "You said they have history."

122

He shook his head.

"No," he said. "You said they had history. I agreed. And let you assume the rest. You got a dirty mind, Ace."

"Must be the company I keep," I said.

He laughed.

"…No doubt."

Down the road, the palatial mansion came into view; then was hidden by pines as we rounded a bend.

"Man, you're obsessed with Desiree's lovers, aren't you?"

I didn't answer.

"What would you do if I gave you the entire list?" he asked. "Track 'em down and kill 'em? There were a few, you know."

I felt a fury rising that I barely contained. And Hicks went on.

"You've had a few, yourself. One night stand here. …A blow job there. …Floatin' from one airhead to another. …A married woman here, one there. If I had to compare, I'd say your list was way longer than hers."

I wanted to deny it, but I couldn't. I had hit a lot of stuff over the years. Even if Hicks *was* telling the truth, it didn't matter. One lover, besides me, was one lover too many.

"Yeah," he said as he pulled the car up to the front of the plantation style house. "I wish I could do half as good you do, Ace."

Who did he think he was talking to? I wondered. If he knew my business, I knew a little about him, as well. And Hicks was babe magnet.

He laughed when I told him that.

"Anyway, there weren't as many as you would think. And there were none after you."

I shrugged, pretending to blow off the entire matter.

"Go on in." He nodded towards the door. "He's expecting you. Probably got a place set for lunch."

"Fatten me up for slaughter, you think?"

We laughed.

"Yeah. You watch yourself in there, Ace," he warned. "Old Royce ain't no joke."

"Alright. Catch you later."

I got out, and watched the car as it cruised down the narrow lane, then rounded a curve and was hidden from view by the pine trees along the road. Turning, I walked to the door and rang the bell. When no one had answered after a while, I tried the handle and the door gave to my nudge. Warily, I walked in. The moment conjured images of old horror movies.

As I closed the door, I was startled by a tall, good-looking brother standing behind it. I grinned, realizing it was my own reflection in the full length mirror.

"Hello," I called from the foyer.

When no one responded, I decided to make myself at home. I was impressed with the style and luxury or the place. The sheer enormity of the living room was impressive in itself, but the collection of artifacts from the four corners of the world, told a story of a man who'd used his time here wisely. He had sampled just about all that life had to offer.

Grudgingly, I allowed a twinge of admiration to temper my envy. If I was to receive the nickel tour, it had begun appropriately, in this room.

I was struck by the beauty of one article in particular. It was a ten inch high statuette carved from ebony. A woman, whose form reminded me of Desiree. Her arms spread wide, imploring the heavens. Her palms and eyes reached skyward, in search of an unseen deity. Her face impassive and feet together, she was stark naked; and ultimately enchanting, as her long braided hair trailed down the middle of her back.

I took the statue into my hands. Its beauty and perfection were so compelling that I had picked it up before actually realizing it. Mesmerized, I studied it from every angle; moved my hands along its length.

I imagined its contours were those of the woman it so resembled. I closed my eyes recalling memories of intimate caresses. Nights of passion stolen while unsuspecting others went about their own affairs. I felt her shudder, involuntarily responding to the movement of my fingertips upon her flesh. I heard her voice as she struggled to maintain composure. All the while, her body implored me to continue.

"Put that back!"

I was too shocked to be embarrassed, although I had been caught fondling a piece of wood as if it were a real live woman. I nearly tossed the statue back onto the table, but it slipped from my grasp. It juggled between hands, as it turned end over end in front of me. Finally, I managed to control the artifact, and put it back in its place.

The old woman brushed pass me to inspect the statue and any other items I may have tampered with. When she was satisfied everything was present, unmoved or at least unbroken, she glared up at me.

"Didn't your mama teach you no better manners than that?" she asked.

"Uhh...Yeah."

"Then why don't you use them?" she pressed.

All of a sudden I was six years old again, and had just broken my mother's favorite vase.

"I don't know?" It was a question because I wasn't really sure she expected me to answer. Anyway, it had bailed me out a number of times when I was a kid; even as an adult. Maybe it would be just as effective now.

It wasn't.

"What kind of an answer is that?" she demanded. "Are you just plain rude? Or are you too stupid to know that you don't go messin' with folks things when you visiting?"

The old woman went on for nearly five minutes, it seemed. She said something about home training and never having nothing worthwhile.

She had gotten around to "I got a good mind to take a switch to you, myself," when Dillon interrupted with a cackling laugh.

"You tell him, Massie," he said, winking at me.

Massie drew a breath to continue her tirade, but was cut off again.

"Well, I think the boy has learned his lesson, my dear. He was only curious. No harm done. Now, is there?"

Massie huffed. "It just ain't right."

The old man laughed again. And Massie left the room. But not before giving me a long, hard, eye-rolling glare.

I stood in the middle of the floor, dumbfounded. I had been set up. They had pulled the best good cop/bad cop routine I had seen in years. I knew exactly what they were doing, and I was still shaken up.

I watched the woman the way folks watch their neighbor's pit bull when they go to visit. It's not that you could actually do anything if the dog decides you've worn out your welcome. It's just that you'd like a choice of which side of your behind he gets to chew on.

I turned to Dillon

"Thanks," I said.

"No…Thank you, Mr. Edwards. I haven't seen Massie as happy as this in years."

I was more than a little confused.

"That's happy?" I asked.

The old man laughed again. And it was infectious.

"I suppose it is," I agreed.

"Of course, it is," he said. "Now, won't you join me in my office?"

He led me to a set of double doors just off from the living room. I assumed this was where we would have lunch and politely interrogate one another.

As we entered the room, I noticed a full length portrait of Deputy Hicks. He wore a three piece suit, with an impressive watch chain hanging from the vest pockets.

Hicks was tall and lean. And he was more handsome than in real life. The artist had caught something of him I'd never noticed. His hazel eyes seemed to follow me around the room; to penetrate into my heart.

"Wasn't I something?" asked the old guy.

I looked at him, then back to the portrait. It was him! The resemblance to Hicks was uncanny. I had never noticed.

The old man nodded.

"My nephew got everything. He's more like me than my own son was. Why, he even got my name."

Royce Hicks.

Everybody called him Hicks. Even Dillon. I figured it just cut down on confusion.

Hicks' mother was old Royce's sister-in-law. When the woman's husband, Royce's brother, died, Royce just sort of filled in. Hicks had access to money, but none of his own. And for some reason, he was never included, in Dillon's business deals. Regardless, he was a small town deputy with connections; could have been sheriff. The old man was getting on in age. He could run the town. Why was he still, just a small town deputy?

We stared up at the portrait, not speaking for a time. We were both lost in thought. I reckoned he was recapturing lost youth. I was pondering Hicks' role in life; and those green eyes. Eyes the exact color of Desiree's daughter's.

"You a drinking man, Mr. Edwards?" he asked.

I turned to him and smiled.

"On occasion." I answered

"Good! I think this is just the right occasion."

He presented a twelve year old scotch with such a flourish that I was nearly compelled to salute the bottle.

We took seats in a pair of overstuffed leather easy chairs, with a small round table between us. Smoke from fat Cuban cigars lingered just above our heads. This was the lap of luxury, I thought. And I knew it when Massie entered with a large rolling cart of food.

The lunch she had prepared was more than four men could eat in a seating. It was a banquet of seafood and meats, with vegetables; raw and cooked; on the side. The bread was still fresh and warm. She had also fixed a big pitcher of lemonade that sweated beads of water just like it was made for a T.V. commercial.

Remembering my initial encounter with Massie, I was reluctant to approach the cart. But she put me at ease when she poured a glass of lemonade and handed it to me.

"Here you go, Mr. Edwards," she said. "I hope it's not too sweet. Mr. Royce is partial to sugar."

I tasted the liquid.

"No, ma'am, it's fine," I said.

"Good! Now ya'll go 'head and eat before it gets cold."

She left the room humming a tune I thought I knew, but could not place. Old Royce laughed.

"Mr. Edwards, I have never seen her happier," he said. "You have got to visit more often."

I didn't answer. I was already stuffing a piece of lobster tail in my mouth.

After we ate, we replaced the lemonade in our tumbler glasses with scotch and water; mostly scotch. He walked me around his office showing me books and odd items he had collected over the years. He told me stories from his past.

It seems that Massie was a childhood playmate. He grew up loving her. But times, being what they were, he couldn't acknowledge that love openly. She came into his home as a maid. And even though his wife, Lucinda, had been dead for nearly twenty years, they still continued the charade. Massie was Dillon's housekeeper by day. But by night, she was his lover-and more.

He looked at me through old cloudy eyes. Emerald orbs that had known luster, but were now faded and dim.

"I lost my Lucinda…My only son, John…He…He abandoned me long ago."

I watched his eyes as he spoke. I saw pain. But not regret.

"Do you know what it's like to lose everything in the world, Mr. Edwards?"

I nodded slowly. He had hit home. No one knew as well as I did.

"Massie was all I ever needed," he said. "And I was an old man before I ever knew that."

"What about Desiree?" I heard myself ask.

He sighed. But his expression never changed.

"Desiree McKensie was an extraordinary woman. This town-you and I-have lost a most precious resource. She was one heck of a business woman; the shrewdest real estate investor I've ever known. No one could touch her....." That was high praise coming from a man who had made his fortune in real estate by outsmarting all his contemporaries and the U.S. government. His voice trailed off, and his old wizened eyes stared at a distant point I couldn't see.

After a moment, Old Royce was his charming self again. He poured me another scotch and lit me a cigar. We sat and we talked. Time passed. And outside the window, the day began to fade.

Neither of us spoke of Desiree again. His pain was all too evident. And I did not have the strength to batter an old man at his weakest.

It was well after dark when I poured off the last corner of our second scotch bottle. I sipped at the liquor as my eyes attempted to anchor the images of the two Dillons who weaved before me. The pair of men melded into one. And I achieved the alertness of a man who had drunk himself sober.

"You know something, Royce?" I asked

"What is it, Ace, my boy?"

We both slurred when we talked. But when Royce spoke, he became two guys. And I had to squint to put him back together.

"I believe you're drunk."

He laughed that cackling laugh that I had come to appreciate in such a short time.

"Well, Aish, if I'm not, we've pretty much pissed away some dang good scotch."

I laughed so hard I fell from my chair.

I felt someone lift me by my arms.

"Where we goin'?"

"Just goin' for a little ride," he said

"Ride? Is Royce goin'?"

"Ace."

It was Old Royce.

"The sheriff is gonna take you home, Buddy. Sheriff you take good care of my friend."

"Yeah," I said; then slumped into the back seat of the cruiser. "You fat...."

I heard Royce's cackling laugh. Then the door slammed shut and I didn't hear another thing until I was dragged by my feet from the back of the cruiser.

"What you think you doin', J.C.?"

I slurred the words as the man attempted to stand me up against the cruiser. I slid to the ground. Sheriff Lindsey cursed.

"You ain't that drunk. Get up and go inside."

Lindsey had parked his cruiser outside my apartment. He had provided curbside service, but that was as far as he would go. There would be no door to door delivery.

I stood and wobbled on rubbery legs.

"Shut up, fatty! Royce told you to take care of me, fatso." I began to giggle. "Heh heh heh. You gotta take care of me fatty."

Lindsey was the meanest person I knew. He was always angry; angry at no one and nothing in particular. Just, angry. But he seemed to take extra pride in his anger where I was concerned. And I got a certain pleasure out of inciting his anger. I was particularly good at it when I was drunk. The problem was I couldn't defend myself when I was in that condition. J. C. was a big brother, six-foot-two and about two hundred and sixty pounds. And he put the entire weight of all that beef behind his punch to my gut.

Being so drunk was a mixed blessing. Although I was too drunk to avoid the blow, the pain never actually registered. I sprawled to the ground as limp as a rag doll.

He had moved in for the kill, when a familiar voice cut through the haze.

"What are you doing?"

It was Diana come to save me.

"That's what I want to know." Hicks had joined the party as well.

133

"Ya'll's behinds about ten seconds too late," I slurred.

Hicks helped me to my feet.

"Well, we're here now, Ace. What's goin' on J.C.?"

"Just bringing him home, like the old man told me to do."

Hicks chuckled. "Did he tell you to work him over, too?"

"Naw," said Lindsey, "that was my idea."

"Maybe you'd like a little help."

The two men stood staring at one another. Their hatred was obvious. And understandable. The put-in-place Sheriff ran the town for Dillon. He was the muscle; the enforcer. His tactics kept the soldiers in line and ensured only sanctioned riff-raff was allowed to operate inside town limits. But he couldn't control his own deputy.

Hicks was the spoon fed nephew of the richest man in town. He didn't need; and certainly didn't ask for Lindsey's permission to do anything. He was the loose cannon a tyrant like J.C. just could not stand.

The old man controlled them both, somehow. And because of that, they found a way to-at least, pretend they were on the same side.

"I'm finished," said Lindsey. "Let's get out of here."

Hicks nodded.

"In a minute. I want to talk to these folks about something."

J. C. grunted his disapproval; then got into his cruiser. We watched him drive away.

Hicks gave me a, you-ought-to-know-better glance. Passersby had started to slow down, checking out the scene.

"You sure do take a lot of chances, Ace."

"Old son'a-gun, Dillon, set me up."

He grinned.

"It wouldn't be the first time. But I doubt it. J.C. just likes roughin' folks up. You know that."

Dee was holding me up. She'd be alright. It wasn't a new experience for her. I'd been falling down drunk a number of times in my life. It seems Dee was present for most of those events.

"Let's get inside," she said. "What do you want to talk about, Hicks?"

He shook his head.

"It'll keep. See ya'll later."

Dee helped me into the apartment as Hicks drove away.

"That guy's ever'where," I said.

Dee snorted. "Humph. Lucky for you. Lindsey could have…"

She stopped short of saying, "….killed you."

We stared at one another; then dismissed the idea. J.C. was capable of murder. He'd done it before; so the rumors said. And there was no reason to believe he liked Desiree any more than he liked anyone else in town. But I just couldn't imagine Desiree having sex with that ape; especially oral sex. She'd have died first.

We added one more suspect to the list, anyway.

I yawned and staggered into the kitchen. "I'm goin' to bed," I declared while bending over in the refrigerator. I came up with a chuck of old salami.

"Uhn uh," she said. "We still have work to do."

She took me by the arm and guided me out the door into the passenger seat of my car. By now, I had lost my buzz, and I was pretty sleepy.

"Where we going?"

She closed the door and got behind the wheel.

"I got a lead," she said. "We're going to talk to a guy named Bob."

"Bob Miller?"

She nodded.

"You know him?"

"Yeah," I said. "I've seen him around. They call him Uncle Bob. Kind of a sleazy guy with a lot of cash and no obvious employment."

"Well, sleazy is right. Totsie told me where to find him."

"So, where we going?" I asked.

She started the car and we pulled off. "To Bubba Ray's."

It was 'gentlemen's night' at Bubba Ray's. That meant all nude strippers. These babes would do anything for a tip. Dee's money was just as good as a man's there. And for some of the ladies, it was better than a man's.

I laughed.

"You got an itch I don't know about?"

She laughed herself. "No sweetheart. Strictly speaking, I only scratch one way."

"Oh. I'm sorry," I apologized. "I just thought…"

"I know what you thought. We're going there to find your boy… Uncle Bob, is it?"

"Yeah."

I watched the night go pass my window. And I wondered what sensible people were doing tonight. Perhaps watching television? Or sitting down to a late dinner? Maybe they were pacing the floor, wondering where their mates were. It always came to that with me; somebody done somebody wrong. Then it occurred to me that everybody wasn't like me. Some people were actually faithful to their lovers.

Then it occurred to me that maybe no one was actually faithful to their lovers. That maybe people were more like me than I knew. I once did a young thing who talked about how in love she was with her husband. She bragged about how smart he was, and how lucky she was to have found him. And how all she had ever wanted was to be his wife. In fact, the only time she didn't talk about her husband and their relationship was when we were actually together.

I chuckled to myself.

Dee glanced over at me.

"What did you get out of Dillon-besides a fifth of scotch?"

I shook my head.

"Two fifths of scotch," I corrected. "And six fine Cuban cigars, a mighty tasty lunch and not a single thing else."

Dee was skeptical. "Are you sure?"

"Well...yeah," I answered. "Did you talk to the colonel?"

She nodded. "Yes."

She was making me wait. Maybe she thought I was too drunk to handle her information.

"So...?"

"So, it was interesting."

"Interesting? Is that a good thing...interesting?"

She shrugged.

"I don't know. It was just...interesting."

I was so full of anticipation by now, I shouted. "Diana, what did McKensie say that was so interesting?"

Dee looked at me as if I'd lost my mind. And she said so.

Slowly, she told me Desiree and McKensie had a big argument the night she died.

"Ace, she was leaving him. He said she was leaving town with her child's father."

I didn't respond. And she went on. "He accused her of sneaking off with you. He said it was awful. That he had been awful. He pushed her. She fell. When he tried to help her up she pulled away and tore her dress."

"So, after that she ends up in the river?" I added.

"No," Dee corrected. "After changing her dress she went out to a party."

I could hardly contain myself. This was more than I'd ever hoped for. I knew the colonel did it and all I had to do was go beat it out of him.

"He did it!" I shouted.

"He did not do it," said Dee. "He got drunk. He found himself a hooker. And he spent that night and the next day in a hotel in Savannah."

"You believe that?"

"Yes," she said. "So does the police."

I snorted.

"Did Desiree mention anything to you about leaving town?"

I shook my head.

"We'd hardly even looked each other in the eye, let alone trade secrets over the past couple of years."

"Well, don't you think it's interesting that the colonel thinks Desiree was running off with you?"

"Yeah," I said. "But weird is a better word."

Dee pulled the car to a stop in the dirt and mud parking lot of Bubba Ray's.

"Doggone shame!" I said. "With all the money this place pulls in, you'd think they'd pave the parking lot, at least."

She laughed. "I guess there's not a lot left after J.C. gets his cut."

"You're probably right," I said.

Keeping the local law happy can be an expensive proposition, if your business happens to depend upon their cooperation. And Bubba Ray's business did depend upon J.C.'s utmost cooperation. Prostitution and gambling were lucrative for good business people. But the right people had to be convinced to look the other way. In Hinesville, J.C. Lindsey was the right people.

We tip toed through the muck on the way to the joint's entrance. Dee cursed the entire time. It seems she thought someone should replace her one hundred and fifty dollar shoes. I declined the offer, although; as she put it; this was my story we were working on. I suggested she take it up with B.C., our editor. I wasn't going to pay for them. She continued to curse.

I held open the door, as she stepped into the juke joint. Although, I know her money was welcome in the place, I expected, at least, some reaction to her presence. But there was none. It was business as usual.

I paid the ten dollar cover, and we worked our way to the bar. The place was large for a strip joint. I had seen school auditoriums that were smaller. I figured they needed the space for the big round tables the girls danced on. Besides the tables, there was the stage, a shining brass floor lined with lights and a bar where customers sat to checkout things up close. There were three brass poles, in different sections of the stage. And two brass trapezes suspended from the ceiling equal distances between poles. Behind all that was a mirrored wall where the girls watched themselves, as they performed for the customers who gawked at them.

140

Neon lights; red and green and white and purple; lit the joint. And strobes and spotlights lit the stage. The carpet was hot red, as was the vinyl in the chairs and the arm rest at the bar, and also the crushed velvet wall covering.

Although, the music was loud, it didn't drown out the conversation. After all, even if most of the customers came to the place purely recreationally, others came to conduct business of their own-sort of your underworld office annex.

Dee looked around the room. "I don't get it," she said.

"What's that?" I asked.

"I don't understand the allure for guys. I mean, you get worked up by some woman jiggling in front of you. But you don't get a pay off. No pop."

I laughed. "Well, we don't know that. Guys always believe there's a chance. Besides, look at the way these girls move. You can't get that just anyplace."

She snorted, pointing. "That? I can do that."

I challenged. "They do have amateur night, you know?"

"Brother, you *are* amateur night," she returned.

I laughed.

I counted close to thirty girls working that night, but I was once told that more than a hundred work on nights the soldiers return from deployments to the field or overseas.

The chicks were mostly young hard bodies from all over Georgia, lower South Carolina or North Florida. Smart girls didn't work long before finding a husband among the GI's-or a sugar daddy. Not so smart ones didn't work long before getting strung out on booze or drugs. Competition among the women was grueling. The more talented ones, generally, went on to become housewives. And the others moved on to alcoholism, drug addiction, or career prostitution; or a combination of all three. By then, they were completely lost, and their earning potential, substantially, diminished.

I ordered drinks for Dee and me. After paying, I scanned the room for Uncle Bob. I was, initially distracted by so many women in so many stages of dress, near dress or undress.

Dee gave me a nudge.

"Keep your mind on your work," she said.

"I was just enjoying the scenery."

"Another time, if you please," she scolded. "I'd like to get this over with."

She was saying something about home and a shower, but I didn't get it all. I had spotted Uncle Bob about then. It was no wonder I had missed him earlier. It's a wonder I noticed him at all. He was partially concealed by a six foot chocolate beauty whose shoulder length hair bounced and flowed as she gyrated in front of him. The girl wore high heels that set her up another three inches. Long, tight, shapely legs flowed up from those heels to become thick enticing thighs and hips seemingly sculpted of onyx. The dancer's waist was small and her belly, flat.

She moved her hands through her hair, as she tilted her head back. Lights and filmy smoke silhouetted her beautiful face. She squeezed her eyes shut and allowed her tongue to glide across full succulent lips.

Bob reached up and took her hand. He guided her forward. The girl moved with the beat of the music as Bob's hand led her. The other hand reached out to touch her, and she'd grimaced and she squirmed involuntarily.

I sipped my beer, as I watched them; oblivious to anything else. When they had finished their dance I needed another drink. I turned to ask Dee if she wanted another one, but was stopped by the hand that palmed me.

"Would you like a private?" she asked.

I backed up slowly. I looked pass the young lady and nodded towards Dee.

"That sounds pretty good, sweetheart," I said. "But I'm with someone."

The stripper shrugged. "It's ok. Maybe she'd like one too. I prefer groups."

I chuckled. "Maybe she would. Why don't you ask her?"

The girl turned to Dee, as I ordered another beer. "How about it, Booty?" she asked. "You want me to do a little rump shakin' for you?"

As she spoke, she placed her hand on Dee's thigh, and squeezed.

That was my cue to leave. I paid for the beer and made my way to Bob's table. When I got there, he was just finishing another lap dance with a different babe. Before she left, he slipped a crisp twenty under the garter at her thigh.

"What's up, Big Shot?" I said

"Acie-Deucie! How you doin', my man?"

Bob had a way of messing up people's names when he wanted to. He offered his hand but I remembered where they had been. I offered him a pound instead. He tapped my fist with his and I returned the gesture; then sat down with my beer.

"Acie, what you doing up in here, man? I see you got your girl with you." He nodded towards Dee. "Kind of a step up, huh?" He chuckled.

Uncle Bob had been in the Army for nearly as long as I had. He got in a little trouble, and was kicked out. He had a way with the women. He had done a little pimping, and got jammed up for it.

Bob was the type of guy who could make good girls do bad things. And he could break bad girls down until they just wanted to be good. From a player's perspective, Bob was the bomb. He just seemed to have it going on with babes.

While I respected his skills with women, I disliked Bob, intensely. He was sleazy and pompous. I didn't like that he took their money and squandered it every place. He wasn't smooth or polished-or even caring.

Worst of all, he had history with Desiree. I hated him, as I hated any man who had been with her. She realized her mistake and dumped him shortly before meeting me. It did not matter to me that it was over between them. He had touched her. Made her feel pleasure. And she had touched him. Whispered things in the dark.

It bothered me. It bothered me then, and it bothered me as we sat at the table watching nudes strut and jiggle in front of us.

"I guess you heard," I said.

"Yeah. I always knew she was a little off," he said. "But I never figured she'd go out like that."

"Like how?"

"Suicide," he answered. "It just didn't seem like her style."

"It wasn't."

He gave me a curious glance before responding. "I guess you would know, huh?"

I shrugged. "I suppose. Or maybe you would know."

He grinned. "That was some good stuff though... Wasn't it?"

Before I could respond, another girl had approached him. Bob helped her to sit on the table in front of him. She sat there naked, before him.

"Did you see Desiree the night she died?"

He was touching the young woman intimately. I drew a breath and turned my head slightly. With his hands on the young woman, he looked at me. "Yeah, I saw her." He turned back to the woman. "Fine, ain't she? Look at that body." He reached for her face and pulled her into a long open-mouthed kiss.

The kiss became more ardent as the music began to crescendo. The dancer reached out to pull him to her in a quickening rhythm. She moaned into his mouth, as she kissed him more and more forcefully. She broke the kiss and threw her head back, shaking as if in pain. As he reached for her body, she shuddered, breathlessly moaning, "No. No."

The song ended, but Bob did not release the young woman. They continued into the next song. By this time, it occurred to me that her response to Bob was less a reaction to pleasure than theatrics for the benefit of a paying customer.

Bored, I glanced around the room. Dee sat at the bar laughing and talking with the stripper who had hit on her earlier. The women looked in my direction; then gave each other a high five. I wondered what that was all about. At other tables, girls were entertaining their customers' amorous fantasies. Some people just sat watching their drinks, or like me, watching the action around them.

A pretty brown sister appeared at my side.

"How would you like to do that to me?" She nodded toward the girl on the table top. I smiled. "No thanks," I said. "I'm on a diet."

She chuckled. "Honey, that's not a problem. I'm non fattening; no salt and preservative-free."

I licked my lips. If I was ever inclined to engage in a mock romance in the middle of a crowded barroom, that would have convinced me. I declined anyhow and she went on to the next table. I watched her climb onto the table settling in front of the guy. A faint sense of jealousy touched me as I watched them establish a short-lived rapport.

Bob had kept the girl at the table through another song. When she got up to leave, he paid her and she thanked him with a wisp of a hug.

"So... When was the last time you saw Desiree," I asked him.

He took a drink from his beer bottle

"I saw her Saturday night," he answered. "Why?"

"Because, she may have been murdered."

I thought I saw something in his eyes, but it was gone before I could read it. I dismissed it. Perhaps my disdain for Bob had biased my perceptions.

"Word is she was leaving town. She was taking the boy and leaving with his real father."

He grinned. "Oh, yeah? And you want to know if I'm the baby-daddy."

My eyes narrowed, as they bore into him over the beer bottle I had raised to my lips.

As I lowered the bottle, he went on. "Ace, I done had eight children by s'em different mothas, but that boy ain't one of 'em."

I felt a surge of relief. He gazed straight into my eyes. "You wrote the story. You told the world that she killed herself. So what was it? Was it murder or suicide?"

I didn't answer.

"Did you know she'd had sex before she drowned?"

He didn't flinch. He stared into my eyes.

"With you, maybe?"

I shook my head. "Or you," I said, staring back.

He laughed. "Maybe," he said. "Acie, you're still strung out. Brother, you ain't supposed to get attached to these babes. Especially one like her."

I was starting to get upset. Bob was trying to work on me. He disrespected women. He used them without as much feeling as he would have for a paper napkin. He just ran through them, and now he seemed to think his mind games were going to twist me up, as well.

I allowed a deep chuckle. "You know, Bob, if *any* woman falls for *your* weak game, you're welcome to her. Now, what do you mean by, 'One like her', anyway?" I asked him.

He laughed again. "Like her. Like Desiree. She was a freak," he said. "Just loved to sex; anytime; anywhere."

My hand closed around my beer bottle as he continued.

"If that broad had as many peckers on her as she'd had in her, she woulda been a porcupine."

It happened so quickly he never saw it coming. I didn't even know I would do it until I had. A frothy spray of blood, and glass, and beer showered our table. Bob reached for his forehead as he fell backwards in his chair.

Women screamed and ran for cover. There was cursing and yelling throughout the place. The two big bouncers were on me before I could shake the broken glass from my hand. One of the guys, a blue-black brother with a tight fade and muscles just every where, shouted at me. "Get up!"

Before I could respond, I was snatched by the scruff of my neck by his partner. Though he was brown with straight hair and Latin features, he was all backwoods and country. "Whatchu thank you doin'?" he asked.

He didn't wait for an answer before they began dragging me towards the exit. I struggled vainly to free myself. As I was being snatched and pulled, I heard Dee shout, "Wait! He's with me!"

Someone grabbed her, as well. "Then you can catch some of this behin' whoopin' we 'bout to put on 'im!"

If she responded, I didn't hear it. The next thing I heard was the crash of my body against the wooden door. It swung open and I went sprawling in the mud there in Bubba Ray's parking lot. Diana followed right after. In spite of the situation, I found myself laughing. Besides those $150 shoes, Dee could add one $300 business suit to my bill.

We must have looked a pitiful to mess, because the bouncers started laughing, too. They looked at one another and shook their heads.

The brown one asked the black one, "Wut you thank?"

Blue-black shook his head, still laughing. "Man, f'git them fools."

He pointed at us, "Ya'll get outta here! Go home 'fo Bubba Ray git back an' fin' ya'll been fightin' in his joint. An' I have ta mess ya'll up f'real."

They turned back and disappeared through the doorway. I checked my hand for cuts from the bottle. Miraculously, there were none. I was, basically, unharmed. I couldn't say the same for Dee's outfit. Her suit, shoes, and nylons were all ruined. And while I might have won a debate over her shoes, there was no denying I was directly responsible for the condition of her suit.

"You know you owe me a new outfit, don't you?"

"How you figure that?" I asked. "You're the one who told them we were together. What were you thinking anyway?"

I started laughing again. "He's with me? I'm sure that's what saved my behind."

She stood, her shoes sinking in the mud.

"Funny man. You still owe me a suit, shoes, nylons, a kickin' hair-do, and one trip to Victoria's Secret."

I got the impression Diana was padding the bill. And I surely did not intend to pay for any underwear I would never get the chance to remove.

She attempted to take a step and there was a loud sucking sound. One nyloned foot rose from the mud and Dee, loosing her balance, tipped face first into one of the deeper puddles of the parking lot. It took a massive effort to suppress the laughter, as I stood to retrieve her shoe and help her onto her feet. And now she could add cosmetics to my bill.

This evening was going to cost me a good deal. My sorry budget really couldn't handle the strain of a new outfit for Dee. Not that and my own suits, ties, shoes, and sport coats. I complained as we drove to get her car. She didn't have a lot of sympathy for my financial condition. And she had no sympathy for my car's interior.

"Too bad," she said. "If you hadn't started a fight, I wouldn't have ended up wallowing in the mud back there." To emphasize the point, she tapped her shoes together, dropping hardening mud to the floor. She was a mess. Mud everywhere. And I didn't look any better. This time, I did laugh.

"Did you get any information we can use before bashing that poor man upside his head?"

I shook my head. "No. Not at all."

She looked at me, disgusted "You've had, kind of, a wasted day, haven't you? Basically, all you've done with yourself is get drunk and fight."

Dee was right. Today, she did all of the work. I was in the way. I felt a wave of shame. But I didn't want her to know that. I changed the subject. "I see you got yourself a new girlfriend." I was referring to the girl at the bar.

She laughed. "No. You do."

"How's that?"

"She's your next birthday present," she said. "You don't have any strong objections to the use of leather, do you?"

That question went unanswered.

I dropped her off and, exhausted, I headed home to a shower and my favorite easy chair.

It had been a long day. And I was no closer to discovering Desiree's killer than I had been that morning they pulled her car from the river. Certain details about that morning were coming back to me. Hicks wasn't the least surprised to find Desiree drowned in her own car. He was relatively calm, in fact; apathetic. That seemed strange to me, considering their long and oddly close relationship.

I hadn't considered Hicks a suspect-until now. He certainly had opportunity. The guy was everywhere. He could easily have lured Desiree to that park; then strangle her. If she trusted anyone in the world, it was Hicks. But they were pals. What would have been his motive? Jealousy? There was enough of that to go around. Why not? Everybody wanted her. Why not Hicks?

Because his affection seemed different from the usual guy/girl attraction. He seemed more...brotherly. There was something about the way they acted around each other. It was like they had just been whispering behind everyone's back. They seemed to be laughing at a private joke only they understood.

No. Hicks wasn't the killer. But if he didn't know who was, I'd have bet my Visa balance he knew why. I made a mental note to ask him that question. Then I closed my eyes. I wondered what my next move ought to be. Fatigue and all the alcohol I'd drunk, answered the question for me.

Through a haze, I saw Desiree enter the ballroom. She was as radiant as ever. She wore a gown the shade of blue I had never seen before. It was bright and tasteful, thoroughly enchanting. Her jewelry, diamond earrings with a matching necklace, emanated dazzling flecks of light as she walked.

Though she was well covered, and the dress was not unusually form-fitting, sensuality lingered about her. The air seemed to crackle and spark like electricity in the night. Men were left breathless in her wake, while many women stood envious. Others more self-assured, greeted her warmly. But all kept a close eye on their dates.

I forced myself to look away from her to her escort. He was a tall, straight as a board, broad-shouldered brother who appeared to be very comfortable with the attention Desiree was receiving. He was as graceful as she was. And obviously as much man as she was woman. With Julie at my right arm, I felt my left hand clinch into a fist.

This was Lieutenant Colonel Alexander "Bud" McKensie. He looked every bit the conquering military hero. They looked every bit the perfectly matched couple. They reminded me of a documentary I'd once seen on public television: a pair of mated jaguars stalking through the jungle, sleek and powerful. Everything in the jungle was subject to them. Everything was prey.

Juliet squeezed my arm. Her eyes never leaving the regal-like couple, she asked what seemed to me, the most ridiculous question I'd ever heard. "Do you think she's beautiful?" She had asked it before. And I had placated her with a compliment. I knew she would not be put off as easily this time.

Reluctantly, I turned to her. It was like seeing Julie for the first time. I mean, really seeing her. She was beautiful! Radiant! Her face was open and guileless. Her body, the body that was as familiar to me as my own, was breath-taking. Juliet... My Juliet. ...My lover. The mother of my two beautiful little girls, stood tall and confident in the face of my most critical appraisal.

Desiree was beautiful, and I said so.

"Yes," I said. "Yes, she is. In fact, she is the second most beautiful woman in this room."

Julie simply smiled. I took her into my arms and kissed her. In that moment there was only my wife and me. No one else existed; then, before, or ever after. We were alone, now and forever.

A small cough returned me to consciousness. "Ahem." It was Desiree standing behind me on the arm of her hero-husband. They each smiled at us as if Julie and I were naughty adolescents caught groping beneath the school's bleachers.

Julie giggled, wiping her lipstick from my face. I tried my best to discreetly adjust.

"We're sorry to interrupt," said the colonel. "But my wife insisted I meet the most charming couple at the ball."

Desiree smiled.

"Darling, I'd like you to meet the Edwards's. This is Sergeant Edwards and his beautiful wife, Julie."

The colonel reached out his big hero-hand and we exchanged polite greetings. "Nice to meet you." "Glad to know you." *("You doin' my wife?" "Only a time or two.")*

After our greeting, he turned to Julie with his big hero-grin. He took her hand into both of his.

"Mrs. Edwards, it's a pleasure to meet you."

He eyed her appraisingly as he said to me, "Sergeant Edwards, you're a very lucky man."

He had no idea. Suddenly I was glad I had made love to this pompous jerk's wife. I wanted to tell him I had. Maybe that would teach him a lesson about leering at mine. Desiree was a beautiful woman who deserved better.

"Thank you, sir," I said. And Julie smiled at me.

"Ace... Colonel, would you excuse me? I'm sure my makeup could use freshening"

"I'll join you," said Desiree.

It was an unspoken cue most men are familiar with. But I've never understood how or why women communicate the mysterious powder room herd migration effect. In that moment, it seemed that women throughout the ballroom were all making their way to the closest lady's room.

The colonel and I watched as our wives strolled off to engage in female ritual bonding.

"Well, Sergeant Edwards, should we wait dutifully here, or move along to the next phase of the event?"

I knew exactly what he meant. I might get to like this guy after all, I thought.

"Sir, I think it would be an unforgiveable waste of time if we waited another moment."

He laughed.

"I like the way you think, Sergeant." He slapped me on the back. "Lead the way."

At the bar, I ordered a straight Chivas. The colonel ordered Jack Daniels neat. We clicked glasses, turned them up and ordered another round. By the third round, we had established that I was Ace and he would be called Bud. We were old friends, telling stories about our childhoods, old girl friends, and our jobs.

I liked good-old Bud so much I was tempted to apologize to him for banging his wife. But neither he, nor I were drunk enough to appreciate that kind of honesty. Silently, through a scotch haze, I vowed to myself that I would never again lust after this man's wife-unless, of course, she asked me to. In that case, I didn't have a choice. I surely did not want to let my new friend's wife down. That would not have been friendly at all.

I chuckled out loud.

Bud laughed too. "What?" he asked.

I was just about to tell him when I felt a hand reach around my waist.

"Hi, Romeo."

It was Julie. She had sneaked up behind me and playfully hugged my waist. From the way she smiled, I could tell she and Desiree had found a bar, themselves.

"Hi, Juliet."

I gave her a quick kiss.

Desiree moved to the bar and ordered Long Island Iced Teas for herself and Julie.

"So, what have you boys been up to?" she asked. She smiled an innocent smile at me, and I hid my reaction behind my glass.

"I think Ace was about to tell us a joke," said Bud.

I was suddenly stoned sober, and choked on the scotch in my mouth. I laughed through a fit of coughing, as Julie patted my back in an effort to remove the liquid from my wind pipe.

Bleary-eyed and choking, I said, "I don't think that joke would be appropriate in present company."

Bud laughed and clapped me on the shoulder with one hero hand.

"That's too bad. I'd like to hear it some time though."

Desiree gazed into my eyes. "Yes. That's a shame. I'm sure it'll be quite funny."

Julie kissed my cheek. "Don't count on it," she said. "He's really not that funny. His jokes are awful, but I love him anyway." She kissed me again;

then wiped the lipstick from my face. We all laughed, and Desiree stared intently.

And the party went on.

The rest of the night was spent pretty much like that. The colonel and I traded rounds and dance with each other's wives. He introduced Julie and me to a group of his officer cronies and their spouses. We were charming and they were cordial. Many of the wives asked the usual questions. *"Where are you from? Do you have children? You're not related to the Boston Edwards's, are you? They're such a bore, you know."*

While chatting with a particularly interesting captain from Texas (she was over six feet tall, blonde and blue-eyed with a twang that dripped honey), I noticed Desiree had slipped off from the crowd with a distinguished-looking older man with green eyes. I later learned this was Royce Dillon. And that he was a business associate to Desiree. It turned out that Dillon was an associate to most business owners in town.

They were seated and held hands. Not hand-in-hand, but they held both hands like old friends might; old women friends. They nodded to one another and smiled as they spoke. The friendship between them seemed genuine, sincere and open. But when he looked at Desiree, I noticed a little something extra. His gaze lingered a bit longer than it should have. His expression was one of bitter-sweet pain, longing.

As she laughed and smiled, I wondered if she was aware that the old man was hopelessly in love with her. I wondered if she cared. Suddenly, I was jealous. Someone should break this up, I thought.

Julie nudged close to me. "I wonder if Bud knows his wife is fooling around," she whispered.

I tensed; and frowning deeply, stared directly into her, now tipsy, eyes.

She smiled, nodding discreetly to Desiree and the old man. "It's obvious that he has a thing for her," she said.

We both looked at the couple; then around the room, checking to see if we had been overheard. When we looked at each other again, we were each vainly attempting to stifle the laughter that burst from our bellies. We left the ballroom snickering and giggling like school girls with fat, juicy gossip.

We laughed all the way home and most of the next day. But for me, the thought of Desiree with Dillon would cease to be funny. Just as the thought of Desiree with any man was no laughing matter.

"Mmmm…. Mama like." – Desiree Simone McKensie

CHAPTER 3

A full month passed before I would see Desiree again. During that time, I concentrated on my job. I was finally adjusting to the area and the people I worked with. We'd accomplished a couple of high profile projects, and I was high with elation. We had done such a great job, in fact, that our company commander handed out three-day passes to my staff and me.

Julie and I had decided to use the time to take a mini vacation. Unfortunately, Sheila became ill that weekend. Not wanting to spoil my downtime, Julie suggested I get away on my own. She said she would nurse Sheila to health, and she and the girls would have a wonderful mother/daughter weekend while I was away.

By now, Desiree was just a small itch in the back of my mind. I had, actually, nearly forgotten the way she had made me feel when she was around. When I thought of her it was like a memory from my far away past. No pain. No longing. No desire. …Just a memory. And, to tell the truth, not even much of a memory. It would have been better for a lot of people had my feelings remained tepid and dispassionate.

But that would have been asking too much of fate. The first night of my vacation found me in a small dark jazz bar in Charleston, South Carolina. I had driven up the coast, stopping from time to time to take in the scenery and enjoy the Southern ambiance and Low Country mystique. I was told this region was called the Low Country because much of it was below sea level.

I was impressed with the slow and easy graciousness of the folks I encountered on the way. Everyplace I stopped, someone offered me an ice cold glass of sweet tea. Most were friendly and downright country, speaking in that Caribbean sounding dialect, I learned was called Geechi.

The food was awesome! I fell so in love with shrimp and grits that it became a favorite of mine for years to come. And fried catfish, collard greens and cornbread.... Man, yes! I learned to prepare Low Country Boil; a seasoned mixture of boiled shellfish, corn on the cob, smoked sausages and new potatoes; and my girls went absolutely wild over it; even Julie.

It was less than a three hour drive from Hinesville to Charleston. But because of my sauntering pace, it was six full hours before I checked into my hotel room. At about three in the afternoon, I threw my things on the king sized bed, not bothering to unpack. After inspecting the room and freshening up, I was out the door to see what I could get into. And there was plenty of southern-style walking around to get into.

I decided to do a little shopping while strolling through town. In the middle of trying on a cool, wheat-colored, linen three-piece suit I asked the salesman about the clubs and bars that I might enjoy. We determined he and I had different tastes, so I wound up stopping a group of trendy looking sisters on the street.

The really hot one sized me up and suggested this spot. She said, "There's this great place with a live band that a guy like you might get into." By "guy like you", I assumed she was referring to my age. I grinned, thanked them for the advice, told them it was nice meeting them, and went my way- but not before getting them to agree to hook up with me for a drink that evening.

We were on our third round of drinks and I was getting pretty comfortable with the second hottest girl in the group. The trophy in the crowd had been flirting with some well-bred fat dude across the little room. When the drink he sent came to the table she decided it was time to follow the money. She told us she would be back after talking to him awhile. The rest of us laughed as we shouted in unison, "YEAH, RIGHT!" I never saw her again.

The women stayed with me for another round; then decided it was time to leave for a place with a livelier and younger set of folks. They invited me to join them, but I realized I would be wasting my time fishing that hole. They told me where they would be if I changed my mind. But neither girl bothered to offer her phone number.

As I watched their sensuous backs melt into the haze and out the door, I pondered the prospect of calling it an early night. I was tired and more than a little buzzed from the scotch I had been drinking. Just then, the waitress came around and asked if I wanted another. "Why not?" I thought.

"Sure," I said. "One more won't hurt. Why don't you bring the tab also?" She nodded. "Okay." And off she went.

She returned and I was settling my bill, when I felt someone ease into the chair beside me. The familiar scent and warm arm draped across my shoulder, combined with the affects of the alcohol reassured me I was in no danger. I turned and Desiree kissed me on the mouth.

She giggled. "Hello, Adrian."

It was a struggle, but I managed to remain calm.

"Where's your husband?" I asked, looking around the bar.

"Relax," she said. "He's out of the country; somewhere playing secret soldier."

I was unconvinced. The coincidence was so uncanny I began to wonder if this was some type of set up.

"You're sure?"

"Absolutely," she said, making a cross sign over the place I assumed her heart should be.

"Desiree, what are you doing here? Are you following me?"

"Of course, not," she replied, laughing. "Don't flatter yourself. Besides, aren't you happy to see me?"

Despite her disquieting appearance, from virtually out of nowhere, I had to admit I *was* glad to see her. We fell into easy conversation until she locked eyes with a strapping stud seated at the bar. The tall corn-fed looking brother flashed a bright straight-toothed grin, and Desiree's eyes lit up with what I could only describe as carnal lust.

I appraised him as he continued his distant seduction. "Kinda young, isn't he?"

Desiree never broke off the flirtation. "Mmmm…. Mama like."

I chuckled at the game she was playing. "Cougar bait," I said.

She released a low throaty growl. "Grrrrrrr. Jealous?"

I shook my head. "Not in the least." And I wasn't.

She turned to me. "Good. There's no need to be. How long will you be in town?"

"Coupl'a days," I answered.

"Great," she said. "Enjoy your night. I'll catch up to you."

Rising from her seat, she gave me another kiss. And she left to do whatever it is older women do with younger men after kissing their lovers goodbye in a dark bar in the middle of the night.

As for me, it had been a long day. I went back to my hotel room, showered and went to sleep.

At five thirty a.m., I was startled from sleep by the loud and flashing hotel telephone. I initially reached to silence the alarm clock, sleepily tapping the button on the little music box. The irritating ringing persisted. Now I was awake and somewhat angry. In one movement, I reached for the phone and sat up in bed.

"Hello!"

The polite digitally generated voice informed me this was my wake up call. Then suggested I begin my day with a delicious breakfast from the award-winning kitchen, delivered by their fast and courteous room service. I placed the phone back on the cradle. I hadn't asked for a wake up call. I lay back in bed, pulled the covers over my head and closed my eyes, trying to return to that gratifying sleep groove you get into just before it's time to get out of bed to start your day.

I was just about there when there came an insistent knocking at the door.

"Now what?"

I swung my feet from the bed and marched to the door. Not bothering to ask who was there, I ripped it open. There she was, standing in the hallway, fresh, fine, casual. ...And glowing.

"Good morning, Adrian," she greeted me with a gorgeous smile and a generous kiss. "Get dressed. We're going deep sea fishing."

I didn't say a word.

"Hurry," she said. "Thaddeus is down in the car waiting."

She turned and walked away. As I watched her bounce her way down the hallway, I stood there half-dressed in boxer shorts and what I imagined was just a stupid expression. When I heard the door click behind me, I didn't even try the handle. Squeezing my eyes shut, I whispered to an unseen tormentor. "Just great!"

It wasn't long before a young woman from housekeeping appeared in the corridor. She noticed my dilemma and dispassionately (there *was* a hint of a smirk on her face) opened the door for me. In less than twenty minutes, I was standing at the front door of the hotel, waiting.

A large black, tricked out SUV Caddy rolled to a stop at my feet. I got in and Desiree introduced me to Thaddeus as a family friend; it was technically true. The young man was even bigger and better looking up close in the early daylight. Physically, he was cut from the same cloth as the colonel. But he was much younger and had none of the colonel's panache; a gigolo in training.

He referred to me as "Old Dude" and I, taking the fatherly, high road, affectionately dubbed him Tad. Desiree smiled cryptically at the irony of the name. Tad didn't get the joke. He was a runner; a young bull that had not yet learned how to pace himself. Unfortunately for Tad, he also had not yet learned the benefit of Dramamine. A fish out of water, so to speak, he spent the better part of the excursion below deck in the throes of a landlubber's distress. And I made full advantage of his malady.

We cruised for two hours; sixty miles to the deep water where the skipper told us we would have the best chance of catching the really big fish. The skipper was an old salt; an experienced sea dog who knew all the big water hideouts. The very capable mate was a weathered red-headed beauty he called Rusty. She was as tall as me, and her aging body stubbornly held on to vestiges of voluptuous allure that rivaled women half her age.

The boat, named "Tavern Maid", conjured memories of the song by The Looking Glass. In my mind I pictured a teary-eyed serving wench in port patiently awaiting our return. She was a speedy, comfortable craft and sliced across a calm sea like the proverbial hot knife through butter. It was an amazingly fantastic day to be on the water.

Rusty had prepared tasty breakfast sandwiches, which Desiree served as we went. The skipper didn't have a lot of rules besides the normal safety considerations. And any puking would have to be done over the rail, into the ocean. Tad was exceptionally obedient.

Desiree nursed him dutifully, stroking his back as he leaned over the water emptying his belly. She gave him saltines to settle his stomach and water to rinse his mouth. I helped by passing her a package of gum for his breath. She stopped dabbing the perspiration from his face to reach for the gum. But her expression told me she didn't really approve of my help. I suppressed the laugh.

Ultimately, her ministrations were fruitless. Though he had nothing left to vomit, he continued to wretch violently. So violently, in fact, I began to wonder if we should turn the boat around and get him medical attention.

Tad had had enough. He resembled a whipped dog with his slumped shoulders and bowed head. He walked as steadily as he could, considering his condition, plus the motion of the sea and the speed of the vessel. Desiree prepared a space for him to lie down. As she did, Rusty and I exchanged glances and quick, skeptical smiles. Tad stretched out, and we wouldn't hear another peep from him for the remainder of the day.

I had staked out a spot on the bow to enjoy the wind and salt spray as we sped along. It wasn't long after she tucked Tad in that Desiree joined me. Looking out at the rushing waters, I gave her a little nudge when she came close. I avoided looking directly into her eyes for fear of speaking inappropriately. I couldn't resist a small jibe, though. I didn't appreciate playing the part of understudy.

"I guess your toy-friend is worn out."

"Yeah," she sighed, wistfully. "They all seem to break so easily. I guess they just don't make them the way they used to."

"No, I guess they don't," I agreed.

She was thoughtfully silent.

"How about you?" she asked.

Desiree was quite a piece of work.

I shook my head, seriously. "No, sister. You play too rough."

"Coward," she challenged.

I chuckled. "Yep," I said, never meeting her gaze.

We were quiet for a time, looking out at the distant horizon. When we finally did look at each other we fell into a fit of laughter so raucous my sides began to hurt. When our laughter subsided, she leaned on me and gave me a small kiss on my stubbled cheek.

I smiled.

The fishing was great! Desiree was first in the chair. Seated at the stern, she manned the rod as the baited line trailed the boat. It wasn't long before she hooked into a magnificent billfish. When the pole suddenly bent forward, she jerked it back, setting the hook. Her face set with the determined exhilaration of a true sportsman, she expertly reeled in line.

Desiree kept the pressure on the aquatic beast, pulling it towards the boat in one movement and furiously reeling in the slack with the next. Bracing her feet against the deck floor, she strained to secure the powerful combatant. She repeated the give and take action over and over, establishing a rhythmic pattern of alternately reeling while bending forward and leaning backwards, attempting to muscle the fish into the boat.

Fighting franticly for its freedom, the enormous animal broke the surface of once calm waters. I was amazed, as in the distance, its gigantic head came up out of the water with a frothy brine spray framing its iridescent body. Rusty let go a shout of excitement, as the fish leapt above the sea, its tail raking the surface. At the apex of its leap the webbed dorsal fin spread like so many fingers of a gloved hand. Shaking fiercely above the water, the fish was trying to throw the hook, but Desiree would have none of it. She pulled back on the rod, ensuring the line remained taut.

Rusty yelled again. "Yeah! That's it! That's the way! Don't let it get away! Keep the line tight! Keep it tight! Keep it tight!"

It was a good hour before the fish's energy was finally spent, and Rusty was able to pull its powerful body into the boat. It was measured, weighed and tagged. After snapshots were taken of Desiree with her catch, the beautiful animal was released.

Desiree's face was beaming with excitement. I was impressed. That was a two hundred pound monster she handled him with expert deftness. I said a silent prayer I wouldn't embarrass myself when it was my turn in the big chair.

I was blessed. Though my fish didn't quite measure up to the one Desiree caught, it didn't disappoint with its zeal to live. It put up a spirited fight in the water and was so active in the boat it nearly speared Rusty in the leg. I was having a great time.

After Desiree and I scored our trophies, the skipper positioned the boat over a fertile reef where we pulled in an array of beautiful reef fishes. The bright sunlight illuminated the deep water. It was so clean we could clearly make out the blended colors down below. We loudly cheered for each other as we reeled in fish two and three at a time from the resplendent, one hundred foot deep ocean floor.

Two hours later, we were exhausted and any primal instinct to capture and kill had been well sated. I was tired, hungry and more than a little thirsty. In all the excitement, I had forgotten to hydrate and the heat of the bright Atlantic sun began to sap my strength. I sat on a bench at the bow guzzling bottled water and wolfing down sandwiches like a man starved for a week. Desiree napped in the wheelhouse, while Rusty moved about, cleaning and securing ropes, tackle and our day's catch. Tad, finally discovering his sea legs, was admiring the well full of fish we had caught while he was recuperating.

Tad was actually a pretty good guy. We talked while Desiree slept, and became friends on the way to port. He was a Charleston native. The only child of an elderly woman who lost her would be husband to his wife; he had grown up with all the world had to offer-except a father. The young man had that folksy charm about him I came to love in Charleston and her citizens.

At the docks, we gave most of the fish to Rusty to share with families in need. We took pictures of our catch before she cleaned, filleted and packed a portion in a cooler on ice for my journey home. Still a little woozy, Tad gave me the keys to the Caddy, and I drove us back to my hotel.

We made plans to get together after we had showered and rested; meeting later to paint the town. Rusty and the skipper continued the tour, guiding us to one hot club after another. With them, we were treated to the seafarer's experience of Charleston. Though this was Tad's town, he was learning a part of the former slave port he was never exposed to on his side of the tracks. We had a ball, grogging and carousing like pirates! The three men graciously shared the two women's attention, dancing and fawning; and stealing the occasional drunken sailor kiss.

It was about three thirty in the morning, after an early breakfast that they dropped me off again. We said our goodbyes, and I promised to catch up to Desiree back in Hinesville. I also made plans to see Tad, Skipper and Rusty in a couple of months for another fishing trip.

Fishing became a tradition with Tad and me. He would come to Hinesville from time to time. We would get together several times over the next few months to fish and chase honeys. The boy had mad skills. He became like family. Julie and the girls loved him.

About a year and a half after we met, Tad's mom phoned to say he had been shot and killed. I rushed to Charleston. Some married guy shot the

171

kid over someone else's wife. And that dude never spent a single day in jail. I was just disgusted.

At the funeral, with Julie by my side, listening to the words of encouragement, I remembered one of our fishing trips. I had caught a small throwback and he teased me about it. "You cain't do no bettern' that, Old Dude?"

"You know, Thaddeus, Tad is short for tadpole, don't you?" I asked.

"Yeah? Ain't nothin' short about my tadpole," he quipped.

"So you say. I heard different." We laughed and we fished-and we drank. He was a wonderful friend and the closest I had ever had to a son. He loved me and was loyal to a fault. I could do no wrong in his eyes.

Though he had adored Desiree, he never even flinched to learn she and I were "tight". He took it in stride. "Besides," he had said, philosophically, "She's married. An' you're married. An' married folk ought to be with married folk."

There was an odd and twisted, ironic truth in what he was saying. But I figured the closer truth was that he wanted to do things on his terms, and Desiree was just too doggone demanding. She wouldn't put up with his flirtations, and Thaddeus loved Thaddeus way too much to change his lifestyle. And all that was just fine with me. It was a perfect arrangement. We all got all we could get-and a little more.

Though, she was all but inconsolable at hearing of Tad's death, Desiree couldn't bring herself to attend the funeral. She said she didn't want to remember him that way. She wanted her last memories of him to be of the happy times. I held her as she wept.

Poor Tad...

Squeezing Julie's hand lightly, I fought back the tears. He had never had a chance. I would really miss that boy.

Following our chance meeting in Charleston, Desiree and I began to see each other increasingly more often. Of course there were the weekend rendezvous while Bud was off saving the world; or debauching with his killer cronies and warrior groupies. Besides the in-town hookups, there was also the occasional "getaway". She would rent elaborate villas and hotel suites, while I booked myself in austere digs to match my meager government budget.

In order to cover my tracks, and finance my travel and expenses, I would align our trips with temporary duty assignments. As an excuse to be away from home so often, I found journalistic reasons to attend conferences and training courses. Leaving Lisa in charge, Desiree planned her work in the shop to coincide with these travels. Because, it was important to her that the boutique should lead fashion trends, Desiree traveled to the toniest cities to buy the beautiful garments. Though these were normally seasonal trips, it was not unusual for her to make additional off season junkets in order to replenish stock.

If anyone made the connection that our absence and availability coincided, they never said so. Like Clark Kent and Superman; if one was missing, so

173

was the other. I attributed the lack of attention to the fact that I, at least, just wasn't that interesting. And I worked very hard to avoid being caught. But it's so often true what they say about "the best laid plans".

With Bud's considerable resources, should he become suspicious, I felt it was best we not overexpose ourselves. It had become an expensive, yet necessary custom to keep separate rooms. Since military people get around, neither of us could be sure we wouldn't run into some busybody who knew one or both of our spouses. We were very careful on the streets and in shops; less so in restaurants. But in the dark corners of smoky little saloons, caution was all but abandoned. It was there we cuddled; relaxed and passionate in our devotion to each other's emotional needs.

On one trip to New Orleans, while shopping in the mall, Desiree spotted Bud through the store window. She, gasping loudly, stopped in her tracks. Grabbing my arm, she ducked behind a rack of clothes.

Caught off guard, I stumbled behind her. Agitated, I nearly shouted. "Have you lost your....?"

Desiree shushed me. "Be quiet! Bud is out there!"

She was pointing outside the store.

"Get out of here!" I said, straining against her grasp to see into the mall. "What is he doing here? How did he find us?"

She pulled me back down. "Keep still! I don't know why he's here. Stay down-he hasn't found us yet. And we *can't* let him find us here together."

"Well, if he comes in here, he will find us together," I said. "Let's just pretend we ran into each other while I was shopping for Julie."

"Please!" she snapped. "The man's not stupid. Think! We've got to do something. If he catches us, he will kill us!"

She was nearly hysterical.

"What do you expect me to do? We're trapped."

She looked disgusted, thinking. Taking my hand she hissed, "Follow me!"

She snatched a pair of dresses from the rack. And with a clamp on my hand, Desiree hurriedly dragged me towards the ladies' fitting room.

"What? I don't care if he does catch us. I'm not wearing a dress," I said.

"Hush!" she snapped. "And keep your head down. C'mon!" We scurried to the fitting room.

Once in the little room, she regained her composure. She began searching through her purse; then retrieved a Benjamin.

After peeking outside to see if Bud had entered the store, Desiree gave me a big kiss. "Stay here for one hour, Baby. Go back to your room and wait. I'll catch up to you after I get him out of town."

I was beginning to feel humiliation rise up in me. "I ain't stayin' up in here like some scared little mouse. What can he do?"

She was very calm now. "Darling... He has a conceal carry permit. And you had better believe he is carrying. Do you want to die?"

That question was like a splash of cold water in my face, but bravado wouldn't allow me to back down. "Bud is reasonable. It's not that serious."

She leaned into me and kissed me again. "It's what he does" she said. "And he's good at it. Besides, even if he doesn't kill us, he may leave me. Adrian, I can't be alone. I need him. Please do this for me."

That did it. I couldn't allow her to be harmed if I could prevent it. I relented. Taking the dresses with her, she left me with instructions to wait until the salesgirl came to rescue me.

Outside in the store I could just make out Bud's voice, as he greeted his wife. She greeted him, cheerily, in that sing-song voice of hers. I imagined her smiling up at him; then kissing him. My pride was bruised. It was an effort to stay hidden like some cowering rabbit. Then I thought of the weapon he would be wearing. He was a very large guy. It was probably a very large weapon. I determined I would remain hidden-for Desiree's sake. It was only the chivalrous thing to do.

It was the longest hour of my life. I expected the door to come open anytime; followed by a hail of cheater killing bullets. When the knock came at the door, I was barely able to suppress a shriek of, "Please, don't shoot me!"

"Yes? Come in," I said, displaying courage I did not feel.

The door swung open. It was an attractive young woman whom I assumed was a store employee. She smiled. "You must be Adrian," she said.

Oh just great! She knew my name! "Yes," I replied. "Who're you?"

She didn't answer the question. "Your friend asked me to guide you out our back door. She said she would call you later with a weather report."

I grinned, appraising her for the first time. "Will I be needing…Rainy weather equipment tonight?"

She returned my grin. "Never can tell…. You just may," she said with a sexy little body swivel. "I'll be at my house, all warm and cozy, and….." The grin left her face. "….Very, very dry."

Suddenly, she wasn't so attractive. She was all business. My grin faded. "Oh. Okay…." I said with a sigh. "Lead the way."

She didn't budge. "Your girlfriend said you would give me a hundred dollars for helping you."

I remembered the hundred dollar bill in Desiree's hand as she left the room. I challenged the woman.

"Are you sure she told you I'd pay you?"

She never batted an eye. "Yes, she said you'd pay. ….And not to take you anywhere until you do." Desiree told me later, that she had said no such thing; the girl had already been paid.

"Of course, she did," I said as I reached in my back pocket to retrieve my wallet. I gave her the C-note. A shame. You just can't trust anyone, these days.

The girl simply took the money; then without another word, showed me her back. I followed closely; but not too close. I was still being chivalrous.

I waited in my room the entire day, hoping Desiree would call to say Bud had left town. When she didn't call or come to see me, I decided not to risk going out and running into them. So the trip wouldn't be an entire loss, I concentrated particularly hard at the conference. I also decided to enjoy myself as best I could. And that meant partying extremely hard. I headed to the one place I was sure I wouldn't have a lot of trouble accomplishing the task.

I hoped that, by now, the dangerous couple would have gone back to Hinesville or stayed inside, to bond in an impromptu honeymoon. While, roaming the French Quarter, I connected with a thick-ankled little conventioneer from Idaho. A medical equipment saleswoman since her divorce, she had become her company's top producer in less than two years. No wonder... In her mid thirties, she was only now blossoming into the hotness which had skipped her in her teens and twenties. With her newly discovered beauty, she attacked the world with the exuberance of a wide torrent, finally bursting forth, after years of swollen obstruction. Whatever she lacked in skill and ability, she surely compensated for in zeal.

I had just walked into the bar when I noticed the woman strutting her stuff in a wet tee shirt contest. Though she wasn't particularly equipped for the competition, you had to admire her guts. Her co-workers loudly cheered her on, but it was a dismal defeat, none-the-less. Seated with her friends, laughing and playfully fending off their aggressive advances, she took the loss in stride.

Catching her eye, I approached the table. I offered to buy her a drink and after introductions, we were getting along like we had known each other for years. Her colleagues didn't seem too keen about our new friendship. They would alternate between attempts to feel her up, taking veiled shots at me and harassing the acne-plagued young man with them. I didn't care. I wasn't trying to do them.

The office stud would challenge me on cool points at every opportunity, calling me names like, "ground pounder" and "grunt". They needn't have gotten so agitated about me. I wasn't their rival. I was only a novelty. And if they were patient, in time, they would each get a chance to nail her. Each of them, that is, except the pimply faced boss's kid. The only thing he would get is an early promotion with perks, an exorbitant pay raise and an exclusive country club membership as a cherry to top it all off. And they had no idea; all the while groping their colleague and pestering their eventual boss.

The disc jockey played an eclectic mix of soft rock, country rock, rhythm and blues and big hair band ballads. It was a loud, but mellow atmosphere that I found myself wishing would last forever. The girl at my side was becoming more comfortable, leaning against me and giggling as I whispered tidbits of nonsense into her ear. In less than an hour's time, she had moved from a questionable no to a definite maybe. Her companions were finally accepting defeat. They were beginning to concentrate on other distractions like drinking contests and the latest office gossip.

179

With one arm across her shoulders, I gave her a small kiss on the cheek. Just as she turned to return my kiss, I noticed a group of military types enter the bar. I had initially thought they were troops from the conference. I was going wave to get their attention when I recognized the tall straight hero silhouette of Bud McKensie. A wave of panic went through me when I realized Bud and his combat crew had me trapped here, and there was nothing I could do. I wasn't a match for just one of these guys. Now I was about to face off with; no less than seven; U.S. government trained and armed patriots.

A deafening "HUA!" boomed over the music; over the tinkling glasses; over the drunken voices and the reveling laughter. Bud spotted me. "Ace!" he shouted, with a great big grin on his face. He marched the distance across the bar in three long strides. Wide-eyed, I watched as an equally, wide-eyed, Desiree came into view behind him.

"Boy, what are you doing here?" The colonel had reached my table and I was, now standing, nearly at attention. Bud reached for my hand. I returned the gesture. My hand disappeared inside his big hero grasp. If Bud suspected anything, he was the best poker player I had ever seen.

I told Bud about the conference and introduced the girl with me. He leered at her and winked at me; then called his men over to meet me. They were a friendly, loud bunch. The term, "Canned Heat" ran through my mind. I may have been the only person in the room, besides Desiree, who had any

180

idea of the level of pain and destruction these good brothers could bring to bear. I suddenly felt very proud; and oddly safe.

Desiree shook my hand. "It's good to see you, Sergeant Edwards. How is Julie?" There was an icy edge to her voice. It was not missed by Bud.

"Call me Ace," I replied. I felt her hand tense. "She's fine, Dez. Thanks for asking. Let me introduce you to a friend of mine."

The women shook hands, exchanging cool greetings. Bud watched intently. I was enjoying this tremendously. We all took seats, and I celebrated the New Orleans night.

Later that evening, Bud cornered me. He told me I should be a little more careful about fooling around on my wife. He told me his wife was a talker; a terrible gossip. And it was obvious, by her attitude she did not appreciate my cheating on Julie. He said he had never been caught because he did all his dirt overseas around folks he could trust. It was an uncomfortable subject, but I didn't dare say anything to interrupt Bud's train of thought. I liked the way he was thinking. And as long as he continued to think this way, I didn't have anything to fear from him.

After the crowd began to thin, I escorted the seasoned ingénue to my hotel room. She didn't want her colleagues to see me leaving hers. Giggling, hugging, kissing and holding hands, we staggered together, the entire way to the room. With her, I was anything but chivalrous.

It was several days before I returned to Hinesville with the expectation of resuming a normal life without Desiree. However, that prospect seemed even less appealing to her than it was to me. Despite our close call, we agreed to continue seeing each other. We resolved we would be even more careful. She had failed to inform me that she always left Lisa her itinerary, should an emergency arise. Bud knew this, and would surprise her from time to time. That was a very important piece of information to blithely disregard. It could have ended very badly. Desiree expressed to me that it did end badly. I had no idea what she was talking about.

The week after I returned found us in a quiet little, off-the-beaten-path, restaurant. We were in the process of fence mending. We never even made it to the entree. It started with small talk; then somehow escalated to the fact that I was able to enjoy myself despite being separated from her. She said something about a frumpy little, bad dressing house frau. I defended the girl. If we were keeping score, Desiree was winning on points. All things considered, in a perfect world, she couldn't lose me.

"That's not the point," she said. "Why didn't you stay in your room, out of sight?"

It had slipped out before I thought about it. "Because I'm a grown man- not your little pull-me-out-when-you-feel-like-playin'-with-me-puppet!"

Her mouth fell open. It appeared that she was about to reply, but thought better of it. I was instantly sorry for what I had said.

She closed her mouth. Now it was impossible to read her beautiful face. She slowly removed the napkin from her lap and placed it neatly over the elegantly prepared house salad. She drew a long deep breath; then released it.

"I think we should leave," she said, quietly.

I reached across the table to stroke her hand. She allowed me to touch it briefly before sliding it from the table onto her lap. She stared into my eyes. I got the message. It was time to go.

After paying for an expensive meal we didn't eat, I escorted her to her car. She walked stiffly by my side, outside of arm's reach. I opened the door and helped her into the car and received a frosty "thank you" for my troubles. When I settled into the driver's seat, I noticed something not quite right.

I sniffed the air a couple of times. "Did you just...."

Desiree cut me off. "Did I just what?"

She had lost her doggone mind. "Nothin'," I said.

"That's right-nothin'," she snapped. "Don't be blaming your bad habits on me. Start the car and let down the windows."

I looked away and shook my head, slowly. ....Then I did as I was told.

"Well... I guess the honeymoon is over," I muttered. ...And pulled the car out of the parking space.

"I guess so," she countered, sharply.

I couldn't be certain in the poor light, but I thought I might have seen the hint of a smile on her lovely face before she turned to look out her window.

183

In time, Desiree and I drew closer. The New Orleans episode had become a source of many hours of jokes for us both. I would tease her about her reaction when she had spotted Bud in the mall. She teased me about being ripped off by what she called a "post pubescent floozy" in the shop dressing room. I laughed with her, but it wasn't funny. That little girl had me at a disadvantage and violated me. I was tempted to go back Louisiana and get my money back. That caused Desiree to laugh all the more.

"That wouldn't be judicious," she said. "Besides, it serves you right for cheating on me."

I wasn't quite sure what to call what it was I had done to her, but I was pretty sure it could not have, legally, been called cheating. I left that thought unsaid. One other thing I was sure of was Desiree would not have seen the humor in it.

I thought of Bud and our conversation that evening. I liked the guy. It seemed to me Desiree didn't know him as well as she thought she did. Bud cheated. But he had well defined rules. It didn't seem logical to me that a man who spent so much time from home actually expected his wife to remain faithful. Perhaps he knew about us, and was being philosophically open-minded about the affair.

I found myself hoping when I was out of the picture they would find a way to be honest with each other. At least, then, I had no delusions about our future as a couple. She wasn't going anyplace. They were a matched set. Even the girl from Idaho commented on how well-suited for one another they seemed to be. It was that comment that had sealed the deal, ensuring she and I would spend an extended evening together-becoming well-suited for one another.

Desiree had said she needed him. She certainly didn't need him financially. She had shared with me that she was independently wealthy. She was made so by a series of very lucrative-and I suspected somewhat shady-real estate investments. She had said her connection with Old Royce would guarantee her a comfortable living for life. All she had to do was continue to maintain her highly respectable dress shop and the deals would always be made available. She didn't offer to explain the details of the arrangement. And there was something that sounded so distasteful to me I did not even want to know. In this, I intended to remain, blissfully ignorant.

Regardless of what Bud suspected; or even knew; he never interrupted another tryst. And Desiree and I became so tight that I began to think of her as exclusively my own. I did my best to establish an equitable balance, with Desiree, work and my family. It wasn't easy. And I wasn't fooling anyone. If either would suffer from lack of attention, it certainly was not going to be Desiree. She never complained about the arrangement. Nor did she have reason to. The curious thing was, Julie never complained either.

Though she never admitted it, I suspected she had a secret companion of her own. She spent a good deal of time with charity work. There were even weekend conferences and symposiums where she said she would go to learn how to better serve those in need. I was sure there was another reason for her zealous pursuit of noble activities. Whatever the reason, she didn't interfere with my own pursuits. And it was fine with me.

Everything was great! ....Until we lost Tad. Somehow things changed after the kid was killed. Desiree and I drifted apart. Our time together was less frequent; the durations, brief. We seemed to find reasons not to be together. Instead of weekends and mid-week getaways, we would squeeze in half hour lunches and twenty-five minute quickies now and then.

Julie and I became closer. We laughed more often. And I knew a peace I had never imagined. It was the, proverbial, "calm before the storm".

Late one night, or early one morning (depending on your perspective) in a nearby *cheaters' inn,* Desiree gave me a bit of news that would change my life forever.

"Adrian, I'm pregnant."

I was standing in the mirror, tying my tie.

"Quit playin'," I said. I watched her reflection over my shoulder in the mirror. She was sitting on the bed, preparing to leave. Her smile was warm. She appeared relaxed. Except for her hands, which fumbled with her lipstick case, she seemed perfectly calm.

"I'm serious," she said.

Watching her in the mirror, I untied my tie and started over.

"Really?"

"Yes," she replied, her face without expression.

My hands were shaking. For the third time, I started the tying process.

"You're sure?"

"Yes," she said.

My tie was a mess. Grinning, I turned and knelt before her. I took her hands into mine. "Sweetheart, that's wonderful!" I was elated over the news. In the beginning, it would be a great big mess. But once we had weathered the worst of the storm, we had a chance at a pretty good life together. It was the best thing I had heard in a while. I would have another chance to have a son.

"Yes, Adrian," she agreed, smiling. "It is wonderful." Then she was sad. She, slowly, stroked the back of my head. "My husband will be very happy. I'll finally give him the child he's always wanted."

All of a sudden, the room was extremely warm. Something in my mind changed. I would never be able to adequately explain what happened in that moment. It was like walking through a translucent barrier and emerging different; something less than I had been. And I knew I could never recover what was left behind in the transition-or better still, what was taken from me in the process.

I thought she misspoke; or that I had heard her incorrectly. She was already referring to me as her husband. She was nervous, I thought; confused. Looking to reassure her, I soothingly corrected her. "Baby, I'm not your husband yet. We've got a lot to do before that happens; a lot to face up to. But if we stay strong together, we can overcome the challenges."

She was holding my face in her hands; and bent to kiss me. I was so proud of her. "Adrian... I adore you.... I love you."

I took her hands and kissed them. Looking into her eyes, I confessed the contents of my heart. "I love you, Desiree." I said it with a great big grin on my face. "I love you more than I've ever loved anyone in my life."

She removed a hand from my grasp and placed it on her belly.

"Adrian, Darling," she said softly. "You're not the father.... This isn't your child."

I stood and backed away slowly. This must have been some kind of bad joke. Taking a deep breath before speaking, my chest hurt and I was shaking from confusion and anger. I was outside my body, watching the scene unfold. I saw the following moments occur before they had, but I was powerless to influence the outcome. "Desiree, darling, you're having my baby. How could it not be so?"

She stood and came to me. With her hands in my hands, she said, "Because it's not so, baby. I'd do anything not to hurt you, but I've got to tell you the truth."

Trembling, I took her into an embrace. I was trying to reconcile my love for Desiree with my anger at what appeared to be a horrible betrayal. "I'm trying to work the math here. You're telling me you were with someone else, other than me while Bud was away?"

She pressed herself out of my embrace. "No," she said. "That's not what I'm saying."

I was becoming, increasingly, angry. "Then, what are you saying?" I had shouted it.

Desiree flinched. Her eyes went wide and a flash of fear went across her face. In a moment, her fear turned to anger. It was a mistake to lose my temper with her. I realized I would lose any chance of reasoning with her if we were to become estranged.

"I just don't want another man raising my child." I sincerely loved her. I wanted her to have my baby. I wanted this baby.

"Listen to me," she said. "I'm sorry. This is not your baby."

"Isn't it possible?" I was asking for a lifeline. "Couldn't it be mine?"

She snorted. "The immaculate conception is possible. But it didn't happen here." Now she was being glib. "This is my baby. ....And the father is whomever *I* decide. Not you; not Bud; nobody can change that."

I reached for her. She drew away. "Don't touch me," she snapped. "Do us all a favor, Adrian. Save yourself. You do not want to get involved....."

I stopped her, walking through her upraised hand. "I am involved. I've been involved since the first time I saw you. You're having my baby and I'm going to prove it. There are tests."

She kissed me; then allowed a small laugh before leaving my arms. "It's just my luck to get involved with a mule of man, like you. As for those tests; think about it; you really don't know who and what you're dealing with here. Thaddeus's death could have been the result of jealous rage; or something much more sinister. Think."

189

We stood staring into each other's eyes. We were silent that way for a while, each of us remembering. Poor Tad. What had she gotten him into? What had I gotten myself into? I shook my head slowly. She nodded, never losing eye contact. Finally, she broke the silence.

"The results are whatever I say they are."

"You could do that?"

She nodded. "That and more," she whispered. "Adrian, it's already done." And with a last kiss, she walked out the door.

The first sun rays of a new Georgia morning had begun to spread across the town like the cloak of a dark evening shadow. From the open door, I watched the day brighten, and felt a melancholy descend upon me with a crushing heaviness. My family would be waking. They would expect to find me; father and husband; rising sleepily from beneath the comfort of the floral print bed covers we had spent so many hours shopping for on one drizzly summer afternoon.

The thought of being discovered; of losing; sickened me. Fear and self-loathing clutched my heart. I shut the door and leaden feet carried my numb body across the floor to the bedside. Fully dressed, I slipped beneath the rented covers of the motel bed, into the therapeutic unconsciousness of sleep.

The bailiff escorted me to the judge's well appointed office. I had just been released from the Biloxi jail after a six week's stay. There were Diana and the judge sitting very comfortably-and too friendly, I might add-sipping scotch and waiting for me. Judge Albert F. Johnson had more compassion for me than I deserved. I had completely lost it, forty-four days earlier, standing in front of his bench in the Mississippi court room. I couldn't help it. There I was damp, drunk and bloody (it wasn't all my blood), trying to explain away a public intoxication and disturbing the peace charge.

I was doing pretty well (at least, I thought I was), when my eyes focused on the name plate in front of him. *Judge Albert F. Johnson.* The "F" stood for Frank. I stopped talking and began to laugh. Albert Frank Johnson. I never knew his first name. He was a friend of Diana's. She always referred to him as Frankie. I was out control now.

"Frankie!" I shouted it and the court room broke up in boisterous laughter.

"Albert? That's your first name: Albert?"

He was very cool. "Yes."

"Albert F. Johnson?" I was hysterical.

"That's right, Mister Edwards."

"A. Frank Johnson!" People in the court room were eating this up. "A. F. Johnson! A. Fat Johnson!" By now, even the arresting cop and the three guys I had been fighting had gotten in on it.

With one swing of his gavel, Judge Albert F. Johnson threw the book at me. When he was finished I owed fifteen hundred dollars in fines and court

191

costs, thirty-five hundred dollars in property damage and he tacked on an additional fourteen days to a thirty day sentence. That last one was for contempt of court.

"Get him out of my courtroom," he said.

As the bailiff was leading me away, the judge called after me, "That's Frank, Mister Edwards. Enjoy your stay in Biloxi."

That was a month since the morning Desiree told me she was pregnant; then left me alone in that motel room to deal with it. When I finally arrived home; two days later; Julie and the girls were already gone. I tried to find Desiree but she had left town, also. I had cornered Colonel McKensie in his office, and nearly got my brains beat out for my trouble.

"I like you, Ace," he said. "But you've got a problem. As far as my wife and I are concerned, you never touched her. She and I are having a baby and we're very happy about it."

I drunkenly, swung on him and missed badly. He fluidly moved out of range and countered with a right cross to my temple. I went down in a heap. It was a blessing that the two military police NCO's arrived when they did. I was about to get up off the floor and settle the whole thing right then and there. They took me away.

"Direct Sergeant Edwards off post, please," he told them. "Put your clipboards away. This scuffle never happened. And you were never here."

The cops looked at each other, then agreed.

"Ace, get some help," he said. "You haven't lost anything here. None of this will adversely affect you. You've still got a career. You can recover your family."

"You're trying to steal my baby," I said, struggling against the MP's.

"The truth is, you tried to steal mine, pal," he replied. "Ace, don't push this. You can't win."

They took me away. And three hours later, I was on the road headed to Louisiana. I was going to get my woman. I was going to get my unborn child. Somehow, the closer I got to Louisiana, the more the plan changed. And now I was in this Mississippi judge's office with Diana, preparing to eat the kind of crow only close old friends could serve up.

"Come on in, Ace!"

Frankie got up and shook my hand. He dismissed the bailiff. A moment later, he was pouring me a drink.

After we were all seated, he asked me, "So, Ace, how do you like my little jail?"

Diana hid her grin in the glass she was holding.

I took a sip. "I've seen better, Frankie. The mattresses are a little thin."

"It's not meant to be a resort, Adrian," he said sensibly. "It is Adrian now, isn't it? They tell me you've had a name change since you moved to Georgia."

I heard the ice tinkle in Diana's glass. She was enjoying this more than she had a right to.

"It wasn't. It's Ace. And I didn't."

"Well, you didn't get married while you were in our jail, did you?"

Diana snorted into her glass.

"No. But I did get a coupla interesting proposals. One wanted a divorce from his husband... Some judge he said was cheatin' on him...Try'n,ta play straight."

Diana set her glass on the desk. She had had enough of our machismo. I supposed she had determined we had played to a draw, and we could both be satisfied there. I wasn't satisfied. I had a couple of mama jokes I had worked on in the jail, and I wanted to try them out on Frankie.

"Alright, boys," she said. "That'll do. Why don't we get down to business?"

Frankie picked up some papers off his desk. After scanning them, he sighed officiously. "Let's see. We have public intoxication, public urination, diving into the Gulf from the casino balcony and there's the matter of the fisticuffs."

Diana stared at me as Frankie read the report. "Public urination.... Really?" she said.

Frankie went on. "Ace, you know, you hurt one of them boys pretty good. If he hasn't got any now, he may never have children."

Diana had been watching me. She turned to Frankie.

He answered the unasked question. "Ace kicked him in the groin."

Diana gave me a little "that's my boy" look; then asked Frankie how long it would take to clear this all up.

"Well, basically, he's free to go," he said. "Ace, I had your car sent back to that *back water* town you've been hiding in for the last several months."

A judge in Biloxi, Mississippi was calling another small town in the south *back water*. That's ironic. I was almost compelled to defend Hinesville. But I thought better of it. *Playing the Dozen* with Frankie wasn't going to get me out of this any sooner.

"Thanks, Frankie," I said. "Is there anything else?"

"Just a couple of things," he said. "There's the matter of a Mrs. Smith. She was stopped two days ago, driving your car. She says she's your wife? Are we looking at bigamy now?"

A wide-eyed Diana waited for my response. I shook my head, "No".

"Good," he said. "Though, I do suppose we could nail you on Mann Act violations. But we'll let that one slid. We get more than our share of those around these parts."

"Interstate prostitution?" Diana asked.

Frankie nodded, disgustedly.

She relaxed. The law was meant to suppress sex trafficking. Neither of them thought I was capable of white slavery, pimping. I suppose it was already established that I was more of a client than a provider. Of course, Frank could have gotten me on other charges if he really wanted to.

I nodded. "Yeah, she's with me."

I remembered it all now. I had driven to Saint Luke, Louisiana, searching for Desiree. Unable to find her, I went back to New Orleans to get information-and my hundred dollars. Mrs. Smith didn't have any information or money, but she liked to gamble. And I bet her if she took a ride with me to Biloxi, she could make me forget all about the money she had conned out of me. I was hesitant to admit I knew her. I didn't want Frankie to add kidnapping to my charges. Although, I had pressured her, I concluded she told him she was with me of her own free will.

"You can collect her on the way out-or leave her." He was talking to Diana. "She's still got a few days to go on her sentence. She was.... Unruly."

Diana gave him a bulging envelope. "Let her finish out her time. Afterwards, put her on the bus." She rolled her eyes at me.

He took the envelope, placed it in his desk drawer and locked it; then stood to dismiss us. In the open doorway, he told me, "Ace, your driver's license is suspended in Mississippi. You can't drive in my state. You can't fly. You can't take a bus. Not a taxi. Not even a pedi cab. If you're caught on a bicycle or even a skateboard, I'm going to send you away for a long, long time. You are in Diana's custody. She's in charge. She'll be doing *all* your driving while you're here. Is that clear?"

We stood toe to toe. He reeked of cheap cologne and expensive cigars. I wanted to object, but I didn't. Frankie and I had known each other for

196

many years. He was serious; he would put me in prison and throw away the key if I gave him a reason to.

"And how long is that arrangement for?" I asked.

"Until I say different, sport." He was grinning. "I'd like to take credit for that one. But I can't. It was you friend, Deputy Hicks's idea. He said it would do you good to walk for a couple of days. He said you would understand."

I did understand. Hicks… That guy was like a nonfatal virus. It might not kill you. But it would likely be a nuisance for the rest of your life. Though he had bailed me out a time or two, I would need to do something about him. It just made sense. You don't praise the disease for the cure. And it seemed to me that Hicks might be-at least, in part-responsible for some of my problems. I'd have to figure it later. But, right now, I had more immediate issues to deal with.

We said our goodbyes to Judge Albert F. Johnson. Old Frankie had done pretty good for himself. We shook hands and I thanked him for being easy on me. He laughed when he said he was glad to help an old friend. I wondered if our other school mates were doing so good. When he and Diana kissed goodbye, I looked away. It just didn't look right. It looked…incestual?

A few minutes later, Diana and I were in the luxury rental car headed to her V.I.P. hotel suite and my, apparently, sub standard, by comparison single servant's quarters.

"You and Frankie seem to be getting along pretty good after all these years," I said.

She stopped at the traffic light. "We do alright," she replied.

"Want to talk about it?"

"No," she said, more tersely, I thought, than necessary.

The light changed and as the car moved along, I watched the pedestrians out the window fall away like still pictures in a slide show.

Diana and Frankie had a sweet little romance several years previously. I thought they would get married some day. It just never worked out that way. Though they weren't the young lovers they had been; they had obviously stayed in touch over the years. For my sake, I'm glad they did. When they located me down there on the gulf coast, Frankie had himself placed on my case. Although I had to admit a pang of jealousy, my heart felt for her aloneness.

"Well, I hope it works out for the two of you," I offered.

She turned the wheel. "You'd probably do better to concentrate on your own problems, buddy. They really kicked the snot out you this time."

Diana was referring to the, ever elusive, but ubiquitous, they. She had rescued me from "they" more times than I could count.

"Yeah, they did," I agreed. "Thanks for bailing me out, by the way. How much do I owe you?"

She shook her head. "It's been taken care of. Your deputy friend worked it out with Frankie."

"Oh." Something about the fact that Hicks had stepped in to clean up my mess bruised my pride. I wondered about Desiree. Was she thinking about me? Did she care that I was broken? I longed to see her.

"I spoke to Julie," Diana said. I didn't respond. "You do remember Julie, don't you? Pretty girl...? You're married to her....? Had a couple of little girls for you...?"

She was being mean.

"How is she?"

"She'll be thrilled you're so concerned." Diana had determined to punish me for this mess. I didn't respond.

"She's fine. She told me you had lost your mind."

I said, "I can see how she might believe that."

Diana let out a small laugh. "Well, your behavior may seem strange to her, but I know better. For you, this is all completely normal. You've always been a selfish, inconsiderate whore of man."

I didn't flinch. Diana didn't scare me. If I disgusted her so much, she didn't have to be here. I told her as much.

She didn't back down. "Careful, Adrian... Right now, I'm the only thing between you and the hoosegow. I own you, pal. For the next few days, you are my personal step-n-fetch-it."

I laughed. "Good luck with that, sister. It ain't happenin'.'

"You *could* go back and consummate your little jailhouse marriage." Just then, we passed a police car. Diana pressed the center of the steering wheel. The horn blew loudly. I reached for her hand and the car swerved.

"Okay," I said, raising my hands. "I give."

She pulled the car to a stop in the hotel parking lot.

"What's next, madam?" I asked, resolving myself to the role I had been cast.

Diana released a small smirk. "I'm going for a swim."

We were outside the car, now. She began walking to the hotel entrance.

"Great!" I said. "But I need swimming shorts."

"*I'm* going for a swim," she called over her shoulder. "*You....* Get the bags....Boy."

She threw me the keys. "Stay in your room. I'll call you when I need you."

Dee was out of control.

I located a cart, loaded the luggage onto it and wheeled my burden through the hotel lobby unto the elevator and to the room Dee had told me she was staying in. When I knocked at the door, it was opened by a very attractive young woman wearing only a towel. She was dripping wet, patting droplets of water from her beautiful face with a second towel.

"Yes," she said, smiling. "What can I do for you?"

I returned her smile. "I'm here to deliver Diana's luggage," I said. I tried to peer over and around the young lady. "Is she here?"

Pulling the door to block my view, the girl stepped into the hallway closer to me. I didn't budge.

"I'm sorry," she said, rubbing shoulder-length, sun-goldened hair with her towel. "There's no one here, but me. Perhaps you have the wrong room. Would you like to come in and use the phone to call her?"

The scent of apricot shampoo wafted from her hair. It lingered powerfully in the brief space between us.

"I don't think that would be a good idea," came the familiar voice.

I looked around to see Dee standing in the corridor wearing a perfectly fitting, turquoise two-piece bathing suit. I'm sure my eyes lingered a little longer than was appropriate. Her body was so perfect. Her skin was dark. And it was so tight. The muscles of her flat belly rippled beneath that skin. She was in a word, "breath-taking".

"Is that your friend?" the girl asked.

"That's her," I replied.

"Well, enjoy your stay," she said. Then with a taunting glint in her eyes, she backed into the room and shut the door.

I watched those blue eyes and that beautiful gulf-sun baked face disappear into the room; then turned to Dee. "You set me up," I accused her.

She laughed. "Come with me," she said. Then, turned and walked down the hallway to her room (the real room this time). And I, leading the cart, followed.

As I carried the first of her bags into the room, Dee was just fastening a very colorful sarong about her generous hips. I set down the bags and playfully reached for her waist in an attempt to draw her to me. She slapped my hand away.

"Keep your hands to yourself," she said.

I laughed. "You always were cruel, Dee. What could it hurt? Why waste all this sun and sand and atmosphere?"

"You are a spoiled, greedy little boy. And while enabling your tired little dysfunction, my support does not extend to the abuse of my body and affections. Do you understand that?"

I wasn't laughing now. "I guess I do," I said.

"Besides," she said. "I'm meeting Frankie at the pool."

That one stung a little.

"I went shopping," she said, all business. "You'll find a complete wardrobe, shoes and toiletries in your room. Those clothes you're wearing are ruined. Give them to housekeeping to burn."

I took note of the shopping bags and packages on her bed; then looked at myself in the mirror. They weren't that bad, I thought. "I like the outfit I'm wearing," I said.

Dee shook her head in disgust. "You're expected to dress for dinner. I'll call for you in two hours. Be ready."

She was really getting on my nerves now. "Okay."

Before leaving the room, she pressed my room key into my hand, along with a crumpled ten dollar bill. It wasn't exactly a tip. At the door she turned with further instructions. "Bring in the rest of my bags, unpack them and neatly put away my things."

She had nearly closed the door, when she added as an after-thought, "Oh. And, please try to resist the urge to walk around the room with my underwear on your head."

That was probably the most uncalled for statement Dee had ever uttered. I had to give to her big props, though. The girl was in great shape. Among the sheer white or black lace, tiger stripes and leopard prints, there was not one padded or push-up bra; not even a pair of over-sized granny bloomers.

It took me the better part of an hour to put Dee's things away. My heart wasn't into it in any way. I was alone now for the first time in some while. Folding and hanging Dee's clothes, I began to reflect on the past couple of months. To be honest, I'd made an enormous mess of my life. I had betrayed the love of my life. I had all but abandoned my little girls. I would father a child, whom, in all likelihood, I would never even see. I'd helped to ruin Desiree's marriage. And I was, potentially, a deserter from the United States Army. Now here I was enslaved; bound in indentured servitude to my only friend in the world. I was *not* having a good day.

I finished my task and rolled the cart to its place in the lobby. My room was in an irregular hallway in one corner of our floor of the hotel. I opened the door to an oddly narrow and deep broom closet outfitted as a guest room. It was obviously the residue from the construction of the gigantic suite Dee was occupying. I had about an hour and fifteen minutes before I expected her to call. It was just enough time to wash off the past several weeks and get in a much needed power nap.

I had just finished tying my necktie when the knock came at the door. Instinctively, I peered through the peephole. There was a tall young man wearing the uniform of a service steward standing outside.

"Room service," he called. I hadn't ordered room service. I thought Dee must have had a change of mind. My mood began to lighten. I opened the door and the steward wheeled in the cart.

"I didn't order room service, bro'," I admitted.

He grinned. "Compliments of the lady, sir." He tipped his head towards the door.

I turned to the door and there was Desiree, standing; beautiful, smiling and glowing. My mood elevated instantly.

"Hello, Adrian."

"Hello, Desiree." I was happily, stunned; resisting the urge to whoop.

The steward finished setting up the table and moved toward the door. Desiree placed a bill in his hand as she stepped aside, clearing the way for him to leave. She gave him an appraising glance before stepping into the room. As the door closed behind her, we stood motionless for a while, watching each other without words.

Finally, breaking the silence, I said, "It's good to see you."

"It's good to see you, too," she said.

I wanted to take her into my arms, but we had unresolved issues. It was a very difficult moment for me, and I could sense the discomfort she must be feeling.

She looked around the small room. "Nice digs," she said, sarcastically.

I looked around. "Yeah... Welcome to my private dungeon. It's part of my penance."

Desiree chuckled. "Your girlfriend has some sense of humor."

I didn't understand. "You mean Dee?"

"Yes," she said. "She stole your suite, you know?"

"My suite?"

She was looking around as if searching for the source of some offensive hidden odor. "Yep," she said. "Your suite."

I laughed. "Yeah, that's my girl."

Desiree laughed. "She's good."

"Yeah, she is," I agreed. "Wanna change rooms?"

Sighing, she shook her head. "No. This'll do."

"You're sure?" I pressed.

She seemed to consider it; then nodding, committed to her decision. "Oh, well... I'll have my luggage sent up." Looking around, skeptically, she said, "I have no idea where we're going to put it."

Dropping the subject, Desiree inspected my new clothes hanging in the room's alcove. "Your girlfriend may be a room thief, but she's got great taste in clothes."

She pulled out a navy blue blazer. "Here. Put this on. We're going to the casino."

I shook my head. "…Can't. I'm on house arrest."

"Those instructions no longer apply," she said. "You're in my custody now… …To do as I see fit."

"Is that right"?

"That's right," she said, shaking the jacket in the air. "Now come over here and put on your coat."

She slipped the coat on me and smoothed the shoulders and back. I shivered as she did.

"Turn around and let me see you."

I did.

She appraised me. "Wonderful!"

We stood, with her adjusting the jacket at the chest and shoulders.

I resisted the urge to reach for her.

When she was satisfied it fit properly, she looked into my eyes.

"Aren't you going to ask to kiss me?" she asked.

I took her into my arms. "No. I'm not," I said. Then we kissed.

I broke the kiss. "Dinner's getting cold," I said.

With her hands on my face, she breathed into my mouth, "Yes, I know. We'll have to heat it up."

By the time we turned our attention to the serving cart, the meal was well beyond reheating. We were ravenous, but determined to wait and dine in the hotel's restaurant. I just sort of nibbled at the edges of our meal; a piece of bread; a slice of meat; while Desiree freshened up from her trip.

In the elevator, on the way to the casino, I asked Desiree how she came to be in Biloxi. She was leaning on me, holding on to my arm. Laughing, she gave me a little squeeze.

"This *is* my stomping ground, you know. I don't know the judge, personally, but I do know someone who does."

I was astonished.

She shrugged. "Small world," she said.

"In deed, it is," I agreed. "So he called you-out of the blue?"

She shook her head. "No. Not, exactly. We were looking for you."

"We?"

"Uhn huh. We." The elevator began to come to a stop for other passengers. "Can't we talk about it later? Let's have some fun. I promise I'll tell you everything."

The doors began to open. "Okay," I said. "I'm holding you to it, Desiree. No playing around. I want to know everything."

She squeezed my arm again. "Of course, Honey."

Several other gamblers entered the car on their way to the nightly shearing at the gaming tables. Desiree slipped her hand into mine. With a cryptic smile, she watched the numbers above the doors blink on and off as they marked our descent to the lobby.

And that was my last lucid memory of the next week or so. From the moment we hit the lobby, we embarked on a ten-day debauch, oddly reminiscent of the bender which had landed me in jail more than a month earlier. We partied from the casino tables of Biloxi to the bars and dog track of Mobile to the beaches of Pensacola to the after-hours jazz dives of New Orleans and back to that ill formed hotel room. Because of the baby, Desiree was careful not to drink alcohol. But her condition did not quell her energy at all. The girl was an indefatigable reveler. She seemed intent to extract as much living from every moment as life would allow. Though I was having a great time, I couldn't shake the feeling we were just one step ahead of calamity. It wasn't that I was concerned about Bud. She had made it clear she wasn't leaving him. He hadn't shown any inclination towards violence yet-except to defend himself when I tried to attack him. When Desiree heard about that she laughed. "I knew you were too good of a lover to be any good at fighting." I didn't know how to appreciate that little comment.

No, Bud didn't seem to care what she did, as long as she came home eventually. So, I didn't expect him to care what I did. Regardless, I had an awful sense I was being stalked. I shrugged off my misgivings and allowed myself to relax, forgetting for a time, my life's personal limbo.

Finally, our energy thoroughly spent, we crashed in the hotel room. There were shopping bags and clothes and fast food bags and pizza boxes and bottles and cans strewn all around the small compartment. The place was a wreck. My heart felt for the chambermaid, whom we sent away when she tried to clean up around ten-thirty that morning.

When the knock came at the door, well after two in the afternoon, I sleepily dragged myself from the disheveled bed. Clumsily crawling across Desiree's sleeping, half dressed body, I fell from the bed to the floor with a loud thud.

Rolling over, she pulled at the covers. "Baby, somebody's at the door," she mumbled.

Picking myself up off the floor, I rolled my eyes. "I know, Babe. I got it." I groggily stumbled to the door, opening it without thinking.

Dee stepped into the room. She took note of my state of half-dress: shirtless, wearing only a pair of boxer shorts.

"You really ought to be more careful," she said, glaring at Desiree's slumbering form in the bed. I reached for a pair of pants to slip into.

Desiree stirred. "Baby," she said testily, "turn the television down. I'm trying to sleep."

I stepped into the slacks.

Dee was beside herself. "The tele…." She drew a breath. "Your husband's on his way up," she said, smiling.

While zipping the pants, I held my breath and shot a glance at the door.

Desiree sprang straight up in bed, pulling covers to her body. Dee laughed. "Television that."

I began breathing again and finished zipping my pants.

Desiree regained her composure. With a dangerous smile, she said, "You are a very mean woman, Diana."

Dee laughed again. "It would do you good to remember that, Dez."

Desiree smiled. 'It's Desiree," she corrected.

Dee was unshaken. "I know your name, sister. I know all there is to know about you."

"Oh, I doubt that," countered Desiree, smiling. "But, point taken, anyhow."

Dee smiled. "Good. How's my boy treating you?"

Desiree stretched, allowing the covers to fall. "Very well. Thanks."

Dee gazed around the room. With obvious disgust, she said, "Glad to hear it." Her eyes locked on Desiree. "I need to speak with him."

I frowned. I *was* in the room.

Desiree looked at me. "Would you like me to wait in the hall?"

Dee's eyes remained locked on her. "That won't be necessary. It'll wait until tomorrow." She turned to the door and stopped. Turning back, she said, "You will be gone tomorrow-won't you?"

The women's eyes met. "I should be," said Desiree.

"Fine," said Dee. She gave me a kiss on the cheek and left.

"Well," said Desiree, "I guess the honeymoon's over."

I was standing, staring at the door. "Yeah, I… I guess so."

I barely felt the pillow hit me in the back.

Dee's visit was ice cold reality, preparing us for the pain of separation we would endure in the upcoming months. We would never again touch the way we were now. There would be no more intimate embraces. We would never again share deep breathless kisses; or the warmth of our bodies lying close to one another. It would come to feel as though someone had ripped my heart from my chest. The remaining hollow was a tender; gaping; bleeding wound.

In the moment, neither of us fully realized the impact of losing… us. Silently, we lay in bed. I held her. I could hear her breathing. The moments passed. Then she spoke. "Adrian?"

"Uh huh?"

She didn't move. "Say something."

I drew a deep breath and released it. "I think it's all been said," I responded.

She didn't reply. A moment later, I could tell by the steady rise and fall of her chest she had fallen asleep. And I soon followed.

Desiree left at dawn the next morning. And in her departure, I was left with more questions than answers. She did make one thing clear, though. She did not intend to give me up.

"Why can't we keep things the way they are?" she asked.

I told her things couldn't remain the same. I wanted her, and I wanted our baby.

"Can't we, at least, try?" she pleaded.

"You don't know how much I'd like to," I told her. "But our baby deserves better than that. I deserve better. You deserve better. Better than the way we're living; this life we're living."

She released a heavy sigh. I took it as an indication of her boredom with the prospect of what I described as a "better life". "Adrian," she said. "It's true the baby could be yours. But Bud is never going to allow you to have it-or me for that matter. He has contacts who will do and say anything he wants. You could never really be sure it's yours. Even I wouldn't know the results of an examination if he chose to hide it."

I watched her carefully. I had come to know her pretty well by this time. She was lying. I got the sense that I had been sleeping with the enemy. I let the matter drop. I would have to find another way. I believed that. I believed she and the child would, eventually be mine. It just never worked out that way.

Once again, Desiree left with the sunrise. Dee and I would remain on the gulf coast several days more before leaving. She told me we had business to discuss with Frankie which concerned my immediate future. I had no idea what I would do with rest of my life. However, since I was, essentially, a deserter, I assumed my future involved hard labor; making little rocks out of big ones.

To help clear my thoughts, I took a walk on the beach, where I watched the day begin. The air was still, and the stench of rotting fish and stale salt hovered with it. Breathing was a chore. The sun had barely risen, and the day was already miserably hot and suffocating. I found walking in that heat, on the shore's loose sand, strenuous beyond imagining. My mouth was dry, and faintly offensive with the taste of the preceding week's excesses lingering there. Sweating profusely, I sat in the sand in order to cool at the water's edge. Somewhere in the distance, I could just make out the smooth voice of Marvin, saying, *"If I Should Die Tonight"*. Farther down the beach, I watched the silhouette of a fisherman cast his net from the pier. Venders were setting out over-priced sun glasses and tee shirts; bathing suits and ball caps; straw hats and beach towels for tourists to purchase. Just inside the gulf's horizon, the shrimp boats were deploying, preparing for the day's snare. A squadron of six or seven pelicans glided in precision formation just above white-capped waves that seemed to reach for them in an attempt to drag them to the water's depths. I watched the gulls swoop into the water; then fly off with their catch. A tiny blue crab, uncovered by the waves, scurried for safety in deeper waters. The engine roar of a pair of C-130 Hurricane Hunters faded in the distance as the planes made their way out to sea in search of threatening storms. The beckoning peal of a faraway church bell sliced through the sweltering morning air, surprisingly, comforting me like the cooling waters of a refreshing and gentle mountain stream.

I thought of the mess I had created of my disastrous little life, and in spite of it all, smiled.

"Je ne sais quoi, Frankie. Je ne sais quoi." – Diana Flanders

CHAPTER 4

It is amazing the affect a shave, shower and a nap can have on a guy. I felt great! And, thanks to Dee and my new wardrobe, I looked great! No one would have guessed my entire world was in the toilet, and everything good in my life was on the verge of being flushed away. Diana had left a message for me to meet her and Frankie in "her" suite. Though, I suppose I should have felt some trepidation, I didn't. It was my mess and I would stand up and own up to it.

She answered my knock at the door. "It's so good of you to join us," she chided.

I grinned. "I wanted to look my best for the hanging," I said. "Nice selection in clothing, by the way."

"Hmph!" she snorted.

"Hello, Ace." The Honorable, Judge Albert Frank Johnson was seated at the dining table in the room. On the table, were several stacks of papers.

214

"Hi, Frankie! How've you been?"

He stood and we shook hands. I hadn't had a drink all day, and I noticed no one was drinking here. Their mood was somber and official. I determined to behave myself, hoping they had figured out a way to get me off the hook with my wife and the Army. I didn't know what their plans were, but I planned to go to Georgia and get my baby. I said so, and Dee told me to sit down, relax and listen to what Frankie had to say. I decided to chill out, and for once in my life, try to be smart. It was a good idea.

Without preamble, Frankie dived into it. "Ace," he said. "What you see here in front of you are your options." He indicated with spread hands; then pointed in succession at the four stacks of paper.

"These are your promotion papers."

I was astonished. "Promotion!"

Dee placed a hand on my shoulder. "Be quiet, Ace! Let him finish."

"Thank you, Dee," he said. "That's right, Ace, promotion. Trust me, if you take it, you will earn it."

I was practically, salivating. "Okay."

"These," he pointed to the second stack. "Are your discharge papers-early retirement, full benefits."

I nodded. That was closer to what I had expected.

He continued. "These are your employment papers."

"Employment?" I asked.

"Yes," said Dee. "We've got jobs in Hinesville."

I turned to Dee. "We?"

She shrugged. "You can't be trusted on your own. No one would hire you without me. We're a package deal, it seems. If you accept it, we'll be newspaper reporters."

That was reasonable-for me. But, Dee was diverting the course of her life for me. She had wagered her future that I could, and would accept rehabilitation. She was making quite a sacrifice. I should have appreciated her more than I did.

Frankie went on. "And these…" He hesitated, patting the stack with his hand. "Well… These are your divorce papers."

It wasn't reasonable that I would be stunned by Julie's decision to divorce me, but I was. The air went out of me. I could hardly breathe. My belly ached. I felt my eyes begin to water. "How…. How did… How did I do?"

Frankie looked up at Dee, who was still standing at my side. She nodded. He took a breath. "In a word… You got reamed, Ace. You didn't give me *anything* at all to work with."

I nodded. "Okay," I said, referring to the stacks of papers. "So, how does all this work? Why are you doing this for me? And how much will it cost me?"

"Fair enough questions," he said. "It's understandable you'd be curious, my friend." I already didn't like his answer. His expression of "my friend" was an affectation which said I was anything but his friend. It was condescending and, not a little irritating. He was speaking in a tone of voice that I suppose was meant to be soothing. It wasn't. It felt as if he were speaking to a child. Dee must have sensed my ire, because she placed a gentle hand on my shoulder. "I will explain how all this works, and how it all is interconnected, momentarily. I'm not doing this for you. Until you decided to throw your little tantrum in my town, I hadn't even remembered you existed. Dee challenged me." He smiled at Dee. "She bet me I couldn't work a little barrister magic and save your sorry bacon. As for the cost: You would have to sell your soul to afford my fees-if you had one."

Frankie was obviously good at what he did. And he was right; I definitely couldn't afford his caliber of legal assistance. But, I wasn't about to sit there and let this joker talk down to me. Frankie was turning out to be pompous and arrogant. And these were his admirable traits.

I had had enough of his trash talking. "You're kind of a jerk, aren't you, Frankie?"

He leaned forward. "In your position," he said. "Somebody else would be more appreciative than you."

I leaned forward. "There's only one hitch in that," I said.

"And, that is?" he questioned.

I leaned back in my seat, allowing my shoulder to rest against Dee's thigh. Thankfully, she didn't move. "I *ain't* somebody else. And ain't *nobody* else in my position."

I felt Dee moving, and heard her attempt to stifle her laughter. I thought I may have over-played my hand. Frankie looked as if he was going to pack

217

it all up and roll out. He looked at Dee. "What is with you two? Why do you indulge this guy so? I've never seen anyone in a more self-defeating; self-destructive spiral. He's nothing but trouble. It's only a matter of time…"

At least he wasn't leaving. I needed him, he knew it and I knew it.

Dee laughed. "Je ne sais quoi, Frankie. Je ne sais quoi. He's just got that…" She shook her head. "…Somethin'."

She moved to the couch. "You're right. He's not any good." She looked at me, smiling. "Not *any*. But, we've come this far." She sat and crossed her legs seductively. "Let's help him, anyway."

Frankie didn't speak. I didn't speak.

After a time, Dee stood. "Well," she said, picking up her purse. "I feel lucky. I'll be in the casino. Come join me when you fellas are done. Work it out, boys. 'Bye."

We stared at the closed door.

"Huh," Frankie grunted. "Now there's a girl who knows how to make an exit."

I echoed Diana's assessment of myself. "Je ne sais quoi, Frankie. Je ne sais quoi."

We looked at each other and laughed. From across the table, he offered me his hand, and I shook it. I found myself respecting the guy; really seeing him for the first time. Through this episode, we would become good friends.

"I appreciate your help, Frank," I said sincerely. "Show me how you're going to 'save my bacon'."

I was out of trump cards, and everyone knew it. I was now at the mercy of the entire world. To extend the gambling metaphor, I had been running a bluff and everyone at the table was calling. It was time to show my hand, and I didn't have as much as a pair of deuces.

Frank confessed. "I was kind of bluffing myself, Ace. You're, actually holding some pretty good cards. You just don't know what to do with them. That's why I'm here. I'm going to show you how to play your hand." He indicated the papers. "Let me show you what I'm talking about."

I nodded. "Okay."

"We're going to start with your divorce." I winced. He was compassionate. "I know it's painful. I've seldom seen anyone experience one without, at least, some discomfort. It's normal. It will be a major life change. But, with counseling and a strong support system, you'll adapt."

I agreed.

"The thing here is there's no way to argue you aren't the offending party; the affair; potential paternity; abandonment." It was a litany that depicted me as an absolute monster. He began to explain the terms. "That's why we are forced to make some extraordinary concessions. We want to do it quick and clean. That way we cause as little pain and ill will as possible. Once you've established a track record of responsibility; proven yourself; we can revisit and negotiate a more equitable arrangement for you."

I nodded. "But, you're saying I'm giving up all my rights. I'm banking on the chance of getting a better deal somewhere down the line?"

"That's exactly it." I was skeptical. He called this a good thing? He went on. "Look… Your wife doesn't hate you. She's, understandably, extremely angry. Although, she wants you to suffer for hurting her, she loves you. She can't control that. She loves your children. She conceived them, in love, with you. She wants to forgive you, but your actions just didn't give her any room to do so."

Frank was a natural born salesman. He was very good. I was buying everything he was selling. And after a while, I began to think of our divorce as a necessary and beneficial leave of absence.

"So you're saying we give her a cooling off period?" I asked. "And you think she'll take me back in a few months or so?"

He shook his head. "No," he said. "No. No. I apologize, if I misled you. It's important you understand that the marriage is finished. There'll be no going back. The best you can hope for is joint custody of the children, and a reduction in child support and alimony."

I drew a breath. It wasn't the best arrangement of my life. But, realistically, I couldn't expect any better. So, I signed the papers. And he placed my copy in an envelope, and handed it to me. The others, he placed neatly in a briefcase on the floor, at his side.

"Okay," Frank said. "These are a bit more… Say… …Complicated."
He was referring to the other contracts on the table. He explained that the
other three contracts were interconnected in a way which wasn't exactly
conventional. That's why it required someone with, not only a judge's skill
and knowledge, but his particular influence and connections. The gist of
the matter was that I was getting, what amounted to witness protection
treatment.

"Here's how it works," he said. "When you decided to have an affair with
Mrs. McKensie, you unwittingly, drew a wild card."

He had no idea how right that statement was.

Frank told me that with the affair ending in the way it had, my stock had
increased tremendously. "Consider this," he said. "You're the scumbag
who's been cheating on his wife with the wealthy wife of a real, live, *bona
fide*, American hero."

To hear him say it was shameful. I chuckled. So did he. Frank got the
joke. I was a scumbag. But I was an envied scumbag.

"Yeah," Frank said. "I think you're starting to follow me."

"I believe so," I said. "Go on."

"Okay," he said. "So, things are going along fine. No one is getting
injured. No one's complaining. Everybody understands where they stand.
But, here's the problem for all concerned. There's a shift in the dynamic.
She gets herself knocked up-and she's keeping the baby. Something I'm
not convinced is all together accidental, by the way."

221

I shook my head. I hadn't considered it.

He shrugged and continued. "Alright, now there's an innocent, unborn child involved. And on top of that, you begin to catch feelings. You throw away your marriage and career, in order to pursue a custody battle you can't possibly win."

This sounded so bleak, I wanted crawl in a corner someplace. "Alright, Frank, you've lost me. I'm not hearing any good part yet."

He held up his hand. "I'm getting there," he said. "Here's the change: Your girl friend goes from beautiful, wealthy socialite to spoiled, home wreaking rich girl. She and her hero husband have the world laid at their feet, but they choose to take advantage of one of the Army's hard working, under paid enlisted members. Why does he want to raise another man's baby? The world begins to question his virility. Maybe he's actually, more image than stud, after all."

My mouth was open. I shook my head. "You sold that load of garbage?"

He never cracked a smile. "Sometimes, it's more difficult to sell the truth than it is to sell a lie." he said. "It's all in how you present it. Look around you. I didn't have to sell this. It is the truth. Regardless of what you think of her; or how you feel, you've been taken advantage of. You're living high on some else's dime-for now. But very soon, things are going to get tight. You've got no wiggle room. You'll make enough money to live on-just enough. You'll be the butt of jokes, ridicule. They'll try to run you out of town. Discredit you. Force you over the edge. They'll try to make you hurt yourself-or someone else. Either will do. They'll just want to be rid of you, it won't matter how.

"There will be no part of your life which won't be investigated. You'll be laid bear. No secrets. If you have any, they will be brought to light. There is nothing too personal for exposure. In fact, the more personal, the better, financial records, tax records, medical records, school transcripts; all fair game. Even your birth certificate will be examined for possible discrepancies in claims to your lineage. If there are any inconsistencies, anything they can use, anything that can cause doubt, they'll find them. Would it surprise you to learn your great-great-uncle was a Nazi war criminal, escaped to Argentina?"

I didn't respond.

"It's not true... But that doesn't matter. Only the accusation counts." He leaned close. "This is subtle. And if you survive subtle...." He allowed me to consider the possibilities. "....It gets less subtle."

"You won't know who to trust. You won't know reality from imagination. And after a while, you will second guess your friends, your family, and even yourself."

"How do you know all this, Frank?" I asked.

He smiled. "I'm a judge, Ace," he said. "It's my business to know. I sign the orders for wiretaps and surveillances. It's people like me who give patriots like McKensie the authority to track down and neutralize citizens like you-and those much, much worse. And everything I'm telling you right now, is only page one in the playbook."

I sat there, in disbelief. "Unbelievable," I said.

He nodded. "Believe it. This isn't her first rodeo. She's been here before. The woman's crazy about you, Ace. Or else someone might have disappeared you weeks ago."

"Come on, Frankie," I said, trying to laugh it off. "It's not as bad as all that."

"No. It's worse," he said. "That's right, pal. You're in the big league now. You had to know. By the way, you asked me why I was helping you."

I nodded.

"You're from the neighborhood," he said. "We take care of each other. But it didn't hurt that she paid me a good deal of money to protect you, buddy." He shook his head, laughing. "Favors. Money. Influence. That's how it works. It's all interconnected. You're a newspaper reporter, and you don't know this? They really keep you guys sheltered in that Army of yours."

I shrugged. "I guess they do."

"My friend, you're a smart fellow," he said. "If you've been ignorant, it's because you've chosen to be. That's got to change. It's time you wised up."

"Why should I?" I asked. "Why should I care? Why should want to know about things I can't change?"

"One person can make difference. One person *can* start change," Frank countered. "Thing is, somebody's got to."

The guy was talking about a movement. Did he really expect me to climb on a soapbox? ...To take to the streets, and campaign for justice for the proletariat masses? I chuckled out loud. Boy, did he have the wrong guy?

"You want me to lead a movement, Frank?"

"What...? Huh...?" He was taken aback. "Heck no! I'm a capitalist; not an activist! Leave that stuff to the guys who don't mind being broke. I'm just trying to motivate you to open your eyes, and get little more proactive. You're going to need to learn how to protect yourself."

I laughed. "Okay….good. I'm ready to learn. Talk to me."

"Think about this. Have you ever heard of the Kessler Syndrome?" I shook my head.

"Alright, check this out. The residue of each space shot is up there floating around us in orbit. In the normal course of time, this debris falls to earth, depending on trajectory and orbital height." That made sense. Everything wouldn't fall at the same time. I nodded my understanding.

"Now with each space launch, we add to the debris. This causes a collision hazard. It's conceivable that we'll end up with a dangerous man-made asteroid belt, a debris belt. Well the Kessler Syndrome is the potential domino effect that could occur when a couple of those "foreign object debris" collide. If and when it does, we can all expect a tremendous trash storm from our upper atmosphere. Imagine spent fuel residue, fuel cells, chunks of space craft and just anything we've discarded up there raining down in an unguided free-fall to Earth."

I was becoming impatient. "What's space junk got to do with me?" I asked.

He laughed. "Everything when you apply it to your life. You see, the debris of our lives is floating around out there, the people we've hurt or double-crossed, the unpaid debts, the jilted lovers. It would be an enormous disaster for any of us if the bill for all the indiscretions of our lives came due at one time. If this happened in the wrong person's life, at the wrong time, that individual and everyone impacted by that person-and so on-could experience a free-fall of Biblical proportions.

"You, my friend, have become upper atmospheric residue. And it is important for Mrs. McKensie, and those connected to her, to carefully manage your orbit-or descent. You may not realize it yet, but in all those hours of intimacy, in the midst of pillow talk, she's told you at least one item of grave import. Within you is, perhaps, a reservoir of information, vital information relating to national security. You know where the, proverbial, bodies are hidden."

I shook my head.

"Well, whether you know anything or not, it's in your best interest that everyone believes you do. Never admit to your ignorance. Once you've done that, you will no longer be dangerous debris, but inert flotsam. …And highly expendable flotsam, at that.

"For all your screw ups, you're in the upper echelon now. All you've got to do is survive being there." He just looked me straight in my eye, and said, "It will be rough. But if you do survive, Hoss, it can be a pretty good life."

I was thirsty, and it was as if Frank had read my mind. "You look like you could use a break. What do you say we find Dee and a couple of cold ones?"

"Yeah," I said, thinking over Frank's revelation. "Suppose everything you said is true, Frank."

"And it is," he said calmly.

"Okay," I said. "So how do I survive?"

"You just do what you do best, Ace."

I didn't understand. "What's that?"

"Be seen," he said. "Be seen loud and often. And be seen everywhere with everyone. Join clubs. The Rotary Club. Toast Masters. The PTA. Become a Mason. Become the garden club president.

"Whatever you do, don't become expendable. Don't allow yourself to be marginalized. Remember, out of sight is out of mind. Gone is forgotten. Mute is missing. And expendable is vanished-or worse. Just… Be… Seen."

I wasn't believing any of this. It was like I had stepped into a cheap espionage thriller. I wouldn't believe it. I couldn't believe it. I became fearful for my family. "What about Julie and the girls?" I asked.

He nodded. "Now you're thinking," he said. "Julie did the best thing for their well being. The further estranged from you, the better. So, you can't move back to the Midwest for some time."

"That's why Dee and I are setting up house in Small Town, Georgia?" I asked.

He shook his head. "You're setting up house there, in order to protect your interest. Let the child grow. Let's see what he grows into. And after a few years, Colonel and Mrs. McKensie may see a definite need to come to the table."

I was starting to feel sick. "That's awful, Frank. You're somewhat of a scumbag, yourself."

He laughed. "Thank you, Ace."

It wasn't a compliment. It was cold and calculating to wait for the child to grow into the familiar features of its father. If it was my child, perhaps the McKensies would be shamed into admitting the truth. I didn't stifle my own laughter.

"You're obviously not a fan of condoms," he observed.

"Yeah, I know," I said, chagrined. "I've been irresponsible."

"Yes, you have," he said. "You're going to want to be better in that area, from now on. Beyond the obvious considerations, you're going to want to manage your DNA."

I didn't get it. "What?"

"Don't leave anything lying around that somebody can use against you. You don't want to find yourself in the wrong place, at the wrong time- evidentially speaking," he said. "A smoking gun isn't always the most damning piece in a body of evidence. You're going to need to be creative, my friend, because your enemies will be.

"I'm guessing you don't believe in voodoo and zombies... ....But they do. And that makes them even more dangerous because they've got more to prove. They're out to corrupt everything you do and own. Don't give them anything to use."

He paused, waiting for me to catch up. "You're concerned about a baby which may be yours. Well, there are babies, not yet conceived, with the power to adversely impact your life. This is the "Master Game", Ace. It's not chess. It's not poker. This is not mano-a-mano, and it's not a team sport. In this game, it's every man for himself. Think of yourself as the continent of Australia on a Risk board. You're the most defensible continent in the world, but you've got the least territory of anyone in the game. You can fortify, but you can't advance. If you try, there's a major power ready to eat you up. Patience is the key. We're all trying to win. We're all waiting for an opportunity to grab a little more. So, be patient.

You really don't want to lose at this level. This game is generational and it's enduring. There won't be a lot of do-overs here."

He paused.

I waited for him to go on.

"Just as in the game," he said. "Today I'm your ally. "Tomorrow? Who knows?" He let that statement sink in.

"Are you ready for that beer, yet?" he asked.

My head was spinning, but I was beginning to catch on. I began to stand.

"I'm way ahead of you, Frank. Let's go."

On the way out of the room, I stopped at the door. "What about those?" I asked, referring to the various documents.

He looked at the papers. "Oh, those..." he said. "They'll be alright where they are. They aren't worth the paper they're written on."

"Why's that?" I asked.

"Because their value," he said. "Is in the execution of their contents. Their value is in the ability of all parties to enforce adherence to the agreements therein. For instance, what will you do when they fall into breach? And they will eventually. What will you do?"

I thought about it before responding. "I hadn't given it any consideration," I said.

Frank laughed. "Well, you'd better start considering it," he said. "I said you had the better hand. But, what happens when you lay down your unbeatable hand, and the loser decides not to pay up? What happens when he kicks over the table, the pot, chips, cards and all? Then it's a free-for-all, one great big scramble and grab. That's right, eye-gouging, hair-pulling, groin-kicking and biting. In the midst of all that, if you don't already have a plan in place, even the most iron-clad contract won't do you any good."

We were walking towards the elevator.

"Listen," he said. "Imagine yourself: Ambitious. …Wealthy. …Beautiful wife. …And the ability to send silent death throughout the world. That's your contract. That's the contract McKensie has signed. That's the contract all the players on your board are adhering to. They make the rules, and then they break them when it suits their needs. Then, depending upon the strength of their position, and their resources, they dare anyone to fuss about it."

As I listened to Judge Johnson explain the facts of life in a way I'd never heard them before, I began to wonder about the contents of his own contract. I kept that thought to myself. I *was* beginning to catch on. The most binding agreement was the one left unsaid. The information Frank shared was fascinating-and valuable. Every part of me wanted to write about it. But, knowing Frank, as I did, I knew he wouldn't hesitate to have me Shanghaied for breaking his confidence. I imagined waking up, a beaten and half starved heroine trafficker in a very unaccommodating prison, in some highly orthodox country with strict laws against drug distribution and an exceedingly slow judicial process. Yeah. You could say Frank and I had an agreement.

231

The single most significant unspoken agreement in those contracts, on the table in the room, concerned Desiree. The job, the retirement, the promotion; they were all contingent on my staying away from her and relinquishing my claim to the baby. Well, regardless of the consequences, I wasn't going to give up. I was determined not to go "gently into that good night".

When the elevator doors opened, Frank was all talked out. We stepped onto the car. Before the doors could close completely, a pretty young woman stopped them and joined us.

Frank greeted her. "Hello, Miss Jacobs."

"Hi, Judge," she said with a smile. "Where're we headed?"

Though she looked entirely different fully dressed, I remembered the young woman I had met in the corridor nearly two weeks previously. I nodded and smiled. And she did the same. The doors closed, and the car began its descent.

We were on our way to the crowded casino, an expensive restaurant and a noisy bar. We were on our way to do what I did best. We were going to be seen and we were going to be loud.

It took us a while, but we finally located Dee at the craps table. She had collected an impressive entourage; not to mention enough chips that she could have financed our partying for the next two evenings. Shaking a pair of dice above her head, she shouted over the noise of the gamblers, the music and machines. "Hello, boys! Did you fellas get anything accomplished or did you spend the entire time up there chicken fighting?"

An impatient gambler called out to her. "Come on, lady, we're waiting on a number. Roll the dice, already!"

"Alright," she laughed. "Keep your shirt on, Handsome." She extended her hand with the dice. "Here. Blow on these for luck."

He did. And she tossed the bones across the table. They rolled out and came to a stop after bouncing against the wall. A four and a one came up.

The croupier called out the number. "Five! Five is the number to make! Place your bets please!"

Someone shouted. "No way, she hits that number!" The dealer passed Dee the dice. She made her bet and picked up the bones. Grinning at Miss Jacobs, she said, "Hey, Jail Bait, why don't you blow on 'em for me?"

"Jail Bait" was only one of several endearing names Dee had for Frank's gorgeous young apprentice, Valerie Jacobs. Jake was the nicest name, but the woman, ten years Dee's junior, was also known, not altogether derisively, as "Furniture"; Frankie's furniture to be exact. It was a reference to a character in the movie, *Soylent Green*. I never fully understood, but I think the *Furniture* moniker had something to do with the way the girl and I met. Dee could be mean at times, but the younger woman took her jibes as nurturing maternal hazing.

Miss Jacobs laughed. "No thanks," she said. "I'll get a pair of my own."

"Alright," Dee said, and flung the cubes across the table. This time they rested on two and three.

"Five's a winner!" the croupier shouted over the racket of cheering and revelry.

Dee collected her chips, cashed them in and we decided to try our luck at the Blackjack table. Dee's luck continued. Mine was horrendous. I lost five hands in a row and decided to try out the bar. It wasn't long before Miss Jacobs relinquished her seat at the table also. From my vantage point, I watched her stroll confidently through the crowd.

She was a tall; blond; tanned natural beauty, the kind of person who had been attractive her entire life. People like her never seemed to think about being good looking. They're just comfortable with their looks, and seem to assume everyone is as comfortable as they are. Like breathing, like air, beauty, to them, is no big deal. It's always been there.

Watching her made me think of Tad, with his smooth confidence, southern charm and classic good looks. I missed him. It was a shame he couldn't have lived to enjoy an evening like this one promised to become. I wondered if his magnetism would have worked on Miss Jacobs the way it had on most women. Probably so, even Dee had scarcely escaped the boy's skillful seductions. I hated it that he was gone; my heart broke to have lost him. But I was grateful tonight, that I wouldn't have to compete with him for Miss Jacobs's attention.

If she wasn't aware that she was a show stopper, the men in her wake surely were. As she made her way to the slots, the gamblers would pause to sneak second and third looks. Working on my eighth or ninth look, I began to wonder whether Frank kept her around for brains or beauty. He didn't seem like the kind of guy to waste resources, so I figured she was probably as smart as she was attractive. That thought made me smile. I finished the scotch I was drinking, and ordered two beers. Unlucky at cards…

I walked up to her, aware we were being observed. I grinned that they were all waiting for me to strike out. She was hot. But she was inexperienced. It would be like shooting fish in a barrel. "Watch and learn," I thought.

"Hey," I said.

She said, "Hey, you", dropped a coin in the slot, and pressed the button.

"I brought you a beer," I said, offering her the bottle.

"Thanks," she said. "Could you put it there for me?" She nodded towards the cup holder next to the machine and dropped another coin.

"Are you having any luck?" I asked.

The machine lit and began to ring as three coins fell from the spout below.

She watched the coins fall into the tray; then looked at me with an ironic smile. "No. Not a lot. How about you? You giving up?"

I smiled. "No. I'm not having a lot of luck either. But the night's young, and I'm a strong finisher in the end."

She snorted and laughed.

"What?" I asked.

She continued to laugh. "Does that really work for you, the double entendre and erotic allusions?"

I was busted. "Yeah," I said sheepishly. "Most of the time. Is it working now?"

She shook her head, laughing. "I'll let you know before the end of the evening. I'll give you enough time to pick up someone closer to your age and skill level. We wouldn't want you to waste your time on a losing proposition."

"Ouch," I said. "That's very sporting of you, Miss Jacobs."

"That's Val, Sergeant Edwards," she said. She lifted her beer bottle and I matched her.

"Ace," I said.

"Ace," she said. "With a name like Ace, one would think you'd have better luck than you're having."

This was *not* like shooting fish in a barrel. Looking around the room for new prospects, I considered what she said. I looked at her and said, "Yeah. That *would* be the assumption."

She looked at me smiling. "Cheer up, Ace. The night's young." She looked around the room. "I'm sure we'll be able to find you someone to play with before it's over."

Our eyes met.

"Do you think so?" I asked.

"Oh, I'm sure of it," she said.

She raised her bottle and I raised mine. They came together with a small clink.

"If you say so, I'm sure we will," I said. And with an unspoken challenge, we tipped our bottles until they were empty.

She held hers up. "How about another one?" she asked.

I set mine down. "Lead the way."

At the bar, Valerie ordered a couple of brews and handed me mine. Before long, we were trading jokes. "So, a gorilla walks into a bar," she said. I busted the punch line. "The zebra owns the place!"

She laughed. "Jerk."

I laughed.

"Okay, Mr. Smart Guy," she said. "Your turn."

"Alright," I said. "Drunk guy, driving, gets stopped by a traffic cop….." She busted my punch line. "Don't give it to *me*! Give it to the horse! He's the one driving!"

I laughed. "Jerk."

She laughed.

We stepped up our game. The jokes got better. Soon we were laughing at everything; the people walking pass; gamblers. Even at the bartender, who busted out a couple of pretty good ones.

Following a fit of laughter, Valerie casually allowed her hand to brush my thigh. "Ace, tell me," she said. "Of all the women in all the towns, in all the world, why Mrs. McKensie? ....Why the wife of one of the most dangerous men in the world?"

I took a sip from my beer, and chuckled. It was a good question, one I had stopped asking myself a long time ago. It was what it was. There are some people who just affect us the way Desiree affected me. It was wrong. It was dangerous. (Though *I* had never considered Bud that dangerous, he really was.)

But when Desiree and I were together, it felt so good! I had the impression Valerie was waiting to hear me say those words, looking for a reason to back away. I wouldn't make it that easy for her. I wouldn't say them.

"A little young to be paraphrasing Bogart, aren't you"?

She grinned. "You'd rather I paraphrased Bela Lugosi, huh?"

I was drinking from my bottle and snorted beer through my nose as she referred to the old Dracula line. Composing myself, I stared into her eyes. She didn't flinch.

"Yes," I said.

"Perhaps I will," she said, "*if* you answer the question."

I didn't fall for that one. "Why do you want to know?" I asked.

"Because, you're my client. If I'm going violate any ethical taboos, I want to know exactly what I'm getting into," she answered. "I don't mind bending a rule or two, so long as I don't get played in the process."

She was smart, and honest. I couldn't fault her for wanting to establish the boundaries. I watched us in the mirror behind the bar. I liked the way we looked. If she had questions, so did I. It didn't make a lot of sense to me that she could be so deeply interested in such a short period of time. I began to wonder just how much she really knew about me.

"Je ne sais quoi, Valerie," I said, "Je ne sais quoi."

"You can do better than that," she said. "I've seen her. I even like her. She's an attractive woman. She's got a lot of style. But I can't see why you'd do.... ....Well, do what you've done."

Her youth was showing. There are qualities in each of us the young *rarely* discern. And there are qualities in the older of us the younger of us will *never* discern until we become the older of us. Valerie was trying to circumvent some very necessary steps in gaining the wisdom of age. She was trying to, very quickly, become the older of us. I wondered how much wisdom she could possibly hope to contain in her twenty-odd years. It is the resilience of youth which enables us to bear the pains of youth, or even make the pains worth bearing. I wondered if, in her search for wisdom, she could survive sacrificing that resilience.

"How did you get involved in this, Jacobs?"

She didn't answer my question. "You're not going to tell me, are you?" she asked.

I shook my head. "I would tell you, Val, if I thought you'd understand," I said. "Where are you from?"

She smiled. "Oh, I thought you knew."

"Knew what?" I asked.

"We went to the same high school," she said. "….more than ten years apart, of course, and *I* graduated from State."

I let the little dig slide, as she subtly chided me for leaving college to care for a wife and child. She had been well informed and she wanted me to know it.

Frank was a shrewd man. Valerie wasn't the only student he had collected from home. He was installing an influence network throughout the nation. Just as he was doing with Valerie, he had trained other young go-getters with grandiose visions of world domination; medical professionals, corporate wiz-kids, oil engineers and scientists. He sought any profession which might prove valuable in the future. But because he was a lawyer himself, he reserved the most rigorous and personal training for ambitious, and gifted, attorneys. Once they had been prepped, they were found positions in which they could thrive, with the assumption they would be available to discreetly, assist in future ventures-professional or personal.

Ventures is what Frank euphemistically called these little life mess-ups like my situation. He wasn't exactly buying influence from powerful men and women in high level positions. He was farming it. He was nurturing influence. The guy was cultivating power in the form of young talented, socially and culturally challenged, politicians and business leaders. He was opening doors and establishing *friendships*. While boot-strapping ambitious young people, helping them make their marks in the world, he was quietly collecting markers on them. Many of them had benefitted quite well from the arrangement. Some would even rise to breathe the rarified air within sight of the White House.

Frank wasn't greedy. A player's marker may never come due, but you never knew when one of these *friendships* would come in handy. I learned later, he was grooming Valerie for the State House. I shrugged. If Frank wanted to take over the world, who was I to complain? His network was saving my bacon.

I remembered those years at our alma mater and the times at The State University. The memories caused me to smile. Then I thought of the odds against Val and me. Our paths were crossed. We were destined to divergent ends. For a moment, the years between us appeared as a widening chasm. But something in her voice caused them to sift away entirely. Staring into her eyes, I reached for her hand.

"Who's hungry?" It was Dee and Frank, fresh from the blackjack table. Dee was flaunting her winnings. We must have looked guilty, because she stopped waving her jackpot to assess the situation. Frank cast a threatening eye on me. "What? Are you two...?"

In unison, Val and I denied the unspoken accusation. "No! No....! Uhn uh! No way....! .....Of course not! No! Absolutely, not!"

Val and I looked at each. "Let's eat!"

Dinner was wonderful! Leaving the hotel, we all climbed into Frank's private limousine. The lights of the party strip faded, and after a few turns we were on a swampy back-bay back road. Away from the coast, the pitch-black night loomed before us, as we made our way over a road I thought might sink beneath us at any moment. The big car seemed to navigate on auto pilot along the treacherous terrain of the dense wood.

In about twenty minutes we cleared the swamp, driving onto a deep woods island. After coming to a stop at the door of an imposing clapboard building, we boys got out of the vehicle and assisted the ladies. No doorman was there to help us out. There were cars everywhere, and people. Loud, but easy-listening music played outside. The intermingled scents of magnolia, deadwood and burning citronella from the numerous torches made for a hypnotic aphrodisiac.

I looked around, appraising the place. I had missed this spot during my most recent debauch. It was the perfect hide-away. I suspected Desiree had been holding out on me, saving this hide out for herself. I filed that little tidbit away. It was just like her to keep a secret getaway. That was just one more reason to be rid of her, not to trust her.

Frank noticed my expression and guessed what I was thinking. "Your first time here, Ace?"

I nodded. "Yeah."

He chuckled. "I'm not surprised," he said. "Welcome to *Île de Meurtre*, French for Murder Island. Don't feel bad. It's hard to hit 'em all-though I know you tried."

I laughed, thinking of Miss Jacobs. "Still trying, Frankie. I'm still trying."

Frank did not laugh.

There was a short line at the door. I looked around while we waited for the people to clear the way. It turned out that *Île de Meurtre* was a favorite of the locals, and they rarely shared their secret with tourists. Murder Island had been an old pirate haunt for smugglers, slavers and cutthroats of all sorts. It was seventy acres of devilish buccaneer history, fable and lore. The island was grave site to, not a few, ill-fated brigands, who had met their demise at sword point, disease or musket ball. Legend has it that even more (deserters) had been lost to the dangers of the swamp or to one of the indigenous tribes, the Biloxi, Choctaw or Chickasaw.

There was no escaping the romance of *Île de Meurtre*. She was a verdant paradise in the midst of some of the most inhospitable terrain on earth. The swamp remained unforgiving, with its snakes and gators, bears, wild cats, stinging insects and sink holes. And if the wild life didn't get you, the hermitic swamp men, who lived by a murderous, centuries-old pirate code of secrecy and plunder, might. But as long you were with a "member", you had a pass to, freely, come and go.

243

Frank warned me that I'd never get back to the island on my own. "Don't go around asking folks how to get here," he said. "It's not safe. Besides, the licensed cabbies won't bring you here. If they do, you and the cabbie could end up in a shallow grave. Or get lost on one of the endless trails to nowhere."

He handed me a black and gold card with the watermark of a cutlass and a musket crossed to form an "X". In the foreground were the initial "I" over a capital "M". Below that, written in Old English script was Île de Meurtre.

"If you can't help yourself, and just have to come here, use this card," he said. "Show it to an independent cabbie, if you can find one."

By "independent" he meant bootleggers, unlicensed cabbies. They were the only cabbies the swamp people let pass through their territory. A client with them was treated like royalty, never got ripped off or overpaid, the price was twice the licensed, but well worth the safety and security. It turned out the independents were better regulated than the licensed guys. They regulated themselves. They operated at the discretion of people like Frank. So long as a cabbie ran a clean operation, he was allowed to do business outside of the law. If an independent cheated or harmed a client, he was swiftly dealt with by the law, if they could find what would be left of him after the other cabbies were done with him.

And, provided they minded their business, no one messed with the independents; not criminal bigwigs; not big shot corporate guys; not government bureaucrats. No one. They each operated autonomously,

244

answering to no authority, but their own informal code. Some kingpin had once tried to bring them all under his umbrella of safety. It didn't work out for him. It was like trying to dam a river with a fish net. In trying to encroach upon the cabbies demesne, he had nearly lost his entire empire. There is a reason they were called independents. They took care of each other and themselves.

I couldn't wait to come out to the island on my own. The time would come when I didn't need to flash the card. And eventually, I was given pass to drive out myself. I had gotten lost the first time I tried, and after a tremendously scary encounter, made friends with a few of the old boys out there in the swamp. Alligator wrestling is not all it's cracked up to be. Shinny is everything it's cracked to be.

Folks were walking all around the well-lighted and elegantly tended lawn and gardens. Some were seated on benches or at tables, enjoying their meals and drinks. Some were paired off, most were in groups. Singles, congregated at the bar on the far side of the expansive yard, teasing and gaming one another-and anyone else who would give them any attention at all.

The restaurant obviously had a waiting list, which Frank dutifully ignored. The hostess greeted him with a familiar hug and faux kiss on the cheek, which I noticed Dee responded to. She didn't like it. I laughed to myself. I didn't care. I reached out and allowed my hand to rest on Val's lower back. She moved closer to me; then playfully smacked my hand away. She frowned and nodded in Frank's direction. He was facing away from us. I grinned and pantomimed, "So". Then she stepped on my foot before moving to follow the hostess to our booth. With a slight limp, I trailed the group.

The meal consisted of crawfish etouffee, a type of crawfish stew, seafood gumbo (the really slimy kind), boudin and rice, fresh homemade biscuits, endless Cajun steamed shrimp and crawfish (heads on), blue crabs and buckets of ice cold beer. After eating, Frank ordered us an aperitif of crème de menthe, and handed out exquisite Cohiba cigars. Diana lounged against Frank, her head resting on his shoulder. She took a puff off her cigar and released a ring of smoke. The circle drifted over her head like a halo; then floated away on the draft created by the slow moving overhead fan. She looked so relaxed, comfortable. For her sake, I found myself wishing we could remain here in Biloxi forever.

I smiled at her through the haze of excess. "You look happy," I said.

Returning my smile, she placed a hand over the back of Frank's on the table. He responded by turning his palm to meet hers. "I am," she said simply.

I nodded, thumped the ash from the end of my cigar, and took a hit, then sipped from my snifter. Swirling the liquid in the glass, I began to wonder what life was going to be like when we returned to Hinesville. No doubt, I would see Desiree from time to time. I wasn't looking forward to it. I would have liked to say I was over her, but it wasn't twenty-fours since we had been together. I stared at Valerie, who returned my gaze with a beautiful smile.

Dee noticed. "Watch out, Jailbait," she said to Val. "That one's knocked up. He's a runner... ....and not very far, at that."

The women laughed. So did Frank.

Frank hit his cigar. The end of it cast an ominous glow against his face in the restaurant's dim light. "Ace, Miss Jacobs is nothing but trouble for you. And let me assure you, as long as you're in this town, you need to stay out of trouble."

They laughed again. But, I thought I saw a familiar glint in Valerie's eye.

I hit my cigar again. "....Guess it's my night."

Frank sat up. "Yup... ....Je ne sais quoi, Ace."

We all laughed at that.

"You're the man of the hour. You ready to do some partying?"

Now he was talking. "What you got in mind, Frank?"

He was sliding out of the booth, reaching for Dee's hand to help her out. "....Got a little after hours joint I want to show you."

I laughed. "Lead the way. .....Those places are illegal, aren't they?"

He drained his glass and wobbled slightly on his feet. "It's okay," he slurred, raising the glass, which Dee took from his hand and placed on the table. "I'm a judge."

I smiled. Yeah, he was. ...And a pretty good one, to boot. He saved my bacon, and quite a few others, I'd guessed. It was interesting that no bill had come to the table, and Frank hadn't touched his wallet the entire evening. He was a judge.

On the way out the door, the hostess, whom I learned was called, simply, Duchess, gave a covered take out plate to Frank. While walking to the driver's side of the waiting vehicle, he told Valerie and me to get into the back seat of the limo. He passed the, near to bursting, plate to the driver, Horace.

"Thanks, Judge," said the appreciative giant of a man.

"It's the least I can do, Horace," Frank said. "I almost forgot to feed you, buddy. We need to remember to get something good for the Duchess."

"Yes, sir," said Horace.

"Do you want something to drink, Horace? How about a beer?"

Horace shook his head. "No, sir…. I'm workin'."

Frank rubbed his now stubbled chin. "Oh, yeah," he said, thinking. "So what do you want to drink?"

"Nothin', sir," Horace replied. "This is plenty."

The powerful man; unaccustomed to rejection; feigned exasperation. It appeared to be a scenario they had perfected over the course of many years. "Horace, what do you want to drink?"

Horace relented. "A large Co' cola would be nice, Judge."

"Great! Now, you're making sense!"

Frank scurried around the vehicle, and dashed into the building. In no time at all, he returned with an exceptionally large cup of cola.

248

"Here you go, buddy," he said, handing the drink to Horace. "Give me the keys."

The big man, with the oddly lopsided chest looked uncomfortable. "I don't know, Judge," he protested. "That might not be such a good idea."

Frank pressed. "It'll be fine," he said. "Get in on the other side and eat. Let Miss Diana in. She can sit between us. If you're scared of my driving, she can be my eyes."

The big fella acquiesced. "Alright, Judge. But, soon as I'm finished eatin', let me drive."

"You got it, big guy," Frank agreed, with a wink to an apprehensive Dee.

"Can you drive?" she asked.

"Sure," he said. "I'm sober as a judge."

He began to laugh. It was an old, stale joke, and I wasn't so sure he could walk, let alone drive. But in my mellow condition, I wasn't eager to kill the warm glow on the evening. Besides, provided we actually reached our next destination, this was a perfect time to get some work in with Val. Frank got in behind the wheel, and seemed to sober right up. I began to suspect he wasn't as drunk as he had given us to believe. Frank was a wily son-of-gun. I would need to be more careful with him. I really didn't want to end up on the Jerry side of a Martin and Lewis relationship.

We left *Île de Meurtre*'s restaurant, lawn and gardens, bars and casinos with as much ceremony as we had entered. But I would return as often as I

249

could over the coming years. Murder Island was just too exciting not to explore.

Frank raised the privacy panel. I guess I wasn't the only one who wanted to make a little woo on the way to the next joint. Valerie and I were sitting opposite to one another. I grinned at her.

"Why are you smiling?" she asked.

"Am I smiling?" I asked.

"Yes," she said.

"Does that disturb you?"

"Yes," she said, seriously.

"Why," I asked, still smiling.

"Because, in your smile, I can read your every disgusting little dirty thought," She said.

I laughed. "They aren't that little. Anyway, I doubt you can, or you wouldn't be sitting there as cool as you are right now."

She, quickly, bit her lip; then looked away.

"Oh," I said. "Maybe you can read my thoughts."

Recovering, she turned to me. "The Judge warned you," she said.

"I'm not doing anything. Besides, though it may be a shock to you, I don't work for the Judge," I said. "In fact, it's my impression, he actually works for me."

"Mr. Edwards…."

I cut her off. "It's Mr. Edwards now. Perhaps I read you wrong. I'm sorry. My bad."

In the dim light, I noticed her brow knit. "Yes," she said. "Perhaps you did."

"Definitely," I said.

Staring out the window, we rode for a time in silence.

After a while, I became bored. I opened the limo's bar, to inspect the libations. "Well, let's see what we have here."

She peered over into the bar. "Is there any gin?" she asked.

I searched through the selection of booze. "Yes," I said.

"Mix me a gin and tonic," she ordered.

"No," I said. "You're drunk enough."

"I'm not drunk. Fix the drink," she said, insistently.

"You're drunk if you think that tone will get you anyplace with me," I responded.

"Fine," she said, in a huff. "I'll fix it myself." She started to move across the car.

I laughed. "If you come over here, you're going to get a spanking."

"I wouldn't like that." She said it with so little conviction that the statement seemed to carry the weight of verbal consent. She changed seats.

"Get back to your side of the car," I said. "This is my seat."

"No," she said, as she reached across me to get to the liquor.

The vehicle made a sharp turn, and her torso pushed against mine. With the feel of her warm firm form against me, all inhibition melted away. I pulled her down onto my lap. I had half expected her to struggle. Instead, she wriggled into a more comfortable position, and leaned into me for a kiss.

Breaking the kiss, she pressed me away. "You do know our different faiths will be an issue, don't you?"

I looked into her eyes. The kiss was as intoxicating as all the alcohol I'd been drinking. I hadn't thought very far ahead. That is to say, I had only thought as far as the end of the evening.

"Oh, yeah, why is that?" I asked. "Is it because you're Jewish?"

"Yes," she said. "That, and…."

I interrupted her. "….And I'm Met…."

"A misogynist," she said.

I was somewhat stunned. "That is not what I was going to say."

"It doesn't matter," she said. "It's the truth."

"Is not," I countered.

"Is so", she volleyed.

"Is not."

"Prove it," she challenged. "You think women are on earth to please you, and for no other reason."

If I thought about it, she definitely had a point, especially, if anyone was to tally my scorecard. Regardless, I wasn't prepared to concede the fact. Her, beloved "Judge" was likely as bad as I was. Only, I had had the misfortune of getting caught. I was in no mood for psycho analysis at the moment. I shrugged off the matter.

I'd met her type before. She had probably spent most of her time in college, learning to drink at frat houses with her Black room mate. She had maybe even sported a permed Afro until she opted for a more traditional hairstyle following college graduation. She had been blessed with stunning good looks and a strong intellect, so she was able to overcome her mistakes where others failed utterly. I wondered what Mommy and Daddy thought of her decision to make her fortune in Way-South, Mississippi? There had to be an issue there. I could have said it, but thought better of it.

For most of us, the only thing between psychosis and relative peace is that thin veneer of sanity in the form of the fantasies we create of our lives. Val's fantasy was her apparent security, her faith in the identity which had been established for her by second generation immigrant parents. Her grandparents were likely victims of Nazi Germany who carried with them, the wounded spirit of the horrid atrocities they experienced in a distant past. I was profiling, guessing based on the little I knew of her. It wasn't fair, but I would have bet anything, I was accurate.

"Are we really going to have this argument, now, Miss Hot-Fun-in-the-City?"

She laughed; then kissed me. "No, we can finish it another time. But we are going to finish it."

"Alright," I said. "But, anytime you're ready to compare ink blots, you just let me know."

She gripped my lapels in her fists, and drew me to her. "Sounds like fun. Why don't we start with lipstick?"

I wanted to answer, but it's extremely difficult to speak with your mouth full of face.

In time, the limousine came to a stop in front of an old house on a dark back street. The home's lawn was in desperate need of attention. And even in the darkness, through the tint of the limo windows, I could tell the house itself would have benefitted from a coat or two of paint. From what I could see, the surrounding houses were in similar state of neglect and disrepair. The privacy window came down. Valerie was seated across from me sipping the gin and tonic I had prepared for her. I drank scotch.

Frank turned to Dee. "That wasn't so bad. ...Now, was it?"

Dee responded in typical Dee fashion. "Sweetheart, it was harrowing. You really drive rather badly, even when you're sober. Let's leave the driving to Horace, next time. ....Okay?"

Dee was tipsy. I was concerned he might be offended by her dry wit. Instead, Frank laughed. "Stop it, Dee. You know you enjoyed it."

She chuckled; then turned her attention to us in the back seat. "So, Jailbait, how's our prisoner? Was he good during the drive over?"

Staring at the young woman, I tensed with the question. Across the car in the evening's half light, the beautiful Valerie returned my gaze over the drink in her hand. "Disappointingly, good," she purred.

Dee and Frank laughed. I thought I noticed Horace's enormous shoulders rise and fall in mirth, as well. Every card was a joker in this deck.

Valerie stretched her legs, as she sat demurely, sipping her drink. She hadn't exactly lied. I had been good. With the urgency and mystic of the first kiss behind us, we mutually agreed to move very slowly. We didn't want to do anything to compromise our legal and professional relationship.

"Once the divorce is final," she said. "....and the dust has cleared from your Desiree situation with the child; there'll be plenty of time to screw up each other's lives."

I kissed her. Though, technically, I was unencumbered, she made a good argument for waiting. "What makes you think we're going to screw this up?" I asked her.

"Perhaps we won't", she said. "But I think you'll agree, our ink blots would indicate differently. Besides, not only does the Judge work for you, but so do I. How would that look?"

Though I didn't voice it, I thought, at this point, we had already violated too many protocols to be concerned with decorum. I did agree, however, that we were both crazy to even consider a relationship with one another, she more than I.

She added a personal touch to her argument. "I don't want to be one of the many women you run through. I want to be special to you. I want to know you gave up something for me. I need to know you waited, that you felt I was worth waiting for. I need to know you value *us* enough to wait."

Valerie was casting herself as the mythological Greek heroine, Atalanta, but I was prepared to throw a few apples in her path. I held her in my arms, and caressed her gently. Turning her face to me, I stared into her beautiful eyes.

"Darling, how many times have you delivered that speech?"

She returned my gaze. "Never before, sweetheart," she, innocently lied.

I remained silent, staring at her with a smile.

She giggled and shrugged. "...Coupl'a times; maybe three."

More like seven or eight, I'd guessed. I chuckled, and kissed her. "Does it work for you?" I asked.

She laughed. "Usually," she said.

"Uh huh," I grunted.

"Is it working now?" she asked.

I grinned. "I'll let you know by the end of the evening," I said.

She changed seats.

"Coward," I challenged.

"Careful," she countered.

We behaved ourselves.

We all climbed out of the car. "Welcome to Gulfport!" Frank said. Given the inauspicious appearance of the neighborhood, it was more fanfare than necessary.

The home appeared deserted. It was dark, no lights shone through the windows. And, if this was a juke joint, it was the quietest one I'd ever been to. Frank led us to the rear of the building. The familiar red porch light cast a feeble glow, barely illuminating the broken concrete steps. The aroma of frying fish and barbeque wafted in the air.

The Judge gave a little tap on the door. It opened slowly. We were greeted by the requisite security doorman. The noise of a raucous party poured out of the house, around the guard, into the night. The fella looked us over for a moment before allowing us entry. All the while, we stood in nervous anticipation, assaulted by the bluesy back street rhythms seeping pass the open door. Once inside, I was amazed at the size of the place. A better than decent country-rock band played on a stage in the spot the front door should have been. The non-load-bearing walls had been removed to make room for tables. The best I could tell, the only rooms left in tact were the bathroom and kitchen. The windows were sealed and covered to prevent light or sound from escaping into the street. All of the exterior walls were covered in a special acoustic enhancing material. They gave the carved out room a concert hall feel I never would have thought possible in a place of its type and size.

We found chairs at a table up front, near the stage. As we settled in among the crowd, our drink orders were taken by a not-too-bad-looking waitress in tight jeans. Dee busted me checking her out, and hollered at me. "Ace, be good!" she shouted over the music.

I laughed. "I'm trying," I shouted back.

Valerie rolled her eyes at me.

"Try harder," shouted Dee.

I changed the subject. "Nice spot, Frank. Has it been here long?"

"Yeah, it's pretty good, Ace," he said. "It's been here a coupl'a years or so. I like to come here from time to time." He laughed. "It gives me respectability with the upper class folks around here."

Dee shouted to Val. "You singing tonight, girl?"

"No," she replied. "Not tonight."

Frank chimed in. "Nonsense!" he shouted. "Of course, she's singing!" He placed his hand on my shoulder and leaned over to speak into my ear. "Ace, you got to hear this! Miss Jacobs has an absolutely amazing voice!"

He waved to the band leader, who gave him a nod. Two songs later, the guy was introducing Valerie to the stage. She shook her head, and covered her face. With some coaxing from the crowd, she took the stage. It was difficult to believe this statuesque beauty was shy to perform before an audience. Maybe Frank and Dee were clowning her. Perhaps they encouraged her as a prank. I suddenly found myself concerned she would fail, and they would hurt her feelings. I prayed she would have the good sense to back down and save some self respect.

I heard her quietly say to the band, *"Ain't No Way"*. I cringed. She was scared, and didn't know how to get out of it. And she was going to try Aretha Franklin? Aww naahw! Dee and Frank were drunk, and being cruel. I couldn't let Val humiliate herself that way. Just as I started to rise to help her off the stage, the music began to play. It was too late. I sat down, resigned to be there to console her following her miserable performance.

I relaxed when she began to sing, and found myself enjoying her rendition. I had to admit she did a passable job with the iconic classic. The audience loved her, though *I* was loath to give her high marks compared to a legend like Aretha. But when she belted out a sultry, heart-rending cover of Alannah Myles's *Black Velvet,* I thought I would loose my mind. It was one of the most sensual experiences of my life. I mean, it was awesome, especially, when she left the stage to work the room! The audience was feeling her passion as she painted a haunting picture of a bluesy country crooner, Southern Comfort, black labeled whiskey and the sticky hot delta summers they knew so well. And somehow, they absorbed that passion, and silently fed it back to her, creating a syncopated connection which begged for its ultimate consummation. Like a voyeur, I watched intently, as she moved from table to table, seductively serenading one hopeful patron after another. Oblivious to the crowd, I nearly lost it completely when she finished her song with a growling moan and a swoon which left her draped, prostrate in my arms, along the length of my body.

The lights dimmed lower, as the bass and percussion faded with the conclusion of the song. I struggled to maintain composure, while helping Val to rise, unsteady on her feet, recovering from her trance. As the room became brighter, the audience ignited with an explosive roar of cheers and applause. Frank cast me a glowering stare.

Dee cheered, but there was an odd expression of bewilderment on her face. Standing, she took the microphone from Valerie's hand, and gave it to the band leader. The girl's face and body were coated with a thin sheen of shimmering perspiration, which her hair and clothing clung to like a second skin. Her energy depleted from the expended effort of physical and emotional exertion, she labored to regain her breath. Wordlessly, like a protective mother, Dee took the exhausted young woman by the hand. Frank and I watched in awe, as the women made their way to the restroom.

I was the first to break the silence between us. "Wow," I whispered.

"Yeah," Frank said. "Didn't I tell you?"

I shook my head slowly. "Brother, you didn't tell me *that*."

"Well, I didn't exactly know *all of that* was in there," he replied.

I took a sip from my drink. "Frank, you hittin' that?"

He side stepped the question. "Dee? Why don't you ask her?"

"Dee," I repeated sarcastically. "Get out of here."

"Miss Jacobs?" he feigned vagueness.

I was patient. "Uh huh."

He frowned with indignation. "Of course, not. I'm surprised you would ask such a question. She's my assistant. That would be highly inappropriate." He sounded like a wounded animal, shrill; and way too many words. He had become tense. Maybe he wasn't with Val now, but there was *something* there. I let the lie slide.

I nodded. "Of course. Forgive me. Sorry I asked."

He shrugged. "It's alright, Ace. No harm done."

I nodded again. "Thanks, Frank."

We raised our glasses, drained them and ordered another round.

The excitement of Val's performance had begun to dissipate, the room was returning to normal. The band left the stage for between sets refreshments. We sat for some time, quietly staring at the empty stage. After my breach of protocol, I didn't dare look Frank in the eye. The silence between us had become conspicuous.

He appeared oddly, disturbed by the event. "She turned you down, huh?"

"Yeah." It pained him to admit the fact.

"Uh huh." I understood.

The silence returned. We sat, each of us thinking, staring at nothing in particular. He had become a father figure to her. Their relationship was sacrosanct. He would never have anything closer than a business relationship. I, on the other hand, represented freedom and excitement. I was danger, damage and challenge. I was the coloring outside of the lines,

261

the stolen cookie from the cookie jar, that piece of cake before dinner. Yeah, it's true, I was also the ruined appetite, decaying teeth, extra weight on the thighs and the whipping if you got caught. But, I was worth it (my perspective).

Neither of us was being rational here. Frank was wrong, she was his employee. And there was Dee to consider. He only wanted what he shouldn't have. Val hungered for the wild side of life, and wanted to taste as much of the bad apple as she could take in one bite. Of course, I was just doing what I do. Without struggling, I was allowing the vortex of mischief and disregard to carry me along until the wind of fate quit blowing.

"Umf," I grunted. "....A shame."

"Yup," he agreed.

"Sorry about that, dawg," I consoled him.

"S'all right, blood," he said.

"'Nother round?" I offered.

"Please..."

We finally looked at one another, and broke up into uncontrollable laughter. Frank was a big fat liar-my kind of guy. At least, now I knew what to expect of him in a tight situation. He was human. Well, he was from the old neighborhood. I felt awful for his loss, but I knew he would recover in no time at all.

By the time the women returned to the table, Frank and I had become good friends. It's a good thing, too. We would bail one another out of a number of scrapes in the coming years. Val was wide-eyed, and appeared as fresh and composed as when we began the evening.

"Drink up, Frankie," said Dee. "We're leaving."

Dee was taking charge.

"We're what?" asked Frank.

"We're leaving," she repeated. "Pay the tab, and let's get out of here."

Frank was dragging his feet. "Dee, I don't think Ace is ready to go, yet."

"He's not leaving, Frankie, darling," she said. "He's going to stay here with Valerie. But *I'm* ready to go.........Right now."

I got the message, if Frank didn't. But, it only took him another moment to catch on. He paid the tab, and Dee hauled him right out of there. They left us the limo, saying it would be easier for them to catch a cab than us.

"Good night, kids," Dee said, hurriedly. "Have a good time."

"G'night, Ace," said Frank, after emptying his glass.

"Night, Judge," I said, shaking his hand. "Thanks for everything."

"Miss Jacobs," he nodded to Valerie, very professionally. "Don't let our client get into any trouble, okay?"

She grinned. "Good night, Judge. I'll keep him safe."

Watching Diana leave with Frank, I began to wonder if he had gotten the better end of the deal tonight. Dee was protecting her interest. She knew what she wanted and went right after it. I smiled at the young and beautiful Valerie, and knew, though she was interested, she was doubtful of her own intentions concerning me.

263

"That was quite a performance," I said.

She smiled. "Was it alright? I was so nervous. I hadn't sung those songs in such a long time. I wasn't sure if I could pull it off."

I placed my hand over hers. "Sweetheart, it was perfect," I said. "So, what's next?"

She took my hand into hers. "You hungry?" she asked.

Remembering the earlier sumptuous meal, I considered the question for a moment. "I could eat," I said.

"Good," she said. "The fried fish here is delicious."

"What kind is it?" I asked.

"You get a choice: Drum or sheep head," she said.

She was playfully, squeezing my hand.

"Hmmm….. Really?" I questioned.

"Umm huh," she answered. "What'll it be?"

"Surprise me," I said, smiling.

"I can do that," she said. "I'll be right back."

She hurried off to the makeshift bar, just off the kitchen. Val hadn't been gone a minute, when I was approached by an extremely large and aggressive yokel.

"Wu'chu thank you doin' here, Air Man?"

It was a drunken townie, jealous of the prosperity and the attention local Air Force members received from the women in the area. He had, somehow, pegged me for a military member, and was taking this opportunity to vent his frustration with airmen. It was a case of mistaken identity. I had seen his kind of rage before, and thought I knew how to defuse the situation.

I was about to respond, but was caught off guard, looking up just in time to see the blur of a huge pair of hands reaching for my throat. He was quicker and more agile than I would have thought possible for a man his size. The guy didn't wait for an answer before catching me at the knot of my tie, and lifting me neatly to my feet.

"Get up off me, Bubba," I croaked with his enormous knuckles pressed against my larynx. "You got the wrong guy. I'm not in the Air Force." The correction didn't come out anywhere near as loud, or as convincingly as I would have hoped. But, that was understandable, considering, I was about to choke to death, if I survived the punch aimed between my eyes. Dangling in the air, my toes raking the floor, I flailed my arms, in an attempt to mitigate the imminent beating I was about get.

Just then, I heard the unmistakable locking mechanism of a revolver, the hammer dangerously clicking into firing position. The snub-nosed, thirty-eight was pointed at the angry guy's head before he or I noticed it. He froze, instantly. So did, I. In the excitement, I wasn't sure whose back-up this was stepping in.

Thankfully, it was Valerie come to the rescue. She pressed the weapon to the back of his head, behind his ear. I was trying to figure out where she could have concealed it.

"That's my date you're grabbing on Billy Bob," she said. "I've got plans for him for later on. And I don't want him broken before I get a chance to do it myself."

I liked the sound of that. Despite my awkward situation, I smiled at the prospect of getting misused by Valerie.

The big fellow stood his ground. "W'udis Air Man doin' here? W'ut *you* doin' wit'im?" he growled, drunkenly. Sweat had begun to stream down his flushed face. His breath smelled of liquor, marijuana and onions. And he spat and shook me like a lifeless ragdoll when he spoke.

Val grinned, pressing the gun more insistently. "Mister, you're as dumb as you look. He's not an airman; he's a soldier. And the answer to both questions is, 'Anything we want to do'. Now put my man down before I give you a six-point hearing test."

His brow furrowed, as he seemed to debate within himself what he would do with me. Finally, sensibility seeped into his dull red eyes. Thoughtlessly, he dropped me like a discarded toy. Gasping for breath, I landed on wobbly feet. I had been punked in front of Val, and I didn't like it. I thought to save face by punching him in the nose. It was only a passing thought, however. Just then, Horace and the bouncer were at our side. They rushed the drunk, and he was through the crowd and out the door in a blink. For all the excitement, the event occurred in only seconds, and most of the people in the room had missed it completely. Those who had not, applauded briefly. Then went right back to whatever they had been doing.

Valerie hugged me and helped to straighten my clothing. "Are you alright, Baby?" she asked.

"Yeah…. Thanks, sweetheart. It's a good thing you stepped up," I said. "I was gonna really hurt that ol' boy."

"I know, baby," she said, straightening my tie. "He sure is lucky you didn't kick his butt." She kissed my lips; then brushed her fingers across them, saying, "Oh, honey, your lip stick's smudged."

She smiled.

I laughed. "Thanks".

We kissed. The gun went back to its hiding place. We smudged more lip stick on my lips. And we sat down to our fish sandwiches and rum shooters. She chose the sheep head. She was right. It was delicious.

Horace returned to ensure we hadn't been harmed. He was mortified to have been behind the action. "Mister Ace, are you alright?" he asked.

I looked up at the big man. "Yeah, Horace. I'm fine. Thanks, buddy. Why don't you have a seat and relax?"

He shook his head. "No, sir. I'm good. I'm sorry, Miss Valerie."

Val smiled. "It's okay, Horace," she said. "You did great. That one was on me. Get yourself a fish sandwich and something to drink. We'll be leaving soon."

He smiled. "Yes, Ma'am," he said.

Horace ordered a sandwich, and took a post near the door with an unobstructed view. He was intent to maintain watch over me. And he never took his eyes off me from that moment until he dropped us off at the hotel, some two hours later. Val explained that she and Horace, both, had a little experience in situations much worse than this one tonight. It was a just the cost of being a part of Judge Johnson's entourage. You never knew whether an attack was an attempt to send a message to Frank through his people or simply a random personal altercation.

"It pays to be ready for, just about, anything," she said.

Val's cred' with me was going up. I was beginning to see in her, much of what I saw in Dee. No question about it, she was definitely from the old neighborhood.

For most of the night, I had enjoyed the benefits of the Frank's protective network. But just now, it was conceivable that I had witnessed; first hand; one of the liabilities-and survived. I wasn't ready to abandon my old classmate, yet. I would remain aware, however, that if he was taking a chance associating with me, I was risking as much, in my association with him.

I tried to close the juke joint, but wasn't up to the task. I thought the crowd would have thinned out at this early hour of the morning. But, if anything, the bar became even more congested. At last, I'd had it. I didn't think I could get any drunker, and I definitely wasn't in the mood to eat another bite. After two, maybe three (could have been four) rounds of vodka shooters, Val and I were in the limo, prepared to return to the hotel. Looking out the car window, I took note of a crowd gathered in front of a building on the corner of the street. It was an old church in much the same condition as the house we'd just left.

It was nearly daybreak; that dusky foggy twilight before the sun rises to burn away what little residual coolness was left behind from the night season. There were droves of people, migrating wraith-like from one end of the block to the other. Some were entering the church, while others were leaving and headed towards buildings in the middle of the block. It was a surreal tableau, in this half light they all seemed to meander aimlessly, as people without will. Through an alcoholic haze, I imagined them as zombies returning to ghoulish haunts, after sating their hunger for human flesh in some ghastly ritualistic feast.

"Where are they all going?" I asked Val.

"Some are going home, some to jobs," said Val. "Others are going to church. And still, others are going to the juke joint, it never closes."

I watched a man and woman stagger into the church. They were familiar to me as a couple I had noticed in the bar.

"The members of the church used to boycott the bar," Val said. "They wanted it closed. It was too close to the church. They called it a 'blighted eyesore, driving the neighborhood to irretrievable moral decay'. The judge intervened. With his help, the church's membership grew to three times its original size, as did the juke joint's-oddly enough."

I laughed.

So, Frank had found a way for both establishments to, not only survive, but to thrive. It wasn't, yet, Sunday, but people flocked into the church continuously. They never closed, neither did the juke joint. They found synergy, indeed, symbiosis. They shared patrons, and the church's pastor benefitted tremendously from the arrangement. So did the owner of the juke. And, I was guessing, so did good old Frank.

As we drove pass, I heard muted music of a church band; organ, drums and tambourines. Voices of a choir were raised in worship. I let down the window to listen more closely to the familiar melody. My eyes closed involuntarily, as my mind drifted back to a time when church attendance was a regular event in my life. I thought of Sunday mornings as a child, hurriedly shining the Buster Brown shoes I had neglected to shine the night before. I could taste the peppermint my mother would give to me in order to halt my fidgeting during services.

"We can go inside, if you like," Val said.

I opened my eyes, considering her offer. "I'm not sure it would be a good idea."

"Nonsense," she said. "The judge stops in every time he visits the bar."

I learned later that Frank attended the church regularly. He, the church's pastor and the bar owner kept a regular tee time at a local golf coarse. In this way, they were able to meet, in order to maintain the balance of their tenuous relationship. They kept the fourth spot open for potential business prospects.

Watching Valerie, her beautiful long legs stretching across the limo seat, church worship was really the last thing I wanted. Raising the window, I declined. The sound of the choir faded. The bodies, the buildings, the street; they all drifted into the distance. I reached for Val. She rejected my advances. Too tired to object, I closed my eyes to sleep. I had accepted that the night's magic had apparently finally come to an end.

"Well, I'm not going to let you go alone." –Valerie Jacobs

CHAPTER 5

It was raining the morning we left Biloxi. As we drove east along Highway Ninety, I watched the face of the storm front roll landward from the gulf. Squalls moved across the waters like the opening and shutting of drapery. The spacing between showers seemed to match the gaps between the dashed lines on the pavement. I closed my eyes, resting, preparing for the miles which loomed before us.

Valerie, and Horace, my temporary protector, were charged with delivering me safely to the appropriate authorities at Fort Stewart in Georgia. Valerie and I had spent a relaxing three days off shore on a client's yacht. I had just about had enough of her icy presence. I was becoming impatient, frustrated with waiting. Since the night of our encounter with a jealous local, she had become formal and aloof. I had had the impression we were starting a relationship, but she was giving me little indication of it. I longed to explore the limits of our relationship. I needed her to express her passion more deeply. She was cordial, but careful to withhold any substantive affection, which I might construe as a signal to press more aggressively.

If Valerie had become unresponsive, it was with good reason. The afternoon following the little dust up in the late night bar, Frank went right off. He had called my hotel room to ask me to meet him in judge's chambers late in the afternoon. When I arrived, I was asked to be patient, as he was in counseling with employees. A half hour later, Horace exited the office. He had the look of a whipped puppy. His huge shoulders slumped, his head hanging even deeper, he mumbled a quick greeting and rushed out the door. It was surprising to me that Frank would give Horace a dressing down. He had earlier said to me, of the driver, "Horace ain't nothin', but good". He loved the guy.

I was let into the office, and there was Valerie seated, rigid and tight-lipped, before Frank's desk. Her brow was furrowed deeply. She blinked rapidly, fighting to hold back the tears that threatened to escape angry eyes. When she greeted me with a terse, "Mister Edwards", I guessed she had been severely chastised by Frank.

Frank was even less jovial than poor Val. Shuffling papers he had been examining, he motioned me to take a seat. After I sat, he dismissed Valerie.

"That will be all, Miss Jacobs."

She adjusted in her seat, and opened her mouth as if she would speak. Instead, she nodded and lowered her eyes. "Yes, sir," she said, in a small brittle voice.

"Don't get lost," he said without lifting his eyes. "I have work for you."

"Yes, Judge," she said.

Frank, stoically, watched her back as she left the room. Once the door had closed, his gaze fell on me. I returned his stare. I wasn't some starry-eyed ingénue or a two-dimensional gun-sell he could cudgel into submission. His stern, disappointed father act wouldn't work with me, and he knew it.

He smiled. "I told you to stay out of trouble, Ace."

Frank wasn't fooling me, he'd heard about the incident in the bar, and he was embarrassed. I had been entrusted into his care, and I had come very close to injury. Dee would never have forgiven him. And it wouldn't have looked good for a client to have been beaten, maybe killed, while celebrating with him and his employee.

I returned his smile. "I did," I replied. "It's not my fault an interactive drama production comes with the drinks in your place."

He laughed. "What makes you think I'm not talking about Miss Jacobs and you? If she hadn't been distracted by you, she may have seen the guy coming."

273

"Not likely. And, what do you care what she does with her personal time?" I asked.

"Ace, she doesn't have any personal time," he replied. "All of her time belongs to me, especially when she's entertaining clients."

"Oh, I see," I said. "You needn't worry that she's earning her keep. She handled the situation like a true professional."

"So, I heard," he said, becoming more agreeable. Changing the subject, he motioned to papers on his desk. "I need you to sign these. They're your freedom pass."

"Should I read them?" I asked.

"No," he said. "Trust me."

He offered me a pen. I looked him in the eye for some time; then took the pen from his hand and signed the papers, unread.

Frank grinned, and I felt a chill along my spine. "Ace, Dee and I are going away for a few days," he said. "I'm going to need to do something with you."

"Okay. ….Like what?" I asked.

"In order to provide you some limits, I'm putting you on a boat, off shore."

I was getting an uneasy feeling now. "Frank, are you having me knocked off over one little brawl?" I asked

He frowned. "What?" he asked. "No, man!" he laughed. "I'm sending you on a little pleasure cruise. You and Valerie are going out to sea on a yacht. I've got to leave on business, and I can't be worried about you getting your brains beaten out before we get you back to Georgia."

"Oh," I laughed. "You had me worried, Frank."

He waved in the air. "Get out of here, Ace."

"C'mon," I said. "You've got to admit, you did come off a little ominously. Down right, threatening."

He laughed. "Sorry, Ace," he apologized for the misunderstanding.

It was my own fault. I'd been a problem for Frank since I'd arrived in his town. It would serve me right, if he wanted to be rid of me.

"Ace, I've been thinking," he said. "Why don't you stay here in Biloxi? You can't do anything in Georgia, you can't do here. You'll have a limousine with a man at your disposal, an expense account, free room and board."

I thought about it. "What would I have to do for all of that, Frank?"

"You'd do what you do, anyway," he said. "I'd pay you to party. Just check up on the nightlife, and let me know who's a little dirty and who's a lot dirty. Let's face it, if you're going to get into trouble anyhow, you may as well be paid for it."

He didn't say it, but I knew he wanted Dee. And according to our previous deal, she went where I went. I had a feeling they'd had this discussion before, and she turned him down. I was beginning to feel like the runner-up in a beauty pageant.

"What about Val?" I asked.

275

He shook his head. "I couldn't make any guarantees in that area. Miss Jacobs would be your supervisor. Officially, she would be off limits to you. We might be able to work *something* out, though."

I was beginning to understand. Val represented a considerable investment. She was his star pupil. He had to value Dee pretty highly, if he was willing to risk Val's professional integrity. A relationship with the wrong person could knock her off pace, emotionally and politically. On the other hand, she was young; and inexperienced in many areas. Like a young race horse, she would need to leave the stall regularly to train and exercise. She would need to stretch her legs, if was she going to realize her full potential. The trick for Frank was to make sure she didn't break a leg in the process.

I frowned with the effort to suppress my laughter. I wasn't going to be Frank's training jockey. I wouldn't let him determine the parameters of my relationships. I didn't want to complete Valerie's maturation process, only to lose her to her career; or some high card, power monger......Or worse, to Frank, himself, once he'd tired of Diana.

He and I, both, knew he couldn't keep me from Val, once I had made up my mind to have her-providing she was willing. But, maintaining a relationship is considerably more difficult than beginning one. I wouldn't take the job. It would be like serving Dee to him on a platter. It wasn't in my best interest. As long as he wanted Dee, and I could keep them apart, he couldn't effectively manipulate me and my relationship with Valerie.

"I don't know, Frank," I said.

He stopped me. "Don't make up your mind right now. Why don't you go on out to the yacht? Relax. And make your decision afterwards."

"Alright, Frank," I said. "I'll think it over."

"Great!" he said.

He rose and came from behind the desk to escort me to the door. We shook hands at the closed door.

"Go on over to the hotel and pack a bag," he said. "Horace will pick you up in one hour."

He lowered his voice. "About our discussion last night.....You know....Miss Jacobs?"

I grinned. "You concerned I might tell Dee about your little crush on Valerie?"

He laughed, nervously. "Uh.....Yeah," he admitted. "There's no need for her to know about it."

I agreed not to tell her, but added, "Frank, I'll lay money she already knows. She most likely knew it before you did."

He rubbed his chin. "You think so?" he asked.

"Uh huh," I said. "Dee's pretty smart. She would have noticed something. Think about it... I did."

"Yeah. You're probably right," he said, his brow knit into a thoughtful frown. "What do you think I should do? Should I bring it up; you know, confess?"

"Are you nuts?" I exclaimed. "Don't do anything! Don't say anything! And don't ever admit it......Even if she asks!"

We laughed; then he looked at me kind strange like. "You know," he said. "Considering all you're going through, you're probably not the one to ask for advice on women."

That was a good one. "Well, you do whatever you want, Frank," I laughed. "You are a judge, after all. You'll figure it out."

"You're a big help, Ace," he said, sarcastically.

He smiled. "Anyhow, I hope you'll agree to stay and work for me. I won't be a judge forever, you know. I think we could make a pretty good team. We could do a lot of good here in Mississippi."

I thought about it. He could have a point, if we could agree upon the agenda. ...And maintain the agreement. Frank and I weren't that much different from each other. There were times, in these few days; it seemed as if we had been thinking with one mind.

"You could be right, Frank," I said. "You and Dee have a good time. I'll let you know."

Frank was ready to jettison our previous plan. Neither of us had mentioned the fact that I was presently a deserter from the Army. I would need to face up to it, get that hurdle behind me. I assumed Frank had an answer for that. After all, he *was* a judge. What good was he, if he couldn't swing a change of venue whenever he wanted to. As I thought about it, it occurred to me that he was extending a courtesy in asking me. He could have used leverage to get whatever he wanted. I had to give him points for respecting me enough to allow me to decide on my own.

I could have taken the job. The last time I saw Hinesville, it was just a backwards blurred image in my inebriated rear view mirror. I didn't have many friends left there, unless you counted Hicks. And I could never really be sure whose side that guy was on.

Frank sent me off with another tidbit of information to consider. Mrs. Smith's husband had been gunning for me. He caught up to some other fellow he mistook for me. Smith would be going away for awhile, and the guy he shot would recover fine. But it looked like I had sparked a feud. That was just another reason to hightail it away from the Mississppi's Beautiful Gulf Coast.

The limo hit a short patch of grooved highway. The road transition startled me awake. As long as I was awake, I decided to pester Valerie a little. During our time on the yacht, we had engaged in several political discussions. I found that in taking the converse argument, I could really irritate her when I wanted to. We'd had a very loud, four hour discussion on nuclear disarmament. It turns out, we were really pretty close on most topics, but we enjoyed arguing so much, we refused to agree.

Now I had goaded her into a debate on education reform. She believed the best way to improve schools was to get parents involved in the reform process. I told her students' grades would improve when teachers were paid their worth.

"You can't just throw money at every problem," she said. "You can't do that, and think it'll solve all of the issues of such a complex problem as this one."

I laughed. She had thrown a considerable amount of money at my problems, and they all seemed to be getting solved.

"That has got to be the stupidest idea I've ever heard," I said.

"Don't call me stupid!" she said. "You're stupid!"

"I didn't call you stupid," I told her. "I said your idea was stupid."

I was just being mean for the fun of it. But, she was in the heat of the argument.

Her face flushed. "You called me stupid. You're losing the argument, so now you decide to get personal."

I laughed. "Well, maybe I did," I said. "…Because, you *are* stupid."

I mumbled that last part under my breath.

Horace laughed. She rolled her eyes at him.

"And you think it's funny?" She was speaking to both of us.

"Mister Edwards," she said reasonably. "If you can't stand losing a debate, perhaps we should just quit speaking."

She crossed her arms, and turned away. "Stupid!" she said.

She was quiet for a moment, before mumbling to herself, "I'm stupid!" she said. "*I'm* the one with the gun, and he calls me stupid. Who's *really* stupid, I wonder?"

Horace and I had been laughing. We stopped. I went back to sleep, but I thought, maybe, I had heard her laugh.......Just a little.

It was late in the day when we arrived in Hinesville. Frank had made reservations for us at one of the local inns. After several weeks in that tiny corner guestroom, my suite was first class. Valerie didn't feel the same. She was used to finer accommodations. Horace seemed completely indifferent to his own comfort. He was concerned Val and I were safe and secure.

We had picked up burgers and fries before checking in, so we all met up at Val's room to eat and talk. It wasn't long before we had started up a penny ante poker game. Horace was a pretty fair card player, nearly wiping us out before we got the good sense to quit and turn in. He had been a professional gambler, before Frank rescued him from prison. He was a good man who had found himself in the wrong place at the wrong time. I never knew the entire story, but he was completely loyal to Frank. And grateful for the chance the judge gave him.

Val was still cool, and pushed me out of the door. Though I had a couple of numbers that might have proved fruitful, I resigned myself to sleep alone. I was sure anyone who may have cared, already knew I was in town. Still, I preferred to keep a low profile, at least for the time being.

Before I left her room, Val gave me a short briefing on the next day's itinerary. At last, she brought me up to speed on how Desiree had winded up in Biloxi. Although, I had just about figured it out, I listened as she

281

explained. It was logical, really. Bud had told his wife about our altercation. Desiree contacted Hicks. And Hicks called Julie. The rest was just a great big snowball, with me ruining myself in every saloon and gin joint I could find from Pensacola to Saint Luke.

Lying in bed, I was apprehensive that things wouldn't go as easily as Frank had laid it out. I felt like a lamb being led to slaughter. This entire deal was extremely unconventional. I found myself hoping Dee would show up to hold my hand through all this. But, Frank assured me everything had been arranged, and Valerie was more than capable of handling any surprises that may arise.

"Valerie may be an excellent attorney," I thought. "But, should we run into Desiree, I would feel much more at ease with Dee at my side."

I tried to relax, and sleep. But it was a long restless night, preparing for my chickens to come home to roost.

We rose early the next morning to grab a good breakfast at the diner. As we pulled into the parking lot people stopped and stared at the limo. The long black luxury vehicle stood out like a fresh pimple on the prom queen's nose. If the car seemed out of place, this enormous dangerous-looking, dark man and young Hollywood beautiful fashion model were otherworldly. They seemed to absorb all the light around them. I had been around them for several days, and even my attention was inexplicably drawn to them.

After we ate we drove up the post's front gate. Valerie explained to the gate guard that we were looking for the office of the Judge Advocate

General. He spoke into a hand-held, brick-sized radio. And after receiving an unintelligible squawking reply, he directed Horace to drive the limo into a parking lot just inside the gate.

We waited thirty minutes. The military police cruiser pulled up next to us. A pair of MP's got out and told us to exit our vehicle. Then Valerie took control. She gave them her credentials and a name. One of the guys went back to the cruiser with her identification. Three minutes later we were escorted to the JAG office. I had been impressed at the polite demeanor of the policemen. But after the guy returned with Val's I.D., they were actually deferential. I began to think that maybe Frank really did know what he was doing.

We were met by a youngish colonel who invited Val into his office. She smiled, and told me to sit tight in the waiting area with Horace. Horace's posture was subtly different. Since we had met, he was my protector. Now, he, almost imperceptibly, held the countenance of a jailer. Twenty minutes later, Val returned with the colonel, and nodded to Horace.

"Trust me," she said to me.

Horace stood, and taking me by the arm, helped me to rise. "Mister Ace, I need you to put your hands behind your back." He said it so gently I thought he might weep. I did as he had asked, and heard more than felt the handcuffs click into place.

The two military policemen who had escorted us entered the room.

"I'm sorry, Mister Edwards," said Valerie. "Good bye."

Horace followed her out the door, as the two cops flanked me; then locked me in a small barren room without windows. They didn't speak, except to give me directions. I wasn't read Miranda rights. I wasn't allowed a phone call. They didn't respond to any of my questions. For all I knew, they might have determined to drop me in a hole and cover it up.

I never knew how long I was left alone in that room, waiting. By the time someone came to see about me I was ready to wet myself. Thankfully, I was given a restroom break and water.

Several hours, later, a couple of guys in civilian clothing came into the room. They asked me questions about espionage, subversion and any organized criminal activity I had been involved in. I guessed this was one of the privileges of attaining, what Frank might call, *upper echelon status*. I didn't know anything, and told them so. As if by silent signal, without conferring with one another, they simply left. I never saw them again (The truth is, they were so generic in appearance, I'd never know if I ever saw them again). From then on, I would run into many others like them.

It was way past dark outside when I was transferred to the correctional custody facility. It was thirty days of intense military discipline and physical activity. When I was released, I would be lean, svelte and sober- and very angry.

Thirty days after Valerie led me, unprepared into captivity, I was released; I had assumed; on my own recognizance. It was sometime after ten thirty that evening two cops let me out of the car at the front gate. Valerie was standing, waiting next to one of the sweetest little red sports cars I'd ever seen.

"Alright, Mister Edwards," said one of the cops. "We'll see you around."

"Thanks, fellas," I said. "I appreciate the ride. Have a good night."

"No sweat. Try to stay out of trouble, man!" said the other.

"You bet," I said.

They waved and drove off.

I turned to Val. She smiled, nervously.

"Hello, Ace," she said. "It's good to have you back."

"Thanks," I said. "Nice car. How's it drive?"

"Pretty sweet," she said. "Especially in the curves."

She held the driver's door open. "Wanna drive?"

"No, thanks," I said. I got into the passenger seat.

She got in.

"It's Ace now, huh?" I asked.

She shrugged. "I thought you could use a friend."

"You off the clock?" I asked.

She chuckled. "Yeah. As a matter of fact, your nickel ran out the moment you left lockup," she said. "Oh, and, by the way, if you ever call me stupid again, you'll pray to be back in C.C."

"Right," I said. "Thanks for getting my car. Where's Horace?"

"He left the day we turned you in," she said. "He told me to give you his best. He's not very good with goodbyes. The big guy gets kinda sentimental."

I didn't say it, but he wasn't the only one. I was fighting back an emotional lump in my throat right then. They took great care of me, even if they did turn me over to the *Federali*. I really did appreciate that she had thought to get my car out of impound, and to have it serviced and detailed.

I was sorry I didn't get to say goodbye to Horace, though. That day at the JAG's would be the last time I'd see him. Some months later, Valerie would call to tell me he'd been killed defending Judge Johnson from an assassination attempt. Horace had done his job well. Frank wasn't harmed in the attack. The big fella had given his all defending the judge and Val, killing all three gunmen before falling himself. When he went to his knees, the judge and Valerie braved the gunfire to rush to him. They held him so he wouldn't die alone sprawled out in the street. Horace died a bloody mess, with friends; in Val's arms, smiling up at that beautiful face. Frank had always said it: "Horace wasn't anything, but good".

"The judge asked me to stay to make sure the Army didn't mistreat you-or worse, misplace you," she said.

I shrugged. "How is he?" I asked.

"Good," she said. "He told me to tell you not to worry. Everything is going according to plan. Dee's good, too."

"That's good. It would've been nice, if you'd let me in on the plan," I said.

"We had to keep that last part from you," she said. "You needed to, at least, *look* like you were suffering. Think about it. You got away with adultery with a fellow member's wife, assaulting an officer and desertion, all scot free. You got a promotion, retirement, and a job. I'd say thirty days in lockup is light, considering."

It hurt to hear it. She had nailed it, except for abandonment of my family. I basically got a new life. I should have been grateful.

"Still," I said. "You should have let me in on it.........If you expect me to trust you."

She looked at me and shook her head. "Maybe, I *am* stupid," she said.

I started to respond, but she cut me off. "Agreeing with me wouldn't be a good idea, right now," she said.

She pulled the car into the inn's parking lot. "Your apartment won't be ready for several days," she said. "And you don't report for work, until Dee gets here. After you sign these final papers I have for you, you're on vacation again. I've got reservations for tomorrow at Hilton Head.......If you're interested."

"You sure you want me around?" I asked.

She laughed. "I guess I could stand it," she said.

"Okay, I'm in! Let's get a drink."

She paused. "No," she said. "Let's eat first."

I was kissing Valerie at the altar when the knock came at my apartment

door. The preacher had just completed the ceremony. We had said our

vows, and were finally legally enjoying one another. The insistent

knocking continued and she vanished from my arms.

My mind struggled vainly, to gain mastery over all the alcohol I'd drunk

during the past twelve, or so hours. Fully dressed, brushing dried mud from

my clothing, and my head throbbing, I forced my body from the bed. All

the lights in the apartment had been left on. I wasn't sure if it was day or

night.

Before I could reach the door, Totsie, the cutie-pie waitress from the Non-

Com club was letting herself into the apartment. I wondered how many of

those keys I had given out. With Desiree's death, and my fights with Bob

and Lindsey that night, it might be a good idea to change the locks.

"Why'd you bother knocking, if you were going to use your key," I asked.

She kissed me, making no mention of the dirt on me and the floor. "I

wasn't going to use it," she said. "You took so long coming to the door, I

had to search for it."

"Oh," I said, stumbling back to the bathroom to clean up some.

Totsie was turning off lights while I undressed and cleaned up some.

When she was done, she undressed in the dark, and slipped beneath the

covers next to me. We had an uncomplicated relationship, typified by our

288

pet names for each other. Because she would never see me until after the club closed, she was my "Last Call" girl. She called me her "One and Only". She said I was only good for one thing, and even that, only once.

It wasn't much of a relationship. But it was enough to upset Valerie when she drove from Biloxi to surprise me one weekend. She had driven most of the night, arriving early in the morning. It was a terrible shock for her. But, she was a sport. Val left the key on the coffee table, took a room at an inn and waited for me to find her. We had been together for nearly two years, working our way to marriage. That had all ended with my infidelity.

She didn't yell or shout, but she did cry. I didn't experience that perverse feeling of power some of us get when we witness someone weep for us out of grief for their loss. I felt sorry for myself, because I believed that someday, hell would surely open up and swallow me alive for the pain I had caused her, and so many others.

Dee was angry, but not surprised. Frank thanked me. He said her broken heart was the experience Miss Jacobs needed to knock off the corners, and smooth her rough edges. Her pain added the polish, the glisten to the stone. She had, at last, attained the wisdom she had sought not so very long ago. All it had cost her was innocence and trust.

For all of her beauty, she had become a, deceptively dangerous adversary. We had remained friends, but I would always have the feeling she was always someplace near, soaring above me…watching and waiting. She hugged me tightly, and sighed as she released me.

289

"You should have taken the job," she said, before leaving. "We would have done great things together."

I didn't doubt that we would have. She left.

The cigarette Totsie was smoking ignited the darkness; then dimmed. "I heard you got beat up last night," she said.

It was after four in the morning.

"Oh, yeah?" I asked. "Well, I heard you're still married." I knew full well she wasn't. She had been married. She had married pretty well, in fact. She caught herself a retired senior NCO with no children or ex-wife. He was soaking wet with life insurance and real estate. He was a great provider, with the good grace to die soon after the wedding, leaving Totsie, considerably better off than she had been.

"Well, I ain't," she said.

"You're *not* what?" I asked.

She volleyed the jest. "I ain't, Sir."

"No," I said. "You're not married."

"I ain't married, Sir." Now she was teasing me for the difference in our ages. "And would it make any difference if I was?" she asked.

I chuckled. "Not any, I suppose," I admitted. "I ain't married either."

She took another drag off her cigarette. "So did Bob beat you up or not?" she asked.

"Bob?" I asked.

290

"Yeah," she said. "They're saying Desiree's boyfriend beat you up, and you were in the hospital."

I frowned at the mention of Desiree and Bob as a couple. My gut hurt where the sheriff punched me.

"Do I look beat up to you?" I asked.

"Who can tell?" she asked. "You're such a mess since she died."

"So I've been told," I agreed, remembering my earlier mud bath at Bubba Ray's. "What do you know about Bob and Desiree?"

She ground out her cigarette in the ashtray on the nightstand.

"They used to do business with Calvin," she said.

Calvin was her deceased husband.

"What kind of business?" I was actually finally becoming interested in something she had to say.

"Real estate, of course." She said it, as if real estate was the only business in the world.

I defended my ignorance. "She owned a dress shop, Totsie."

"Well, Calvin was a real man," she said. "He didn't sell dresses."

"Of course," I said. "Forgive me. So they did business together."

"Yes." She rolled over and kissed me. "They used to buy people's houses who couldn't pay their mortgages."

I listened to Totsie as she educated me about real estate and mortgage finance, Hinesville style. Desiree, Calvin and Bob were members of a loose, informal cartel. Desiree was in position to know which customer was a little financially stressed. If they owned homes, they probably had mortgages.

They had enlisted the help of some low-level bank employees, so they could research the mark's spending habits and monetary weaknesses.

They would work an *insider-man* close to the mark. If he or she had issues with spending or shopping, they're contact encouraged them to spend. If they were married, with a fondness for infidelity, they provided someone to feed their need. Drugs? They gave them drugs. They had learned to exploit people's problems to their advantage. They did anything necessary to distract the mark, and ensure their life spiraled out of control. They pushed, or influenced the mark to financial, marital, or even mental ruined, occasionally death. And it all appeared legal, because it was influence and suggestion; enabling. It could be reasoned that an adult should know not to make the bad decisions these people made.

Once the problems began to take over the mark's life, they really began to work on them. The collection phone calls would begin. Threats from attorneys. A lover would threaten to expose an affair. Careers would be placed in jeopardy. Most people would crumble, divorcing; giving up cars they couldn't pay for; walking away from homes, or letting them go for a fraction of their worth.

They would set up manageable numbers of marks, from ten to twenty at a time. Each mark was different. Some took only a few weeks to crumble, others took years. One thing was certain, though; everyone has a weakness.

Once that weakness was discovered, it was rare for a mark to survive. And they never knew that different people from various walks of life had colluded to run them out of business, bilk them out of vehicles, homes, thousands of dollars, and even relationships and marriages to well-off spouses.

As I listened to Totsie, a wave of anger washed through me. It occurred to me, there was hardly anyone you could trust. To make a scheme like that work, you would need a very intricate web of influential people, with myriad skills. Every profession was suspect, attorneys, bankers, real estate professionals, mental health counselors, anyone in a position of trust.

When capitalism worked at its best, we picked the bones of our consumers' wallets. That was the contract. It was acceptable. But this was something different. This was more personal. This was not taking advantage of opportune circumstances. This was creating the circumstances. This was *rainmaking*, flooding the lake and blowing up the dam protecting the village.

They were selecting people to fleece. Once a weakness was identified, they cut and hobbled their victim. They watched him struggle, then bleed out. Finally, gathering to feed on the carcass. And they'd move on to the next victim, all the while presenting an officious image of servitude and respectability.

I drifted off to sleep, wondering if Desiree had been assigned to bring about my own ruin. And if, she had, why did she rescue me when I was most vulnerable?

I was awakened by the annoying ringing of the phone on the table on the opposite side of the bed. Totsie was still there. She would normally have left by this time. She angrily shouted for me to answer the phone. I took the phone call while she dressed. Before leaving, she would inform me she was done with me, that I wasn't good for anything, at all. It wasn't a revelation. I could have provided her references to that point, if she had asked.

It was Hicks on the phone. Watching Totsie dress and walk out my door, I suppressed a petrifying sense of dread. The last time he'd called, it was to summon me to the site of Desiree's demise. This call couldn't bode any better. It was a summons to the jailhouse. He wanted to question me about the incident at Bubba Ray's.

I asked if a complaint was filed by Bob or Bubba Ray's. "Just c'mon down here, f'me, Ace," he said in a thick southern drawl. "I'll let ya know what's goin' on when you git he'a."

Not having had a lot of sleep the night before, I took my time getting ready. It was a full hour and a half before I walked through the door of the sheriff's office. Lindsey was there, with a twisted sneer which was closer to a scowl. He pulled his sidearm, aimed at me and cocked the trigger. I froze in my tracks.

"Ain't no need for that, J.C.," Hicks said. "He ain't going anywhere. Are you, Ace?"

"Hicks, as long as he's holding that gun," I said. "I ain't even going to scratch."

Hicks laughed. "Sit down, Ace," he said.

I sat, all the while, watching J.C. with that ugly sneer, and just as ugly police revolver. "What's this about, Lindsey?" I asked him.

"Charge him," he said to Hicks.

Hicks sighed and waked over to me with a pair of handcuffs. "You know the drill, Ace."

I extended my hands. "All this over a bar fight?" I asked. "What's the fine? Just let me know so I can pay it. I'll apologize to Bob, and we can all get on with our lives."

Hicks clicked the cuffs into place. "Ace, Bob Miller died at three thirty this morning in the E.R.," he said. "He was being treated for wounds, we assume, were sustained in a fight on the premises of the club, Bubba Ray's."

Five hours later, Dee and I were seated in Bill Cook's office, trying to explain how his reporters ended up in a bar fight in a strip joint, in the middle of a murder investigation. I had been booked for murder, fingerprinted, searched, mouth swabbed for DNA, interviewed and locked up until the paper's attorney had me released. Sheriff Lindsey gritted his teeth so hard with my release you could hear them grinding together. I wanted to tease the guy, but I still wasn't in the clear here.

I was led into the interview office where the lawyer waited.

"Sit down, Ace," said Hicks.

He gave me a cold, dry ham and cheese sandwich and a soda pop. I peeled open the sandwich. No mustard. No mayo. The orange pop tasted that much better.

"Ace, why didn't you tell me you were with Desiree the night she died?" Hicks asked.

I hoped I hadn't flinched when he asked the question. There was a faint sensation inside my head I couldn't quite describe as a headache. I recalled the dream I'd had of her coming to me that night. I didn't think he would have believed the truth before, and was certain he wouldn't believe the truth now. I didn't know if I had been with her. I just didn't remember. He was watching me, waiting for an answer.

"What are you talking about, Hicks?" I asked him.

He pointed to a report on the table. "The results from your DNA test. Yours matches DNA found on her body."

I didn't respond.

He was patient. "You got nothing to say about it?"

I feigned bravado I didn't feel. "No," I said. "Are you charging me with her death?"

The attorney stepped in; telling Hicks his question wasn't pertinent to the situation at hand. I had been charged with the wrongful death of Bob Miller. I had popped him up side the head with a beer bottle. He subsequently died; supposedly from the wound to his head. The truth was that he died from complications related to a reaction to anesthesia administered during emergency treatment.

Hicks ignored the lawyer. "No, Ace," he said, easing my mind on that issue. "Just before he died, Bob Miller confessed to killing Desiree."

"What?" I was shocked.

"Yep," he said. "You solved the case, buddy! You're a hero! We just needed to be sure you hadn't killed the guy out revenge. We're going to let you go."

He knew the cause of Bob's death before hauling me in to jail. What was his game? What was I missing here? I should feel some sense of relief with this news, but I didn't. It was unfulfilling; a thirst, unquenched; a hunger, unsatisfied. Something was just……Off.

"Well, you got your vengeance," Dee said. "Are you happy, now?"

I was examining the package on my desk. "Not particularly," I said. "I wonder what this is?"

Dee grunted something I didn't understand. She was at her desk packing her things. Cook had just fired us for assaulting Bob.

"I pay you to report news!" he had shouted. "Ace, when I gave you that assignment, I sent you to get the facts, and inform the public. I didn't send you out to settle a personal vendetta."

He pointed his finger at me, stabbing the air with each word. "You don't make the news at my paper! You report it!"

I wanted to respond, but I knew he was right. In fact, I'd had enough. I began to feel I had been hiding out at this paper. It wasn't satisfying to something inside of me. I didn't know what I wanted......Or needed, but I wouldn't find it here.

"You're right, Bill," I said.

He stopped short. "What?"

"I said, 'You're right'. I'll tender my resignation immediately," I said.

Dee was staring at me, in disbelief. I was, not only, gambling my job, but hers, as well.

"Oh, no, you don't!" he shouted. "You don't get the satisfaction of quitting here!"

I was very close to losing a job. Suddenly, I began to think about the mounting stack of bills on my kitchen table back at that dumpy little apartment. I couldn't afford to quit my job. And I couldn't afford to get fired this way. I had to change the dynamics of this argument.

I laughed. "Bill, Dee and I just solved the murder of a one of this town's most prominent citizens. Although, the investigators initially ruled her death a suicide, we proved it, a murder. And *I* got the killer to confess. Maybe I should ask for your job."

Bill's mouth fell open. Diana was looking at me as if I had gone mad.

"You're both being let go," he said, with considerably less wind in his sails than before. "Pack your things."

I offered him my hand. "Thanks, Bill," I said. "We could use vacations. See you in a couple of days."

He didn't take my hand. "Dee, he is delusional," he was appealing to Diana. "Please get him out of my office."

Dee had stood, and appeared to have a problem maintaining her composure. "Come on, Ace. Let's go."

I rose. "It's been nice talking to you, Bill," I said, smiling. "See you in a few days."

"Get out, Ace!" he shouted.

We left the office, and nearly turned around when we heard the loud sound of something crashing against the wall in there.

"You just got fired," Dee said. "Don't you think you should be packing your things?"

"No," I said. "Bill knows what he has to do. You can afford not to work. You have royalties from book sales. I have people depending on me. I can't leave this job without unemployment insurance." Besides, I thought to myself, the information Totsie shared must be worth something-on a literary level, anyhow. I hadn't told Dee about that stuff, yet. It could endanger her life.

Desiree, dead; Totsie's husband, and now Bob; it couldn't all be coincidental. They were all connected. With his contacts, I would have bet money Bill was involved in some way. We would need the time off to do the research for a story, or a book, possibly.

I was opening the package that had been delivered while I was in jail.

"Have you thought about what you're going to do with your time off?" I asked her.

She didn't respond.

"I'll bet Frank would be glad to have you visit for a while."

Dee sighed in exasperation. She stopped packing, and looked at me.

"What's in the box, Ace?"

I had just removed the wrapping, and was opening the box. "Hmm," I said, peering into it.

"What?" she asked.

"Women's shoes," I said, holding up a pair of white strapped high heels.

"Oh m'goodness!" she exclaimed. "Ooh! Lemme see!"

Dee had dropped what she was doing, and snatched the shoes from my hands. She examined them.

"Ace, these are Salvatore Ferragamos!" she said.

"So?"

"So," she said. "These are thousand dollar shoes! And they are beautiful!"

I was amazed anyone would pay that much money for so little leather. "Thousand dollars, huh?"

She didn't hear me. "They're the wrong size, of course. And they're knockoffs-or stolen, the numbers don't match. So, they're probably only worth six hundred."

"Dee, they're not your shoes," I corrected. "And how do you know they're knockoffs?"

"What do you mean, they're not mine?" she asked. "Whose are they? What are you doing with them?"

I shrugged. "Good questions," I said; then repeated the question. "*How* do you know they're knockoffs?"

She frowned. "Huh? Oh!" She pointed to numbers stamped inside each shoe. "The serial number. Every pair has one. Only, this pair has two numbers. There's one in each shoe."

She gave me a shoe. I examined the number: 83.5300. There was something familiar about it. I took the second shoe, and held the shoes so that I could see both numbers at once. 83.5300/33.9500. 33.9500/83.5300.

Then I noticed it. "Huh!" I grunted.

"What?" Dee asked. "What did you see?"

I wrote down the numbers, took up the paper and shoved it in my coat pocket. Packing up the shoes, I headed for the door.

"Feel like reading?" I asked on the way out.

Leaving her *breakup box* behind, she hurried after me. "Why? Where're we going?"

"The library," I said.

"Why? What did you see?"

"Lat, Longs," I said. "The numbers are latitudinal and longitudinal coordinates. It's a treasure map." I laughed. "We're going treasure hunting, Dee!"

At the library, we searched through the reference section until we found what we were looking for, the World Atlas. Taking several books from the shelves, we selected seats at a secluded table. I explained to Dee that we were looking for coordinates that matched the shoes' "serial numbers". The coordinates would most likely appear as they did in the shoes, left shoe/right shoe. But, we couldn't rule out other variations, the code could be more intricate.

It wasn't very difficult to find the geographic location. We chose the most probable grid coordinates, but needed an address. The information was in these tomes someplace. We were each experienced in methods of research, so I was confident we wouldn't have trouble locating what we needed. However, it took us a couple of hours to narrow down likely locations. If we had been more experienced at this type of research, we may have found it sooner. We searched volume after volume for addresses which might match the grid coordinates. The library was nearly ready to close when we found what we were looking for. If we were right we would be looking for a bank in a town several hours away.

"Great!" I said. "Bogart, Georgia, that's where we're going."

"Ace, it's late," Dee complained. "The bank is closed. It's not going anyplace. We can get a start in the morning."

I shook my head. "Dee, we've been here too long already," I said. "We've got to get out of town now."

She frowned. "Why?" she asked. "What haven't you told me?"

I sighed. "I'll tell you everything on the way. Let's go."

Before leaving the library, I made three phone calls. The first was to Lisa, Desiree's assistant. The next was to Bud. The last, Totsie. I wasn't able to reach either of them.

I told Dee what I knew and suspected. She was driving, and nearly drove into a ditch, responding to the news. "How do you know all this?" she asked.

"A reliable source," I said, grateful she didn't press for the name of the source. "They were all connected to Desiree and her shady real estate deals, in some way. Now she and two of her partners are dead. Bud, Lisa and Totsie are in danger.....And; if I'm right; because of those shoes, so are we."

"What do you expect to find at that bank?" she asked.

I hadn't told Dee about the dream of Desiree without shoes. I couldn't tell her we were following a tip from a ghost who had sent us a clue in a pair of cute little expensive pumps. I could hardly think it, let alone, form the words to say such a thing. I couldn't tell her I expected to find several thousand swindled dollars, in loot Desiree had embezzled from Old Royce, who'd likely paid her lover to kill her. I couldn't tell her our shady friend, Deputy Royce Hicks had either killed Bob, or had him killed in the hospital. I couldn't tell her Desiree had targeted me as a mark from the beginning, and now I was being played for a patsy. I couldn't tell Dee her long time boyfriend, Judge Albert F. Johnson and his beautiful assistant had likely set us up, and couldn't be trusted. I didn't want to believe any of it.

I shrugged. "Leverage," I said. "Names, money, a confession maybe."

She nodded.

What I didn't say is "We are looking for anything we can use to keep us from winding up on a growing list of corpses".

Latitude: 33.95.00 degrees, North/Longitude: 83.53.00 degrees, West were the grid coordinates for the First Georgia Bank on Monroe Boulevard in Bogart, Georgia. Four hours and fifty odd minutes, northeast of Hinesville. After a restless night in a cheap motel, I walked up to the teller with no idea what I was asking for.

"May I help you?" asked the attractive young woman.

"Yes," I said. "My name is Adrian Edwards. I'd like to make a withdrawal."

"Certainly, sir," she said, smiling like a debutante. "Can I have your account number?"

I passed her a slip of paper with the grid numbers on it. She typed in the number. After typing it the second time, she frowned. She tried it again.

"I'm sorry, sir," she apologized. "We don't have that account number. Could it be a different number?"

"Oh. Of course," I said. "That's my other account." I gave her the other number. "Here. Try this one."

She typed in the numbers. The computer didn't accept that one either.

"I'm sorry, sir. We don't have that number, either."

A line of fidgeting customers had begun to form behind me. Dee was seated, impatiently waiting for me across the lobby. Nervously, I glanced over to her. She sensed my discomfort, and grinned before burying her face in the magazine she was holding.

"Sir, perhaps there's a mistake," the kindly young woman said. "Would you like to speak to our manager?"

"Umm, No," I mumbled. "Maybe I've got the wrong bank."

Standing outside the bank, I was befuddled and humiliated. Dee was angry, but didn't speak, and I was grateful for it. It wasn't surprising to me when a pair of police cruisers pulled into the parking lot. It wasn't surprising when four of the largest, meanest looking cops I had ever seen got out of the cars. It wasn't surprising when they asked for our identification. It wasn't surprising when they searched, and handcuffed us. It wasn't surprising when they shoved us into the backseats of separate cruisers. It wasn't surprising that we were taken to the police station. It

305

wasn't surprising that we were placed in cells, and held for several hours, in isolation. It wasn't even surprising that, without a single word, they took us from the cells, and drove us out of town to the deserted boondocks.

But, it was surprising that they let us out of the cars, took off the cuffs, and drove away, leaving us standing on a deserted air strip. It was surprising when the sleek Learjet aircraft came into view, landed and taxied right up to us. And it was, most definitely, surprising when the door opened, and the beautiful, smiling Valerie Jacobs stepped through the door.

"Did you call for a ride, Mister?"

I turned slightly to Dee in the crowded elevator. "Why didn't you tell me she was getting married?" I whispered to her.

"Now's not the time, Ace," she whispered back to me. "Besides, you don't care."

"You should have told me," I said.

"Shh….She asked me not to."

I frowned. "Did you see the size of that diamond?" I asked.

"Yes," she said, smiling. "It's beautiful. Good girl."

I heard a woman's snigger in the back of the car.

Valerie had flown in a client's private jet to bring us to Biloxi from Bogart, Georgia. She and Dee chatted and sipped champagne while I lay back and relaxed, listening to music and enjoying the luxury accommodations. Except for the enormous engagement ring, reminding me we weren't a couple anymore, it felt like old times. Valerie had matured quite a bit in a few years. To see her now, compared to when we had first met, was like the difference between a string quartet and a symphony orchestra. She was good before. But now, she was complete, full-bodied and, like the stone on her finger, multifaceted.

The tone announcer sounded. The light indicating our floor number illuminated. A moment later, the elevator came to a stop, and we left the car for our rooms.

"Relax," said Dee, as we searched the hallway. "She's not married, yet." I found my room. "Did you see the size of the ring?" I asked.

She laughed. "Yeah, wow!" she exclaimed. "Isn't it beautiful?"

"Yeah, it is," I said.

She had stopped outside her door, grinning. "Did you see that big smile on her face?" she asked. "She sure looked happy, don't you think?"

Dee opened the door with her key, and stepped into her room. I stood, outside my door, perplexed. My key wouldn't open my door. After getting a replacement, I let myself in the room for a much needed nap. I hadn't told Dee of my suspicions concerning Frank and Val. The fact that Val had met us following our release on that airfield was evidence of her involvement in a setup. I stretched out on the bed, closed my eyes and tried to relax. At least we were safe.....for now.

It was too soon that the phone rang, waking me from my rest. Frank asked me to meet him in his suite. He kept a room in the hotel now. I freshened up; then walked down the hallway to the room. Once inside, we all greeted, and took seats. Frank had ordered a sumptuous buffet from room service, which arrived just as I'd settled down comfortably with my scotch. Suddenly, I was hungry, but wasn't quite ready to separate from my liquid nourishment. So I ate a mixed meal.

The atmosphere was tense, like four people seated at a poker table. Everyone was holding their cards very close. I wanted answers, but didn't know where to begin. Sipping from my glass, I hoped Dee hadn't shared with Frank all we knew. Suspecting his information might prove more valuable than mine, I decided to wait him out.

At length, Frank sighed. "Well, we may as well get started," he said.

He produced an attaché case, and drew a clutch of folders from it. Dee and I gave each other sidelong glances.

"Ace, I assume since you found your way to that little bank," he began. "That Mrs. McKensie has expired."

I tensed. "Yes. Several days ago," I said. "It was discovered, yesterday, that she was murdered."

"That's unfortunate," he appropriately, sighed. "She knew you pretty well. She said that in the event of her death, you'd find your way to Bogart, somehow. The up side is her demise makes you a very wealthy man."

I was stunned. "What?"

"Yes," said. "You're heir to an amount, somewhere in the neighborhood of one hundred million dollars or so, locked up in several off shore bank accounts........Plus interest, less my fees, of course."

I had expected to find several thousand dollars in the Georgia bank. But, I couldn't even conceive of a figure the size of the one Frank mentioned. I began to laugh. "Of course," I said. "Get out of here, Frank. What's going on? Why did you bring us here?"

Dee was laughing also. "Yeah, Frankie," she said. "Stop playing. People have died over this woman and her games. Don't, you get started."

I stopped laughing and shot her a warning stare. She was right; people had died. And we could be next. Whether Frank was telling the truth or not we were in treacherous waters. We would need to be careful until we knew what was going.

He lifted a form and gave it to me. Glancing over the it, I recognized the familiar signature. I had signed the papers. On the line entitled, Beneficiary was the amount not less than One Hundred Million dollars ($100,000,000). My eyes began to water, and my hand to shake.

It was a considerable amount of money. It was good money if I could hold on to it. I could give it back to the people who had been cheated out of it, if I could find them. There would be tax concerns. And someone would be looking for it......And me.

"I can't keep that money, Frank," I said.

"Sure you can," he said. "It's your money. She left it to you-with stipulations we'll get into later."

He didn't understand. "It wasn't her money, Frank," I said. "She stole it from people who've already killed for it. They'll kill all of us."

Dee was in the beginning stages of *gold fever.* "Why can't we keep the money?" she asked. "Ace, think of the good we could do with it."

"Dee, even if we could get away with it," I said. "It doesn't belong to us. She swindled that money from some good people."

Frank shook his head. "Ace, you're a global player, now," he said. "But, you're thinking like a small-timer. Take the money. You've lost so much in that town. Julie; your family lost so much. I don't know her, but she's my home girl. Do it for her. I can help you hide that money forever.….You, too, for that matter."

"No, Frank," I said.

He shook his head. "What is it? Help me understand," he said. "What do you care about that ten-block patch of dirt in Georgia? .….Or its den of thieves?"

I sighed. "Frank, I left my name in that town. I've owned property with my name on it. That means something to me. I don't want my name erased," I said. "If I take that money I'll have to run. Even if they never catch me, they'd surely go after Julie, and use her against me."

Dee shook her head. She was disgusted. "With that much money, we could protect Julie and the girls." She appealed to Valerie. "Val, talk to him. Make him understand."

I looked at Val. She smiled at me. "No, Dee," she said. "He's right. It's too dangerous for his family."

Frank rubbed his chin. He shook his head. "I don't get it, Miss Jacobs," he said. "There was a time, I was concerned you'd tell him about the accounts, steal the money and run away with him. I wouldn't have thought you'd take a conservative position when faced with the opportunity to have Ace and wealth."

She shrugged. "I admit, I was tempted," she confessed. "But, now that I'm faced with a choice, I don't want the responsibility. It's not our money. It belongs to Ace. It's *his* decision to make."

They all stared at me, waiting for my final decision.

"Listen," I said. "Here's what we're up against. Frank, you get your....What? .....three percent?"

"Six," he corrected.

"Six?" I asked.

"Six."

"Six! My gosh!"

"Yep."

"Okay," I continued. "Now, here's what I'm thinking: There are several types of dirty money. Relatively speaking, we're not talking about a great deal of money. It's just enough to overcome our sense of reason. This is runaway money. You keep running until it's gone; then you get caught. There's runaway and hide money, and you can hide until you're found. But, then there's hide in plain sight money. That's untouchable money, the kind that changes international borders."

I looked at the forms. "This is bad money," I said. "It's not safe, and we'll never be safe until we give it to the people who are most comfortable with it." I smiled. "......Minus a small finder's fee, of course."

Frank grinned. "That's my boy!"

Once I had explained my reasons for turning over the money, Dee agreed wholeheartedly. It wasn't a big deal. Knowing Dee as I did, I knew she would have eventually, reached the same conclusion. I'm glad she had challenged me. Defending my position, against her objections helped to strengthen my own resolve. I had to admit, it did feel pretty good to be filthy rich, if only for a few minutes. As for Val, it was sickeningly gratifying to know she had been tempted to steal in order to runaway with me. I doubted she still felt that way.

Frank shuffled other papers. "These....," he said. "...Are a bit more personal; confidential." He glanced at the women. "Would you prefer we went over them in private?"

I shook my head. "No. We've all got skin in the game, now," I said. "They have as much right as I do to know why we're here."

"Okay," he sighed. "I had some people look into Mrs. McKensie's past."

I nodded. "Alright," I said. "Go on."

"Alright. Mrs. McKensie was born in a little hamlet in the swamps called Saint Luke, in southern Louisiana." I nodded. I had been there a number of times.

He went on. "She was the daughter of Claudia Simone. Father, unknown.......at least, officially. Unofficially? They say Claudia took up with a wildcatter, a fortune hunter named Royce Dillon."

I heard Dee audibly draw a breath. I frowned, intently. I would have liked to say I was surprised, but once you knew it, it was obvious. Val's eyes began to water. Frank continued.

"Claudia went away to New Orleans to find work when Desiree was an infant. The woman simply disappeared. Not a trace was ever found of her," he explained. "The child was raised by her grandmother and aunt. It was a poor town." He shrugged. "They...survived."

I nodded.

"Is her mother still living, Frank?" I asked.

"I don't know, Ace."

"How did Desiree wind up in Hinesville?" I asked.

"Well, Ace, things get a little sketchy here," he said. "Somehow, she learned who her father was, and his location. She made her way to Hinesville, a beautiful, skillful, and angry seductress with an agenda. Desiree found and seduced her half-brother; an act of vengeance directed towards the old man."

313

Dee and Val listened quietly. I watched them, their chests rising and falling with emotion. Their faces were distorted with anger.

"Her little girl in Saint Luke?" I asked.

"John's," he said. "Her brother's."

I placed my hand over my eyes. Dee sobbed. Val sat quietly, stone-faced.

"That's most of it, Ace," Frank said. "There's something else. Your friend, Hicks, had a DNA test done."

"Yeah, they tested me," I said. I hesitated. I didn't want Dee to know the test suggested I had been with Desiree the night she died.

"I'm sorry, Ace." he said. I held my breath. My heart stopped in my chest. "The little boy isn't yours. The examination results support an affidavit Mrs. McKensie signed when she established your trust fund. The father is Robert Miller."

Robert Miller. Bob.

"You're my friend, Frank," I accused him. "That information could have saved me some grief. Why didn't you tell me earlier?"

"I'm sorry, Ace," he apologized. "But, she was my client. It was privileged information. Plus, it was expensive information, and you just couldn't afford it."

Though I didn't like it, I understood it. I nodded.

The room became deathly silent. They were all waiting, watching to see what my reaction would be. I stared ahead, seeing nothing at all. I didn't know how to respond to the news. I didn't know what I was feeling. I didn't know what *to* feel.

In a few moments, the humiliation began to seep into my being. Suddenly, I was very ashamed. I had been used by Desiree. She had played me, and I was embarrassed for the way I had felt about her. For years, I had believed we would get back together. For years, I had believed her child was my child. Now, I was finding out Desiree had been cheating on her husband…..and me. I thought of Julie and the girls. I thought of Valerie and the way I had mistreated her. I didn't want her to see me this way, as a pitiful chump. Her witnessing it wasn't the same as her hearing, second-hand, that I had fallen hard. This experience could define our relationship for years to come.

Frank must have guessed what I was feeling. "She was bad, Ace," he said. "And she was very good at it. Let's face it, she just came from bad seed."

I nodded. "Yeah."

"There's more," he said.

I flinched. The events of the past couple of days were catching up to me. How much more could there be? I couldn't take anymore. Valerie came to my side. She placed a hand on my shoulder.

"It'll wait, Judge," she said.

He paused, looked up at her. It appeared he would admonish her for interrupting, but instead, nodded. "Right. Let's take a break," he said.

"It's just the legalities. The finer points. We can go over it later. Valerie, get him out of here."

"Yes," she said.

"Raise his spirits a little," Frank said. "But, don't be overly supportive. Remember, you're an engaged woman."

Valerie and I smiled. "Yes, Judge," she said. Taking me by the arm, she helped me stand. "Come on, sweetheart. Let's find us a couple of beers."

I smiled a pained smile. "Thanks, Val. I could use one," I said, agreeably. "Are we going to be bad?"

She smiled; then pinched me on the behind. "I doubt it," she said, laughing.

"Oh."

As Val and I were leaving, I thought of the first time she'd come to Hinesville. She and Horace turned me in to the Army for thirty days of lockup. I resented, intensely being ambushed that way. She came to meet me at the completion of my sentence. It was late in the evening, but we found a place to eat and a cozy bar where we could repair our relationship.

We made up, deciding we might have enough in common to, at least try a relationship. Even still, I had maintained a shade of resentment.

"Are you sure you won't come inside?" she had asked.

"Absolutely, sure," I replied.

She upped the ante. "I could make it worth your while."

I chuckled. "No doubt, you could. But you probably won't," I said. "I've had enough of your teasing for one night. What time are we going to Hilton Head tomorrow?"

"Eight or nine," she said. "You're kind of a mean drunk," she observed.

"Yeah," I said. "Some people just bring out the best in me."

She laughed. "Well, I'm not going to let you go alone," she replied. "I'm coming with you. I've got a key to your room, you know?"

"I didn't know that," I said. "Do what you want, but I'm not going to be responsible for the outcome."

That was the beginning of our relationship. Walking her to her room now, I missed being "us".

"This is my stop," she said.

"Okay," I said. "Mine is a few doors down."

Smiling up at me, she leaned against the door at her back. "It's been good seeing you."

I held the hand with the ring on it. "Will I meet him tomorrow?"

She shook her head. "No," she said. "He's out of town until next week."

"Oh," I said.

"Uh huh."

"Well," I said. "I'll see you in the morning."

She sighed. "Yeah," she said, tapping me lightly, twice with her fist on the chest over my heart. "Goodnight."

Valerie opened the door, and with a lingering smile, slipped into her room.

Friday morning: The day before Desiree's funeral.

Frank opened the door, and I pushed through him, into his room.

"Where's Diana?" I shouted, looking around the room to be certain we were alone.

"In her room, I guess," he said. "Why? What's the problem?"

"What's Operation Homesick?" I asked.

"What are you talking about, Ace?" he asked.

"A Special Ops agent, posing as a chambermaid, just left my room," I said. "She told me to ask you about Operation Homesick."

The woman had let herself into my room. I'd neglected to secure the door from key entrance. Beneath what appeared to be a blond wig, she was dark-haired, and decidedly pretty. She was just above average height, with taut musculature which managed to hold in check, a voluptuously, curvaceous womanly frame.

"Who are you?" I asked her.

"Promise," she said. "You can call me Promise."

"Promise," I said. "That's it; Promise? Promise, what?"

"Just, Promise."

"Okay, Promise, it is," I said. "If you're here to eliminate me, Promise, you should have brought backup?" I was only partially joking.

She didn't flinch. "I assure you, Mr. Edwards, I'm sufficient for the task; if that were why I'm here. We're very efficient, our agency doesn't waste resources."

There was an insult in there somewhere. I was thinking how much I didn't want to be expired by a *girl* assassin. I found myself ashamed and angry they didn't have as much respect for me as to send a team; or at least a man; to kill me. I learned later, Miss Promise was Captain Elyria Promise. She was among the elite of the elite in her field. And if she had been there to kill me, I would have joined a long list of very good and capable men to have been so distinguished.

She said she had been sent by a mutual friend. "How can I be sure of that?" I asked.

"Your friend told me to tell you they would have come to see you themselves," she said. "....Except they were 'feeling pretty sick'."

I frowned, remembering the phrase as a code I shared with my assistant. We would use it anytime we were out of place and wanted the other person the cover for us. It generally meant we had unexpectedly taken the day off for a romantic rendezvous; usually with someone not our spouses.

Feeling pretty sick was our way of bragging to one another about getting laid in the middle of the day. I lost contact with her, and hadn't heard the term since I'd left the Army. Now it seems she was reaching out to me through this special operations agent. I couldn't imagine what she was trying to tell me.

"You've got my attention, Promise," I told her. "How is our friend? Doing well, I hope."

The woman was all business. "She's fine, Mr. Edwards," she said. "Of course, considering the circumstances, she couldn't be here, herself."

"So, what is it?" I asked. "What does she want?"

"She says you should ask you friend, Judge Johnson about Operation Homesick," she said. "It could help explain those dreams you've been having lately."

That was it. She wouldn't say another word. She just turned, and left. I'd see Promise again, but it was never for more than a few minutes at a time. She was always so cryptic and inscrutable in our meetings that I was always left with a throbbing headache. I would eventually learn the headaches were induced by Promise, herself.

Frank didn't have a clue.

"Ace, you're about to pay me a tremendous amount of money," he said. "If I'm going to be your attorney, don't you think it's about time you decided to trust me?"

"Why should I?" I asked. "How much more are you holding back from me?"

We stood in the middle of the room staring down one another, each taking the measure of the other. Though we were friends, Frank had made it clear, he was Desiree's lawyer. It had been her hand, which opened and shut the door to the feed source. Any benefit I received from the arrangement was purely collateral. Now, it seemed, since her death, my hand controlled the golden spigot. If money was his only motivation, I needed to know now. There would always be someone willing to out bid me if they thought Frank was worth the price.

"Look, Frank," I said, finally. "You're going to get your money. After that, you can do whatever you want to. But, if money is the only reason you're in this, you may as well bail out now. I'm in the middle of something I can't begin to explain. I don't need any wildcards in my camp."

He watched me, closely. Finally, he spoke. "Alright, Ace," he said. "I'm in. There won't be anymore surprises. Tell me whatever you're comfortable telling me, and we'll figure it out from there."

I told Frank about the dreams and visitations. I told him everything, all about the affair with Desiree, places and people. I told about my "relationship" with Totsie. I told him about the boy, Thaddeus, who's death may have connected to Desiree's business dealings. Now he knew everything, I knew; everything except the part about Diana and me. He didn't need to know that part. He really didn't *want* to know that part.

He thought for a while. "Well, I've never heard of Operation Homesick, but I know someone who may have. You've got a lot going on. Why don't you leave Captain Promise and *feeling pretty sick* to me?"

I agreed.

I was going back to Hinesville to pay final respects to Desiree. I was going back to serve justice for her murder. I was going back to settle the score with her family. I was going back to confront her father. I was going back to make him pay for ordering the assassination of his own daughter. I was going back, because if I didn't go to Royce, sooner or later, he would send someone to me. I was going back because I didn't have any other place to go.

But, before going to Hinesville, there was someplace else I needed to go. The conditions of the inheritance were simple enough. It was written in her own handwriting: *1. Get my daughter to the funeral. 2. Don't let my son grow up without a mother's love. 3. Never let my children find out who my father was.*

I love you, Adrian.

Desiree Simone McKensie

"Mr. Hicks, you may be a big deal here in Podunk, Georgia...." – Sen. H. C. Beckmon

CHAPTER 6

Valerie wanted to join me in Hinesville, but Frank had something different for her to do. Operation Homesick needed investigating. We encouraged Dee to remain in Biloxi. I told her I preferred she stayed close to Frank. She would be safer there. She reasoned that, if she was going to be in danger, she didn't want to wait passively for it to overtake her. She wanted a part in bringing down Old Royce.

The service had just begun when we entered the crowded sanctuary. The procession of ministers had made their way to the pulpit. The reading of the Holy Scriptures was complete, and the family had been seated, Bud McKensie and the little boy, Alex. Desiree's father, Old Royce Dillon, and her cousin, Royce Hicks were seated among business affiliates, friends of the family. The entire family hadn't yet arrived. One member was missing.

With our entrance, there came an audible gasp from the pulpit which rippled successively, pew by pew, throughout the sanctuary. The attendees, who had been seated, so orderly and properly, began to stir extensively. I became concerned the more animated of them might bolt, shrieking, from the church.

The young lady between Dee and myself, trembled as we walked to the royal blue casket at the altar. There, her mother lay in repose, angelically resplendent in death, wearing a stunning white ball gown. Elizabeth Simone, the eighteen year old daughter of Desiree Simone Mckensie, stood bravely, at the coffin, looking down upon the woman whose face and form, she so hauntingly mirrored.

The girl, quietly weeping, leaned on Dee, who offered her tissue as she held her. Elizabeth sniffed, "She used to call me her only love".

"Don't let my son grow up without a mother's love" was the second of Desiree's final stipulations. I glanced over at young Alex, seated with the colonel. Bud accepted the boy, although he had to know he wasn't the father. But, I knew, without incentive, he would never accept Elizabeth. I wondered if Lisa, Desiree's assistant, could help with that. She didn't seem to have had difficulty in stirring him in the past. I was certain she and Bud were lovers. Lisa was the reason Bud could always find Desiree. Lisa was, also likely, the reason Bud never complained about Desiree's many excursions without him. They had to be together; it just made sense. And she was probably the one to send me those shoes following Desiree's death.

Finding us seats near the rear of the sanctuary, I pondered how to go about accomplishing my charge. The first was already complete. The girl was attending the funeral. How could I ensure Alex would have a loving mother? I thought about Lisa. Could I trust she and Bud would remain together? As for denying her children their grandfather, and heritage; I wasn't sure I agreed with it. If I was going to return the money, I perhaps the stipulations didn't apply. I decided not to sweat it. If I had guessed correctly, I might have a solution for both problems.

Royce *was* their grandfather, after all. I could dump in his lap, and walk away. But, he would likely spend his remaining days in prison after I'd gathered enough evidence to prove he had Desiree killed. I smiled. So, why bother?

It was an elegant service, if not a lengthy one. She would have approved. There was music, moments of reflection and speech-making. The attendees-you couldn't exactly call them mourners-were mostly business

324

and political contacts. The rest of the audience consisted mostly of curiosity-seekers. Even I, it seemed, in accepting her passing, had abandoned my grief.

Though there wasn't a whole lot of crying, more than one woman sobbed loudly when little Alex, mistaking Elizabeth for his mother called to her. "Mommy!" he called. Bud scowled at me, presumably for my callousness to have allowed the child to discover his older sister. I wasn't bothered if I was breaking any codes. I was in the mood, now, to make the rules for a while.

While leaving the grave site, following the interment, Hicks fell in step next to us. I noticed several men, strategically shadowing our pace. Dee watched him intently, and drew protectively closer to Elizabeth. Guessing he wouldn't do anything drastic with witnesses around, I motioned the women to walk ahead.

He smiled. I smiled. "Gotta say I'm surprised to see you here, Ace," he said. "I woulda thought you'd of took all that money, and hid out in some third world country. Probably enjoyin' the protection of a company installed des-pot."

I chuckled. "The thought had crossed my mind," I said.

"Don't feel bad about it," he said. "It's crossed mine a number of times."

We stopped walking to allow a group of people to get out of ear shot. The men stopped.

"You miked up?" he asked.

"No," I replied.

"I'll take your word for it," he said, agreeably.

I nodded. "Good."

"I see you brought my cousin with ya," he observed.

"Yep."

"Man! She's even prettier than her mama was," he said.

I agreed.

"I wish you hadn't, though. It complicates things a little more," he said.

I looked at Dee and the girl waiting for me. "How so?" I asked.

"Well," he began. "You've got money that belongs to us...."

I cut him off. "Money you stole."

He nodded. "Yeah... Well....Money that belongs to us. If it was just the money....Well, your showing up like you did here, would go a long way towards showin'..." he paused. "You know.......Good faith."

"...And?" I said.

"...And? But....But, you brought Elizabeth here. No one expected you to bring Elizabeth," he said. "You see, that makes you look unpredictable. And I just don't know what to do with unpredictable, Ace."

I laughed. "Is that your only problem?" I asked. "What about this funeral? What about her mother; your cousin; you either killed or had killed."

"Is that what you think?" he asked. "You think we killed our own blood?"

"Are you denying it?" I asked.

"Doggone, right, I am!" he exclaimed. "Maybe you killed her. Your DNA was on the body."

I laughed. "No, it wasn't. I wasn't with her that night. You know I wasn't," I said. "You used that sample you took to rule me out as the boy's father. You thought the money would follow the blood; that she would've left it to the father, but you were wrong. Too bad for you, it would have been easy to get it from someone already in your employment. You knew I wouldn't bend as easily as your lap dog, so you lied to keep me off balance."

He stonewalled. "Ace, I always said it, you got one heck of a imagination," he said, trying to throw me off the trail.

"A good imagination's important," I said. ".....When you've got friends who'd as soon cut your throat as look at you."

He paused. I'd struck a nerve.

"Well, I didn't kill her," he said, shrugging defensively. "I could tell you who did, but it won't do you no good. You wouldn't do nothing about it, no way. You ain't the type."

"You don't know me as well you think you do, Hicks," I told him.

He laughed. "Buddy, you may have a trick or two up your sleeve," he said. "But, in the end, you ain't nothing but a do-gooder, an eleventh hour hero. And that's gon' mess you up bad someday. Now, why don't you tell me how you're goin' to give me back my money without gettin' you and Dee killed?"

I laughed. "That's all you had to say. Let's go see the old man."

We resumed walking. So did his men. A pair of them collected Dee and Elizabeth. To ease their fears, Hicks assured them they'd be safe. Dee said to me, "I hope you know what you're doing."

"So do, I," I said.

Hicks chuckled. "He, don't," he said.

I wanted to dispute his assertion, but he was right. I didn't have any idea what I was going to do or say. I hoped the situation would sort of work itself out as we progressed along. Why shouldn't it? I had the money. I had the girl. And I had a few valuable bits of information which we might be able to use as leverage.

As a newspaper reporter, I'd done hundreds of interviews. For every subject, there is one perfect question asked in the perfect way at the perfect moment. It's the one question no one can spin the answer to. I really needed that question now.

We arrived at the Dillon mansion, and entered unbidden into the expansive anteroom. Massey, impassively, greeted us in the ornate living room. "Mr. Royce is in the study, Mr. Hicks," she said.

"Thank you, Massey," he said, and left us standing with three of his goons. This is more like it, I thought. Guys. And they're a team. I felt very, respected. But, I had the feeling someone was going to get punked today.

Upon seeing Massey and Elizabeth in the same room that perfect question came to mind. "Claudia," I said, addressing the woman who called herself Massey. "Aren't you going to say hello to your granddaughter?"

One of the henchmen punched me in the jaw. "No talking," he shouted. I barely saw the blow coming, and nearly slipped it. Elizabeth screamed. Dee pounced on him and was restrained by one of the others. Then the guns came out.

"Hey! Hey! Hey!" shouted Hicks rushing into the room. "What's going on out here?"

"He was getting smart," said the punchy guy. "I had to shut him up."

Hicks laughed. "Ace, have you got a death wish?" he asked me. "The old man wants to see you. You can talk to him all you want, but it had better be about giving us our money."

I was holding my jaw where I'd been sucker punched. It wasn't a good time to tell them I didn't have their money. I had given it away, because I couldn't satisfy condition three of Desiree's stipulations. I never could. Though she had never met her grandparents, Elizabeth knew all about them. Mother had told when she was young. Just now, I knew the truth of what Desiree had told her.

According to the young woman, Desiree was sad, she had been drinking. Brushing her daughter's hair, she said to her, "I found my mommy and daddy. Someday I'll take you to see them. They know who I am and they love me. They said they were sorry and glad I found them".

Hicks examined my face. He gave his guy a disgusted glare. "Did you search them for weapons?" he asked. They had. "Good. Wait outside. They won't be any trouble."

He turned to Dee. "Ladies, could you wait here while we talk?"

Dee looked to me. I nodded. "Please," Hicks implored. "Make yourself at home. It'll be alright. We're family, here. We're just trying to work through some things."

Hicks was emotionally conflicted. Any serious harm to us would be a problem for him. We had become friends. You could say we had a fraternal kinship between us. The old man was a little more pragmatic. He would do; or have done to us; whatever was necessary to achieve his ends.

The two of us joined Royce in the study. Hopefully, we would all leave the little library in agreement. It was most important to me we agree that what I had to say was worth one hundred million dollars, and my life.

Royce was standing, studying an oversized globe. He turned to greet me, extending his hand with a smile. "Hello, Ace," he said. "It's good to see you again. It's a shame about the circumstances."

"Good afternoon, Royce," I said. "I'm sorry for your loss."

A sad shadow fell across his face. "Yes," he said, nodding slowly. "Something should be done for her family."

"Royce, we won't get very far, if we continue with this charade," I said.

He laughed a cackling laugh. "You're right, Ace," he said. "We should try to be as honest a possible here. Drink? Scotch, I believe?"

I shook my head. "It's a special occasion. How's the brandy?"

"That, it is," he agreed. "And the brandy's very good."

We all fixed drinks and settled down to begin negotiations. My bargaining position wasn't as precarious as I had thought. Royce produced a sheriff's badge from a little goldfish bowl. Shaking off excess water, he passed it to Hicks and me.

"This arrived by courier just this morning. Can either of you tell me where the fellow is who was attached to it?" he asked.

"No," I said. "Not a clue." Sad thing about Lindsey, he was a good and capable man. "I'm sure he'll turn up sooner or later."

Hicks gave me a suspicious glare. "Are you sure you don't know anything about this?" he asked.

"Yes, I'm sure," I insisted. "Why would I know anything about it?"

Royce changed the subject. "Gentlemen," he interrupted. "Why don't we say Sheriff Lindsey has resigned? He isn't exactly family, now, is he?"

I was ready to get the business of guaranteeing my safety. But, I didn't know where to begin. Royce seemed to have read my mind.

"Ace," he said. "It has come to my attention that you have a significant amount of my money."

I was searching for the right tone here. Royce wasn't a man to trifle with. He didn't get where he was in life by being stupid or weak kneed. He would respect strength and honesty. I determined to deal all the cards from the top of the deck.

"Yes," I said. "I only discovered it a couple of days ago. When I became aware of off shore accounts of such large amounts, I guessed it was your…Shall we say……Misplaced funds? I hope you'll accept my apology for the misunderstanding."

He smiled. "Of course, Ace." he said. "It was just a mistake on the part of my departed daughter. She was prone to pranks, as you know. So have you got a plan for getting my money back to its proper place?"

"I have been giving it some thought," I said. "But there seem to be certain obstacles….."

The cagey old man frowned. "Ace, you're not entertaining the notion of *keeping* my money, are you?" he asked.

There was an icy threat in his tone. I remained cool. "Royce, you're going to get your money. I don't want it."

"Then, what are we haggling about?" he asked.

He would never believe I wasn't, at all, interested in the money. Royce just wasn't built that way. He just couldn't trust a man who wasn't motivated by greed.

"Well…..We're talking about a finder's fee," I said. He smiled. This was bargaining. This was what he expected, and trusted. "We're also talking about Desiree's children; your grandchildren. …And of course, mine and Dee's lives. We'd like to be able to spend the finder's fee. We're funny that way."

He laughed. "Not unreasonable. What are you proposing?"

I drew a deep breath. "I'm proposing a partnership," I said. They frowned.

I raised my hand. "Let me finish….."

They relaxed. "You take the children into your home, and raise them as your own. The Bud will understand. It was Desiree's final request that they were united. And also that you do what you've always wanted to do, marry their grandmother. I'm proposing that you take your winnings off the table, leave Hinesville, move to Saint Luke and raise the family you longed to raise a generation ago."

I thought of Julie and the girls, and wondered if I wasn't asking for more than he was able to provide.

"And your finder's fee?" he asked.

I shrugged. "Whatever's fair."

He nodded, thoughtfully. "You've done a lot of growing up in a few days."

"Let's just say I've been converted," I said. "Or it could be the influence of a hundred million dollars and multiple threats to my life and freedom."

"Oh, we do have a lot to talk about," he said.

Just then, I was no longer sitting in Royce's study. Dazed, I scanned the darkness. Desiree took my hand. "Hurry, Adrian!" she whispered, urgently.

We were standing in the parking lot of King's Ferry Landing. "Come!" she said. "Hurry!"

Not speaking, I allowed her to guide me through the darkness. Just ahead were Sheriff Lindsey and Bob Miller. Lindsey carried the lifeless body of a woman. He placed her behind the wheel of the gold Bentley. In a moment, the vehicle began to roll forward, towards the river. The car plunged into the waters and slowly sank beneath the surface.

"Thank you, Adrian," she whispered. I watched her wade into the river, following the automobile, and finally disappear in its depths.

From the expressions on Royce's and Hicks's faces, I could tell they had seen what I had. It was the haunting effects of Operation Homesick. The Army had been working on brain wave communication technology. They were working on the premise that they might be able to read the thoughts of people by intercepting low voltage brain wave impulses and interpreting those impulses. They had hoped to develop a weapon to effectively, read and manipulate people's thoughts. I had once heard about a cap and a helmet which allowed test subjects to manipulate characters on a computer screen. This was beyond that.

For all their efforts, the researchers had failed to achieve their goal. The technology was hopelessly flawed. They were decades from wireless, brain wave communication. However, in their efforts to tap into the thoughts of unsuspecting targets, they had unwittingly developed technology that, frankly, caused people to "see dead people".

Bud had thought Desiree was running away with me, so he "borrowed" the device in order to protect his meal ticket and dignity. He had not planned on his wife's death, but hoping to learn what we knew, he tuned to the device to Dee's brain wave pattern, as well as mine. He also didn't know the capabilities and limitations of the device. The effects, it seemed were residual. Frank's sources couldn't tell us how long we could expect to experience, what they'd termed the "dead phenomenon".

"I've arranged to have your money placed in an account belonging to Claudia-minus a small finder's fee and the interest, of course," I said. "I'll make the final arrangements for transfer, once we have an agreement. Have we got a deal, gentlemen?" I asked.

Obviously, predicting the implications of the technology he had experienced, Royce became very reasonable. He spoke, impassively. "It might be good to spend a few years, relaxing and watching my only grandson grow up," he said. "Hicks, please bring in Massey."

Hicks was more affected by the experience than I had initially thought. "Get her yourself," he said. "You're giving up; quitting. You've had your time, and now you're letting Ace cut me out. I'm done taking orders from a frightened, impotent old man."

I could hardly believe my ears. Hicks was losing his cool. He had never expressed a desire for succession to the headship of Royce's empire. Now that he had, he could be very dangerous. Perhaps I was trying to negotiate with the wrong man.

Old Royce gave out a cackling laugh. "You young pups," he said. "Yes, it's true, I'm not the man I once was; a result of age and illness. You, however, won't have that excuse when Mr. Edwards, here, has made a gushing young lady out of you."

Hicks was at a loss for words

"Now, go do as I told you," he continued. "Before I take off my strap and whup you like I used to."

Hicks did as he was told.

I stifled the laughter at Hicks's dressing down. And I felt my chest expanding with pride from the vote of confidence expressed by the old man.

Royce turned a winnowing eye on me. "You may have bitten off more than you can chew," he said. "Are sure you want that boy as a partner? He'll cheat you first chance he gets…Been stealin' from me for years."

It was uncanny how the old goat always managed to be in charge. Hicks may have been punked, but with one statement, Royce had done the same to me. I began to wonder what, in the world, I had gotten myself into.

When Hicks had gotten past his desire to end our lives, he admitted his affection for Dee and me. It was a good thing too, I managed to negotiate a deal in which she handled public relations concerns for our growing business. The position came with a generous compensation and expenses package; a full one percent of all profits. She was also provided a half percent voting ownership of all businesses. All of that on top of her share of the finder's fee made her a wealthy woman.

Watching Hicks fume over his losses, I thought he might convince Royce to revert to their previous position. But, our agreement held firm. They would pay a steep price, but it was the price they would need to pay for threatening my best friend. I wasn't in the mood to mess around with them, and now that we were on a level playing field, I wouldn't be intimidated. They had no idea how bad things could get for them.

Diana was a busy woman. I seldom saw her, early on, after Frank and I managed to strike a deal. Combining business assets created formidable economies of scale. She did remember my birthday, though. She located the stripper we had met in Bubba Ray's. But, instead of getting me a night of pleasure, she hired the young woman as a personal assistant. Never mind the girl had no training or natural skill for the position. We battled long and furiously over that one.

"Find her something she can do!" Dee shouted.

"What's wrong with what she's been doing?" I asked, jokingly.

"Send her to school, Ace," she said, reasonably. "Do something worthwhile with your money."

She wore me down. "Okay," I said. "But, the first rumor….The first time I hear any whispers about her strippin' or 'hoin', she's going to go to jail *and* lose a job."

"You're such a jerk!" she hissed. But she got her way. And the young woman became a valued associate.

"Absolutely, right," I said. "That's my middle name. Now get out of my face."

Boy, I loved fighting with Dee. But, she still owed me a birthday present.

It was an effort to transition into wealth and respectability. The first six or seven months following the deal I'd struck with the Royces were the busiest of my life. I hadn't considered the myriad of problems and challenges I would encounter. I found myself constantly traveling between Saint Luke and Hinesville putting outs fire of every type.

I wasn't having a lot of fun. There was always an earth-shaking decision to make, something to sign, or a dispute to settle. And Royce had been right about my partnership with Hicks. I was trying to steer us into a legal operation, but Hicks was desperate to hold on to old larcenous ways. I didn't want any part of fleecing soldiers out of their homes. Though I only held a three percent share of all concerns I demanded we maintain an honest business. I wasn't popular with Hicks; or his cronies who were used to favors, kickbacks and shortcuts.

After two months, and constant arguments with Hicks, I began to receive odd anonymous phone calls. You couldn't exactly call them threatening, only disturbing. They were often, coded psychological messages. Things like personalized license plates on two automobiles with a continuing message: *G1TYR* on one car, and 4ZZ0T on the following (Get your ass out).

There wasn't much I could do about the undercover psycho games. I'd simply have to deal with them. But, Frank sent a solution for my Hicks problem in the person of, The State University graduate, Senator Hiram C. Beckmon. Beckmon a tall, lanky Texan, listened quietly, as Hicks boisterously, expressed his rights as an independent businessman. I'd had just about enough, and was about to suggest closing down all operations, legal and other wise.

Just then, the senator stood to the full length of his six foot six inch frame. "Mr. Hicks," he said, calmly. "You may be a big deal here in Podunk, Georgia. But, I wield the pen with the power of life or death for your little fiefdom. This is a one company town. With one stroke of that pen I told you about, that sucking sound you'll hear will be talent and money leaving so fast, it'll pucker your eye sockets.

"I may not be able to touch you, personally, but, I can close your little hamlet. You'll be a kingpin without a kingdom. Let's see how much weight you throw around then. Clean up your operation, mister......Or lose it!"

I didn't have anymore trouble with my adopted illegitimate brother.

I decided I couldn't work effectively knowing there were wild cards out there looking to settle old scores. On one of her mysterious visits, I asked Promise to find the Smiths and the family of the fellow Mr. Smith had shot. I was able to get them together so that I could make a deal for keeping peace among us. Mrs. Smith was no longer an issue. She had left Mr. Smith two years earlier. The other guy recovered. I apologized and paid him for his pain and suffering.

Mr. Donovan Smith had lost a wife and several years of his life. I was responsible for his troubles, if only peripherally. As an ex-offender, he was

339

having trouble finding work, so I hired him as a driver and body guard. I was able to cajole Promise into finding a paramilitary training course for him. She didn't think it was a good idea.

"He's a thug," she'd said. "He's as likely to turn on you as defend you."

"It's your job to make sure he doesn't," I said.

"I don't work for you, Mr. Edwards."

"No, you don't," I agreed. "But, as long as I'm your Psy-Ops guinea pig, you'll insure I'm safe.........At least, until I become expendable. And at that point, you're likely to be the one he protects me from."

She allowed a frighteningly wry smile. "Alright," she said. "We'll teach him everything he'll need to know to protect you."

She didn't say, "He'll never be a match for me, though." I was betting he wouldn't be as good and capable as her contemporaries. I was betting my life he would remain loyal, and could, at least, deflect the spear, should Promise's agenda change.

I was in Saint Luke once a week, those first six months. Royce was giving me a hands-on B-School education. He explained that Hicks would be an excellent businessman, once I was able to trust him. "He'll make you wealthier than you could ever dream," he said. ".......If you can keep him from swiping your share of the company from you before he does. Ace, I'm betting, in three years, you won't own so much as a townhouse. "

What Royce didn't count on was the residual effects of Operation Homesick. In less than two years, he had completely lost touch with reality.

It seems, because of his advanced age and previous life style he had more ghosts to reconcile than most of us. The time came that he would spend more time with haunting visitations than the corporeal world. Eventually, he was only with us in body. Hicks became a shrewd businessman. And we remained close friends. I couldn't have hoped for a more honest and trusted business partner.

Bud and Lisa were more than happy to let young Alex's Grandmother and sister raise the boy. Bud had reservations about, allowing Royce to take part in his upbringing, however. Those reservations were resolved with liberal fiduciary application. Once the couple had managed to produce a child of their own, their contact with Alex and his family diminished to nil.

For me, the dreams persisted. They were most intense following the visits from Promise, which had become more frequent, by the way. She hadn't learned to laugh, but possessed an engaging dry sense of humor, I found entertaining and challenging. She had become a friend, of sorts. I would have welcomed her visits if they had not left me with such terrible headaches.

I could always tell when she was near. My thoughts would begin to muddle, and the space around me would seem to take on a gelatinous consistency for only a moment. I assumed she was armed with one of her psy-com devices, and was using it to gather data and manage me during interviews. She would never respond to my questions concerning my disorientation during her visits.

It was three days since Promise's most recent visit when Desiree appeared in my bedroom doorway. She stood in my way, preventing me from leaving the room.

"It's been a long time," she said.

"Not so long as you think," I replied.

She patted my belly. "You've gotten soft," she said.

"I let my fitness club membership expire."

She smiled. I'd always loved that smile. Her hand slid to my crotch.

"Perhaps you should renew it," she said.

I stepped back. "I'll consider the advice," I said.

"You should," she said, tipping her head slightly forward. "It's good advice. Take It. It's free."

It wasn't free. Nothing about Desiree had ever been free. There were always costs involved. But this wasn't really Desiree, of course. Desiree was dead. It wasn't clear how or why. And in the long run, it seemed no one really cared. Everyone close to her had benefited from her death; me no less than anyone.

I cared.

The knock at the door startled me from sleep. I opened it to the beautiful smiling Valerie. I stood holding the door, smiling in return.

"You should invite me in," she said.

"Of course," I said, stepping aside.

It occurred to me in a moment that she shouldn't be here. "I was having a dream," I said.

"About Desiree?" she asked.

"Yeah," I replied.

"You're wondering if you're dreaming now?" she guessed.

I nodded. "This *is* your wedding day."

"Yeah....About that...." she said. "The wedding's off. Caught him schtuppin' one of the bride's maids."

I tried my best not to laugh.

"Men are pigs," she said.

I agreed. "Yes. Yes, we are."

"How did you get here?" I asked, hoping, in her present mood, she hadn't driven all the way from Biloxi.

"I flew," she said. "You bought a jet last night!"

"I didn't buy a jet," I said.

"Of course, you did," she said. "I signed for it. It's your wedding gift to me! Congratulations, Mister! We're engaged!"

Valerie said men were just no good, but if she had to have one, she might as well have the one she really loved.   She gave me her hand. This ring was even larger than the one she had replaced. I didn't know I had such wonderful taste in jewelry.

I grinned. "You're stupider than I thought," I said.

She kissed me. "Guess so," she said. "How about it? Want a really stupid girl?"

"Doggone, right, I do!" I exclaimed. "I'm pretty stupid, myself."

We embraced and kissed.

Just then it occurred to me. I bought a jet?

"Sweetheart," I began.

"Yes, Darling?" she replied.

"How did I come to buy a jet?" I asked.

"Darling, it's a very good investment," she said. "We need it."

"Yes, but……" I paused, thinking to select my words carefully. I remembered the old saying that if you can't stand the answer, don't ask the question. "How did *you* sign for my jet?"

She laughed. "Darling, I'm your lawyer. I sign for you all the time," she said. "I have power of attorney. You can buy me anything I want."

"Really?" I asked.

She grinned, nodding. "Uh huh."

"Boy," I said. "I am stupid."

"No, Baby," she corrected. "Just lucky."

She was right, I was lucky. The jet paid for itself ten times over. Valerie went on signing for gifts for herself. It turns out, I had excellent taste in dresses, hats, purses, diamonds and particularly, shoes. She had pretty good taste in cars, too. She wasn't surprised when I drove home in the brand new candy-apple red Corvette she bought me for our first wedding anniversary.

"We make calm, the troubled waters. And if we can't do it, only God can."

- A.F. Johnson

EPILOGUE

Frank married Valerie and me in a small quiet ceremony in his office. Life was pretty good, going along as usual. Frank had become the focus of a paternity dispute, claiming to have never met the young woman. DNA examinations exonerated him of responsibility-but not with Diana. She stood by him, but their wedding would be postponed. She never mentioned it, but I wondered if she ever experienced any residual effects from the Homesick phenomenon. Some people recovered immediately. I wasn't one of them. The haunting dreams would manifest as often as once a month; with just about the frequency my hangovers. It was a manageable arrangement.

I was able to renegotiate the terms of my divorce from Julie. Thanks to her perfect boyfriend, she was happier than she had ever been. Because of my unexpected wealth, the court increased child support, and recalculated her alimony. Julie wasn't getting married anytime soon. At least, Val was able to get me much better visitation terms. I got to see the girls anytime I wanted, provided I remained reasonable in my demands.

I had a spectacular relationship with the girls. Janice adored me, and Sheila thought I was lame and unreasonable about her too-old-and-too-fast-for-her boyfriend. They both absolutely loved Valerie. Their mother had taught them how to shop. But, Val took their education to a whole new

345

level. She was teaching them the finer points they'd need to know when they were older and she gave them charge cards of their own. They had always loved Auntie Dee, and Uncle Frank was lots of fun. They liked to watch him bang his gavel, and throw people in jail. He let them sit in his judge's chair, where they pretended to send bad people away for life.

Though she was a silent partner, Totsie went underground following Bob's death and J.C. Lindsey's disappearance. When she showed up again, Hicks scooped her up. He had a real knack for keeping the money in the family. They made a handsome couple.

Dee and I returned to the paper to finish packing. By then, Cook had simmered down, and offered us our jobs back. I informed him we were never fired. We were tendering our resignations now, and expected severance pay.

"And by the way, I'm a minority owner now," I said. I told him he should post ads in the help wanted section for two reporter positions. And also, he shouldn't hire anyone without my approval.

Needless to say, we wouldn't write the story we went after. Mysteriously, every document; every phone number; scrap of paper or cocktail napkin that had the slightest scent of Desiree's story had vanished. I couldn't prove it, but I was certain someone had searched my home on more than one occasion. Evidence just went missing, in the office and my apartment. Dee had the same experience. I asked Promise if she knew anything about it, and got a splitting headache along with what amounted to an annoying game of verbal tag for my troubles.

Valerie had spent a night in jail, charged with the murder of her former fiancé. The wealthy and very connected investment banker, Raymond Petersen, was found floating in the Back Bay with six bullet holes in the chest. Authorities said he died from multiple gunshot wounds. Val said, "He died of natural causes. He was a natural man who couldn't do right".

Since the dissolution of her relationship with Petersen, her chances of getting to the state house had diminished. We believed we might have a chance of overcoming the racial hurdles, but with his death, there wasn't the remotest chance. A jealous husband had killed him, but the damage to Val's reputation was already done.

Elyria Promise didn't come around as often following my marriage to Val. And when she did, she seemed distracted, her eyes drifting to Mr. Smith as she spoke. I never asked Donovan how he spent his days off. If my suspicions were correct, I didn't even want to know. There was no telling what kind of bazaar experiments she was performing on the poor guy. I imagined she could be uncommonly persuasive, if she decided to enlist him and his store-bought killer skills against his employer. I really wouldn't want to find myself in a position to have to contend with a Smith and Promise team up. That wasn't a problem after Mrs. Smith serendipitously showed up in Biloxi one evening. It just so happens, Promise, Mr. Smith and myself were entering a casino when Mr. Smith's former wife walked pass. From that night on, I didn't get anymore headaches when Promise came around.

A wealthy, Central American, terrorist enlisted Promise's agency to broker a deal with us to find his wayward daughter and send her home. Val wanted us to decline the job, saying, she didn't want any part of that vile murderer or his evil spawn. Frank would say of him, "That dude is the kinda fellow who, with four urinals available, chooses the one right next to you. Makes you wonder if he wants to watch you, or he wants you to watch him. Either way he gets your attention........And it's usually a very uncomfortable experience".

Personally, I understood their ire. But, I tried to impress upon her that we were in it for the money. We weren't in the political commentary business. We couldn't allow geopolitics and our prejudices to affect sound business decisions. Despite our reservations, we took the job.

We solved problems. We found people, and we found things for people. We couldn't afford to turn away business just because we found the potential clients distasteful. When the players came with upper echelon cred, it behooved us to satisfy their needs-within reason. Political expediency was just bad for business.

We were chilling at Il de Meurtre one evening when a prospective client asked if we could solve his problem. We told him, of course, we could.

"What's so hot about you people?" he asked. "All I see here is a Barbie Doll bimbo, an uppity soul sister, and a pair of washed up pimps in Armani."

We laughed. It was good of him to notice. It cost us a lot of money and effort to get the look just the way we wanted. He was right; at first glance we didn't appear to be much. We weren't exactly private investigators. We weren't paramilitary mercs. We weren't grifters. We didn't sell protection. And we weren't debt collectors. Because of our deft touch, we interfaced best with the U.S. psychological warfare community. Diana jokingly, dubbed Promise and her kind "Neuronauts"; and us, "Neurocrats". We couldn't tell him that.

"So what are you?" he asked.

It was Frank who best described what it is we do.

"My friend, we're solvers," he said. "We provide solutions. We make the crooked roads straight. We ease worried minds. We make calm, the troubled waters. And if *we* can't do it, only God can."

The End.

www.ingramcontent.com/pod-product-compliance
Lightning Source LLC
Chambersburg PA
CBHW062013170626
46813CB00001B/147